ASSASSINATION GAMES

ZACH FRANZ

What's past is prologue.

—William Shakespeare

PROLOGUE

Thunder—deep, vast—shook the heavens like an inverted earthquake. *They're coming.*

And like the storm, unstoppable. He could sail to Constantinople, ride the Dakota Territory—they'd still find him. It wasn't their number that outlawed escape, but their network; a thousand contacts from New York to Ceylon, all eager to broadcast his whereabouts. He might survive for days, even weeks. But eventually he'd make a mistake. Then one evening a peaceful sleep would come, from which there was no waking.

Emile Delacroix twirled a cheroot within his lips, soon releasing its lazy trail of white smoke into the Louisiana night. He was surprised to feel no fear. It wasn't, though, the calm of courage. He'd simply given up.

He puffed the cigar once more and surveyed the surrounding expanse, shrouded in the typical semi-gloom of a southern summer. Seas of green grass flashed turquoise with the lightning; massive oak trunks stood firm, oblivious to the growing wind. Beyond flowed the Mississippi, its inevitable current sparkling through the darkness.

Behind, the large house beckoned, its glow piercing his back like a spotlight. He turned its way, refocusing. This went well beyond a single life. He may have personally given up, but the rest of the world still deserved a chance.

Delacroix had never considered himself markedly noble. But faced with such a pervasive and ruthless threat, what was the alternative? He liked to think that anyone else would've done the same. Still, it wasn't a pleasant prospect. He shivered through the humidity.

If only he hadn't accepted their invitation. 'Recruitment' was the more accurate word. In the end, he'd merely been in the wrong place at the wrong time. A young man of means and limited wisdom, disillusioned by the perceived futility of European society. More than anything, Delacroix realized, he'd simply wanted the world to remember his name.

Maybe it still would. For a different reason.

1

It never rains in Southern California. Keith Hardy tossed the lyrics around in his head and took another bite of muffuletta. *It pours, man, it pours.* Fine. Los Angeles could have the metaphor; New Orleans was the real thing.

He rolled down the Ford's passenger-side window, just far enough beneath Tujagues' awning. Another few inches and the soaked skies would've begun splashing his lap. Over thirty years in this place and it was still either mist or monsoon. He could hardly remember a time there'd been a simple, steady shower.

The balance of extremes went beyond precipitation, deep into the city's DNA. Where else could you find the world's best restaurants and its lowest dives? Bourbon Street blocks from St. Louis Cathedral? Amoral games and amazing grace?

This town was never supposed to be home. He'd been born and raised in Baton Rouge; New Orleans was where you went to party, maybe see the Saints. But then he tore a couple tendons in high school, and that dream of edge rushing for LSU faded. Tulane, though, was still offering, with a scholarship to boot. He'd followed the river south, almost like gravity.

From this point, missing out on the NFL was no shock; becoming a cop certainly was. But he'd had a pregnant wife to support, and needed something stable. The department was desperate for an influx of honesty—to this day a deficiency it'd never quite rectified. How he'd survived to make detective was beyond him. All it'd cost was a marriage and the respect of his children.

Hardy took another bite of ham and salami, watched the rain choke Decatur's overworked drains. Sometimes people would ask why he still did it. His answer was always the same: every once in a while, you got to put away someone really bad. There weren't too many jobs that still offered that kind of built-in satisfaction.

He glanced toward the Café du Monde a block south. Its lights, dripping through the car's front windshield, melded with the rest of the traffic clogging the street ahead. What was with this volume? Just before midnight, in a downpour, and you couldn't see asphalt. At least the temperature was cooperating—first week of December and still hovering above sixty degrees.

He saw a figure seconds later, weaving through the vehicular maze with his jacket held high like an umbrella. He gripped a paper sack in his left hand. The man reached the Ford just as Hardy stuffed the last of the sandwich in his mouth. The driver's-side door flew open and the newcomer, trailing an errant flurry of noise and droplets, ducked behind the wheel.

Hardy let his partner, Mark O'Brien, settle before clearing his throat. "You know, you could have brought the beignets from home. They make a mix."

"Not the same, beautiful." O'Brien was Hardy's opposite in most major categories: young, white, married. He removed a pair of paper cups from the bag. "Besides, where would we get the chicory? Staking out a house is hard enough without you snoring for eight hours."

Hardy reached for the caffeine. "Suzie finds it melodic."

"Yeah, well, she's a cocker spaniel. Her standards are low."

O'Brien put the car in gear and began to pull forward. Hardy was rolling up his window when his cell phone buzzed. He fished it out to find the screen flashing an unlisted number. At midnight. *What the hell.* He swiped the screen and brought it to his ear. "Hardy."

"Keith, Craig Scheffler."

He'd been expecting a drunk with the wrong number trying to sell him some watermelon-flavored ecstasy. This was worse. Scheffler was a lieutenant from the first district. They didn't see much of each other, and that was still more than enough. Strong personalities and different work styles didn't mix well. *Why are you calling?* Hardy wasn't feeling particularly civil. "Isn't it past your bedtime, Craig?"

"No time for pleasantries. You dressed?"

"Uh…yeah. In the car, actually. Following a lead."

"What's your twenty?"

Hardy glanced at O'Brien. "Jackson Square."

"I need you at St. Louis One. We've got a hostage situation."

"You've got to be kiddin—"

"Look, Keith, I know I've been a dick in the past. You can run me over the coals all you want later. Right now, I need you."

Hardy took a breath. "Why me?"

"There's one hostage, one suspect. We have reason to believe the latter is Darius Thibodeaux."

By now O'Brien was crossing St. Peter Street on the west end of the square. Hardy thought a second, then quickly shouldered the phone. "Turn around."

Hardy was hazy on a lot of the offenders he'd busted, but Darius Thibodeaux still came through clear. The man had been in and out of custody since he was a teen. Early infractions were relatively mild: disorderly conduct, vandalism, petty theft. But they steadily grew in intensity, until, just over a decade ago, he'd been convicted of armed robbery and assault with a deadly weapon.

The sentence, in light of his prior record, had been severe. But some inexplicable good behavior, and an agreement to testify against a few bigger fish, got him released in eight years. He'd been out on the streets for six months.

Streets that, as O'Brien steered the unmarked sedan north of Bourbon, began to thin. By the time he crossed Rampart onto Basin and officially exited the Quarter, their surroundings actually wore the look of midnight. Few cars and fewer lights cut through the rain. A block ahead, just across the street from the cemetery, the area was completely deserted. Save, of course, the half-dozen police SUV's parked outside the first district station. Thibodeaux had never been the brightest bulb in the pack, but holing up a few hundred feet from your chief opposition took a special kind of stupid.

Hardy was still thanking God for half-baked criminals when they pulled up in front of the station and walked inside. A dispatcher behind a wall of bulletproof glass raised her gaze. They fished out their badges. "Hardy, O'Brien, homicide."

She nodded and picked up a phone. Two minutes later a door off the main lobby swung open and a uniformed officer, squat and sturdy, made his way forward. Hardy had seen his face a few times but couldn't quite put a name to it. "Detectives," said the man. Once he was close enough, he offered a hand. "Sergeant Ed Moses. Follow me, please."

They obeyed and were led back through the door toward a small conference room. It was dated: thin paint covering three walls, a chalkboard the fourth; in the center rested a large wooden table, chipped and stained. Upon it was spread what Hardy assumed to be a map of the cemetery. A quartet of officers stood pouring over this, one seeming to direct the other three. He looked up as the detectives entered.

After twenty-five years on the job, Craig Scheffler could've still adorned the department's recruiting poster—even if he insisted on wire-rims instead of contacts. A perfectly pressed uniform covered muscles that were nearly as taught as the day he'd applied. His six-two frame came close to Hardy's, though the buzzed blonde hair—and matching mustache—veered in another direction.

Moses closed the door as Scheffler stepped forward. "Thanks for coming, Keith."

"You didn't leave me much choice." Hardy turned to his left. "My partner, Mark O'Brien."

Scheffler shook his hand. "Sorry to meet you under these circumstances."

"Forget it," said O'Brien. "What are we looking at?"

Scheffler exhaled. "Multiple witnesses place Darius Thibodeaux at a bar down off Bienville thirty minutes ago. Evidently, he'd had a lot to drink, got into a shouting match with the bartender and hopped the counter. You know how big this guy is; the bartender panicked and pulled a shotgun. Thibodeaux stole it and shot him in the stomach.

O'Brien swore under his breath.

"It gets worse. A couple others tried to intervene; he sprayed one of them in the leg, grabbed a female as leverage. He dragged her toward the door, then outside. Eighth district had a pair of officers on the scene a minute later. They turned onto Basin just in time to see Thibodeaux bust through the cemetery gate with the woman."

Now O'Brien was shaking his head. "You can't make this stuff up."

"Why keep the girl?" asked Hardy. "She would've slowed him down."

"I don't know," said Scheffler. "Maybe he was thinking ahead."

"Are you sure they're still in the cemetery?"

"Almost positive. Eighth stayed on scene until we arrived. I've got officers surrounding it right now. Treme and Conti gates are still intact. Unless they hopped a wall, they're inside."

"And you're sure it's Thibodeaux?" asked O'Brien.

Scheffler nodded. "He used a credit card. Bar also had security cameras; we're confirming the footage now." He grabbed a slip of paper from the table. "Girl is Keila Miller. Twenty-six years old, black, five-three."

Hardy tried to picture her, giving up a full foot and likely over a hundred pounds to a man who could fling her around like a rag doll. "They could be anywhere inside those walls."

"I've got spotters with infrared scopes on top of Basin Street Station to the east and some apartment buildings west. They each have clear line-of-sight, but between this weather and all the graves to hide behind, it's a crapshoot.

"A helicopter?" asked O'Brien.

Scheffler shook his head. "I'd prefer to keep this from getting loud too fast. SWAT and a negotiator are already on the way. Once the press gets wind, this could easily turn into a circus, even with a single hostage."

By now Moses had shuffled toward the other three officers—all younger, probably subordinates. They focused back on the map; Scheffler made no attempt to introduce them.

"What about contacting Thibodeaux?" asked Hardy. "Can you call him?"

"We're still working on getting his number, assuming he even owns a phone. The hostage does, but it's back at the bar in her purse."

"So, we're blind and deaf," said Hardy.

"Yes," said Scheffler, "we are. That's why you're here. I know it was over ten years ago, but you still tracked Thibodeaux and put him away. There are going to be a lot more bodies at this scene in a matter of minutes, and every one of them will benefit from knowing all they can about this guy. Anything you can shed light on—his movements, tendencies, the way he holds a weapon…I want to keep this from getting any worse than it already is."

Hardy was nodding, but he'd stopped listening halfway through—partly because he'd guessed the gist of Scheffler's speech, and partly because he'd had an idea. He motioned toward the hallway. "Can I have a word with you alone, Craig?"

Mild surprise lit Scheffler's eyes. "Sure."

O'Brien was left to mingle with new friends as his two elders stepped into the corridor. Hardy closed the door and faced Scheffler. "Let me go in there alone."

Scheffler almost laughed. "Where—the cemetery?"

"Yeah."

A shade of frustration. "What voodoo queen put that bug in your brain?"

"I'm serious, Craig. You said it yourself—I'm the best man for the job."

"Yes, for consulting from the side and letting the well-armed hostage professionals handle it. Look, Keith, I know how you must feel, but Thibodeaux's no longer your responsibility. There's no blood on your hands here. Early word is the bartender probably won't make it, but that'll simply go down as a random shooting. You did more than anyone else a decade ago. Let that be enough."

Hardy shook his head. "But it's not. Not when I know I can make a difference—"

"You're not going in there!" The bare walls of the hallway stared back in silence, including the thin one between them and the conference room. Scheffler shook it off. "It's impossible, Keith, even if it was my call—which you know it's not. This whole situation is a house of cards. Nobody's going to let a lone gunman blow it over playing hero."

Hardy took a deep breath, putting his palms up in appeasement. "I don't feel guilty, Craig, and this is no ego trip. I just know Darius Thibodeaux. His entire criminal career's been trending toward greater and greater violence, without matching remorse. I don't care how he cooperated in prison, tonight's who he really is."

He looked directly into Scheffler's eyes. "He'll kill her, Craig. Even before the noose tightens, just to spite us. Once we add tactical and air support, TV crews, there's no chance she's coming out of there alive. Thibodeaux's not going to prison again; he knows the sentence a second conviction brings. It'll be a crowded firefight, at best."

Hardy didn't stop for approval. "Or I go in there now, alone. Catch him by surprise. He won't expect a single intruder, least of all me. I can move quieter than a SWAT team, try to get eyes on our hostage before a shot is fired. With any luck, I'll bring her—and him—out alive."

Moment of truth. The course of the night hung on Scheffler's expression, which was unreadable. Finally, half a minute later, he narrowed his gaze. "And if you don't come out?"

"By then your support will be here. Hand over the reins, tell Thibodeaux I was acting alone and you're ready to talk."

"If he hasn't killed her by then."

"That's not going to happen."

"Good. Because if you lose your head, so do I."

2

Five minutes later Hardy stood outside the front of the station, alone. Scheffler had ordered his men already posted around the cemetery to stay in place, but there was no reason for anyone else to escort the detective across Basin Street. The less commotion the better. Especially since, true to form, they'd lost the rain and its covering noise. All that remained of the downpour was a thick mist, clouding the air like a wet blanket.

Hardy adjusted a bulletproof vest, tight over his shirt, and felt one last time for the Glock tucked behind his back. He'd take it out once he reached the cemetery gate. By now, though, it felt woefully inadequate. He'd banished the doubt from his voice inside the station, but it'd always been in the back of his mind; this plan was a longshot. With a hostage and a hiding place, Thibodeaux had the clear strategic advantage. He really could end up getting his head blown off.

Only one way to find out. He took a step forward, then stopped as the station door swung open. He turned to see O'Brien walking toward him—wearing the same vest, likely packing the same heat.

Hardy waited until his partner was alongside before shaking his head. "We discussed this."

"I know. I changed my mind. What are you going to do, shoot me?"

It was Hardy's chance to huff and puff, but he saw the conviction in O'Brien's eyes and knew it was a lost cause. "Think about Sarah. What would she say if she knew you were going in there with me?"

"What would she say if she knew I let you go in alone?" O'Brien smiled. "We've had you over for dinner too many times, Keith. She and the kids love you."

They started walking forward. "I'm not coming to your funeral," said Hardy.

"Good. There'll be enough food on the buffet for everyone."

They strode in silence the rest of the way, banter swallowed up by encroaching fear. They passed a uniform near the gate, who'd been notified of their approach. The Glocks came out. Ahead, the iron handle had clearly been mangled by a shotgun blast. Hardy took one last breath and pushed it open.

Instantly the outside world melted away. It was as if the cemetery's stone walls had successfully resisted the onward crush of time and they were stepping back centuries. Silence hung on the humidity, shrouding each edge and entryway in anonymity. Above, a half-moon started to break through the clouds.

Both men crept forward on a patch of slick grass. Gaining a wide path between vaulted crypts, Hardy motioned for O'Brien to flank the right edge. They moved forward. Hardy could feel his palms moistening around the Glock's polymer. He'd been in this position before, but it never became normal.

Movement, quick, to his left. A figure? He couldn't tell. Shifting off the center path, he ducked past a handful of graves. A slight rustling of feet led him forward. His heartbeat continued to surge as he braced himself against a high stone slab. He could almost hear breathing on the other side.

A long moment of silence, then a deep voice. "Detective?" Hardy almost jumped at the word. "Still on the case, after all these years."

He leaned against the divider, gripping his Glock a little too tight. Conversation hadn't been part of his plan, but he saw no other choice. "Is that comforting?"

"It's predictable. Tonight, they're the same thing."

Hardy heard a whimper from the other side. "Is that Keila? Is she harmed?"

"*Keila*," repeated Thibodeaux. "We hadn't actually been introduced. Thanks for breaking the ice."

"Darius, this doesn't have to end in bullets. If you give the girl up, you'll be in a much stronger position to—"

Laughter, deep and genuine, cut him off. "Are you actually following procedure, detective? Someone must've done a real number on you…"

Thibodeaux's voice trailed off. Hardy heard an abrupt thud on the right end of the crypt. He started toward the noise, then stopped, knowing it was a decoy, and pivoted back to the left edge. Raising his gun, he lunged for the other side. Thibodeaux was waiting for him, hostage in hand. He had no shooting angle.

Thibodeaux shoved Keila forward. Hardy, reacting on instinct, lowered his gun to catch her. She was barely conscious; blood oozed from multiple spots on her forehead. Behind, hands now free, Thibodeaux leveled his shotgun. Hardy threw Keila to the grass, unable to move himself. The muzzle flashed.

He'd been expecting something brighter, then realized much of it had been covered by O'Brien's diving body. Hardy froze. O'Brien convulsed at the impact and was thrown back. He bounced off of Hardy's left shoulder and collapsed to the ground. Thibodeaux saw that his original target was unharmed and aimed again.

This time Hardy had a split-second to react and leapt right, clearing the edge of the crypt just as a storm of pellets blew a chunk off its stone façade. He rolled to his feet. Thibodeaux pumped the shotgun. Hardy reached for his own weapon, then realized it was gone. He must've dropped it in the collision with O'Brien.

O'Brien. No time to think right now. Hardy rushed ahead. For the briefest moment he was back on the football field. Thibodeaux appeared on the far side of the slab, but Hardy was already too close. He chopped the shotgun aside just as an errant spray thudded into the ground. Thibodeaux grunted and the two of them—over five hundred pounds together—careened through the open like a pair of angry bulls.

They crashed into the nearest vault a second later. Part of its brick exterior crumbled beneath the force. Hardy fell back and slammed into the unforgiving ground; a vicious pang knifed through his spine. Immediately he curled off a thick rock and grunted for breath.

Thibodeaux lay beside him, also breathing hard. He recovered quickly, though, scrambling to his feet. Ignoring his opponent, he scanned the grass, then lurched forward. Hardy knew he had to get up. *Now.* His back screamed as he forced himself to his knees. A look where his body had been revealed the shotgun. He reached for it.

By now Thibodeaux had his hands on the Glock; he must've seen it drop. To the right, Keila was coming-to; O'Brien lay motionless at her side. "Darius!"

This, along with a pump of the shotgun, brought Thibodeaux to an immediate halt. Hardy took a few steps forward, his new weapon leveled. Thibodeaux still held the Glock, but raised his arms. He turned around. The hint of a grin stretched his face. "You win again, detective."

Hardy forced his breathing under control. He paced forward, slowly. "Drop the gun."

"Sure." Thibodeaux's shoulders relaxed. "Just let me do one thing first—"

In a blur, he swung the Glock toward Keila's head. Hardy pulled the trigger. The shotgun blast dug into Thibodeaux's side just before he could fire. He staggered back, but didn't fall. He switched the pistol to his left hand and aimed once more, this time at Hardy. Who squeezed again.

A fresh salvo pierced the still air and sprayed Thibodeaux's chest. This time the big man did drop the Glock, then dropped himself. Hardy figured his own weapon was now empty, but kept it poised and rushed across the grass. The closer he got the less he worried; Thibodeaux lay unmoving, covered in a sheen of red.

Hardy turned. Keila was on her knees, trying to right herself. "No." He dropped the shotgun and moved to steady her. "Stay down. It's over." He could hear footsteps approaching. "I'm a cop. Just stay there, you'll be okay." He stood and raised his voice. "This is Detective Hardy! Site's clear! I repeat, clear!"

He figured nobody on SWAT knew his voice, and so didn't blame the half-dozen men who closed in with their weapons still aimed. Then he heard Scheffler a few graves away. "That's him! That's Hardy's voice!"

At this, and seeing Hardy without a weapon, they lowered theirs. Four of them shuffled to Thibodeaux's corpse, the others toward Keila. Hardy left her to them and faced O'Brien. He was lying on his back, eyes closed; he hadn't moved since hitting the ground. For the first time since the shooting started, Hardy felt the terror of their predicament. His heart drummed into his throat.

By now the rest of the SWAT team had reached the area, trailed by Scheffler, Moses, a few other officers and several paramedics. Hardy didn't notice. O'Brien didn't appear to be breathing. His vest was shredded where the bullets had entered, but no blood seeped through the shirt beneath. Hardy gingerly removed the Kevlar, holding his breath until it was clear the rounds hadn't penetrated.

Instantly O'Brien sprang awake. His eyes scanned the scene, slowly relaxing as they settled back on his partner. Hardy was shaking his head. "You're a center-cut idiot, you know that?"

O'Brien winced. "It seemed like a good idea at the time." He gripped his left side. Hardy noticed a patch of red staining his shirt above the beltline. He pulled at the fabric. "It's nothing," said O'Brien. "A scratch."

"A bit more than that." Hardy signaled for a paramedic, then turned back to his partner. "One of the pellets must've found a way through. Worth a few stitches, at least."

"All in a night's work."

"Not for what they pay us."

A pair of EMS personnel made their way over. Hardy stood back to give them room. After another minute Scheffler stepped up. "How is he?"

"Alright, in spite of himself."

The Lieutenant flashed the ghost of a smile. "I know I'm supposed to say 'well done,' but I don't think I have the energy."

Hardy waved it away. "Save it for the next time I piss you off."

3

Four hours later, dawn still a promise on the black horizon, Hardy sat punching out a report behind his desk at the police headquarters building on Broad Street. For the second time in as many minutes, he glanced at the surrounding sea of empty detective's chairs. Why hadn't he quit this job a decade ago? He could've done the paperwork tomorrow, but his body wasn't what it used to be. He needed a hot bath and a full day off. The stakeout would have to wait.

He was just rolling his sleeves up when a soft pad of footsteps sounded from the shadows on his left. Seconds later O'Brien rounded a corner carrying two steaming foam cups.

Hardy had followed the ambulance from the cemetery to the ER. Docs had only needed a few stitches; finding the pellet was more of a nuisance. Eventually, though, they'd cleaned O'Brien out, bandaged him up and sent him away with a pair of Vicodin. The two detectives had just made it back to headquarters fifteen minutes ago.

Hardy stopped his typing and leaned back. "I thought you were going home."

"I was, then my cell rang. Rodney Aucoin. Said he left you a message."

Hardy fished out his phone. Dead. "Forgot to charge it. That's what happens when you turn fifty."

O'Brien set one of the cups down on his partner's desk. "From a machine, but it's fresh."

"Thanks." Hardy took a sip. "So, what did Rod say?"

"He found something. Apparently, part of the evidence brought in from the cemetery. Said we need to see it."

"Okay. I don't know if I can make it tomorrow. We'll go first thing the day after."

"No," said O'Brien. "He wants us there tonight."

Hardy looked up, Styrofoam poised at his lips. "What?"

"His words. Don't ask me why. He didn't elaborate."

Hardy grunted—another privilege of age—and turned to the landline on his desk. He dialed the crime lab. Three rings later a Cajun accent slipped onto the line. "Central Evidence."

"Rod, Keith. Tell me you're not going to make us drive up there right now. What the heck are you even doing at work this early?"

"Keith." Aucoin seemed to ignore the questions. "Heard you're a bit of a hero."

Hardy couldn't help glancing up at O'Brien. "I just pulled the trigger."

"Well, a win's a win. Always glad to see the good guys walk away from this kind of thing."

"Thanks, Rod. Look—"

"I know. I couldn't sleep, came in to catch up on some work. Got here about the same time as the debris from your shootout."

"Yeah?"

"Yeah. And I found something, on a chunk of stone. Must've broken off one of the vaults."

"Why are you telling me this?"

"It's your crime scene, and we go back a ways. I didn't know who else to call."

"What do you mean?"

There was a long pause on the other end. "I can't say—not over the phone."

Hardy was about to accuse Aucoin of theatrics, but something in the man's voice stopped him short. "Alright. We'll see you in ten."

The crime lab lay well north of downtown, in a research park along the shore of Lake Pontchartrain. They traced Gentilly under I-10, then curved onto Elysian Fields the rest of the way. It was an easy drive, especially considering the hour. Hardy nearly dozed off in the passenger seat. Curiosity, though, kept him conscious. What could possibly be important enough to warrant his and O'Brien's presence at five a.m.? And why the secrecy?

By the time they approached the site, half the clouds had cleared out, allowing a handful of last-minute stars to peek through. Both detectives flashed their ID's at the security gate, parked and strode inside. More security checks and a few minutes of walking brought them to the proper door. On the other side, they could each hear the faint sound of Chuck Berry riffing his way through "Sweet Little Sixteen". Hardy glanced at O'Brien, then knocked.

The music quickly faded. Seconds later the door swung open, revealing a barrel-chested man about Hardy's age with red stubble decorating his cheeks. Rodney Aucoin wordlessly waved them inside and shut the door. The sharp smell of bleach singed their nostrils. Hardy almost had to shield his eyes from the fluorescent glare magnified by a sea of stainless steel.

"So?" he asked.

Aucoin nodded toward a metal table near the room's center. They covered the requisite distance to find a clear plastic bag resting atop a sheet. Inside looked to be an ancient cluster of brick and mortar about the size of a thick serving tray. Aucoin donned a pair of plastic gloves and reached inside. "CSU brought this in about two hours ago. I keep thinking it's going to crumble in my hands."

Hardy entertained the fleeting thought that his colleague had gone insane; they'd been summoned for a rock. "Why is this even here?"

Aucoin eased the last of it loose and laid the bag aside. "No apparent

DNA or bullet holes, but it's still evidence of a struggle. These things don't just fall off on their own." He glanced at Hardy. "You and Thibodeaux must've had quite a dance."

"He's always been a willing partner." Hardy slowly pulled his eyes from the slab up to Aucoin. "But I still don't get what's so special about this thing."

Aucoin was already reaching for a flashlight at the far end of the table. "It's not the slab; it's what's on it." He shined the beam down. Like magic, it illuminated what had been all but invisible before.

Writing, etched into the clay. It looked to be a short paragraph, then some kind of list. But the arrangement was messy. "You're thinking this is some sort of message?" asked O'Brien. "How do we know it wasn't just kids breaking into the cemetery?"

"Because this writing came from the inside of the grave." Both detectives turned to Aucoin. Their host continued. "And it's old. I've seen bits and pieces of St. Louis One come in here over the years. These carvings weren't made yesterday."

O'Brien rubbed his chin. "So they're…what, some kind of marker for the original crypt? Maybe the builders left a few notes."

"No," said Hardy, leaning closer to the slab. "The words are crooked, crude. They were carved in a hurry, probably by someone under stress."

"What are you saying?" asked O'Brien

Hardy slowly turned to Aucoin. "Buried alive?"

"The thought crossed my mind."

That was something. These graves were owned by families—often prominent ones—and were used multiple times over the course of generations. If they could determine when the markings were left, perhaps they could find out who was inside at the time.

Even if it were true, though, it was an eighteenth-century murder. A coup for the cold case unit—maybe even front-page news—but hardly the kind of thing that couldn't wait twelve hours. "That still doesn't explain why we're here."

Aucoin nodded, as if expecting the comment. He set the flashlight down and stepped toward a desk in the rear. Retrieving a single sheet of paper, he strode back to the table. "The writing is small, I know." He laid the paper down. "I took the liberty of typing it out."

Both detectives eyed the sheet. It was arranged just like the etching on the stone. What Hardy had thought was a paragraph actually looked to be a stanza to a riddle or poem. He scanned the words, but they meant nothing. The list came next. It consisted of close to three-dozen dates, each about fifteen years apart. They began in 1865 and ended…in the future. Half of them hadn't happened yet. Peculiar, but still meaningless.

He stole a glance toward O'Brien: just as confused. Back to Aucoin. "I'm not seeing anything."

Their host pointed toward the center of the list. "Look a little closer. You recognize any of those?"

Hardy's aching body had begun to protest this unexpected extension of the night. He was in no mood for a cryptic history lesson. "I don't—"

"Yes," said O'Brien, looking up at Aucoin. "November 22, 1963. That date's familiar. But I can't think why."

Then the light bulb flashed inside Hardy's head, followed, almost immediately, by a patch of vague dread in his stomach. He turned to O'Brien. "That's the day Kennedy died."

The room seemed to go quiet for a moment. Both detectives looked at each other, then Aucoin. "Two points for you, gentlemen. Care to guess another?"

Now Hardy didn't have time to be annoyed. His eyes rose straight to the top of the list. April 14, 1865. "*Lincoln*. Were any other presidents killed in office?"

"Garfield and McKinley," said Aucoin. "They're on here too."

"I never took you for a history buff."

"I'm not. But I can use the internet." Aucoin ran his finger down the string of dates. "June 28, 1914: *Franz Ferdinand*. August 22, 1922: *Michael*

Collins. January 30, 1948: *Ghandi.*"

He didn't need to go on. Hardy had suddenly forgotten his aches. He stood frozen beside O'Brien, each of them processing the same immensity. They were looking at an assassination list. But not only that. It was a list written, in all likelihood, *before* any of the killings took place.

"How is this even possible?" asked O'Brien.

"It could be nothing," said Aucoin. "A joke, coincidence."

"Do you really believe that?" said Hardy. Aucoin didn't answer. "Have you told anyone else?"

"No."

Hardy was already walking toward a landline at the back. Deep down he found himself hoping that this was, in fact, nothing—some bizarre parlor trick. But with every step such a fantasy was hammered further out of his psyche.

"Who're you going to call?" asked O'Brien.

"Your boss?" offered Aucoin.

"*His* boss," said Hardy. "This thing'll be far out of our hands before the sun comes up."

Two pages in twenty minutes. John Shaw shook his head and flipped to the third sheet. These were simple notes for a simple lawsuit: eminent domain, open and shut. When had he gotten so slow at case prep?

You know when. Of course he did. But it still didn't make sense. He wasn't supposed to be the nervous one. Not when the man he was meeting would be asking to marry his oldest daughter. It wasn't a step many guys took anymore. Maybe that's what made him anxious, even if he appreciated the gesture.

Pulling back from his notepad, he exhaled and reached for a nearby ceramic mug. At least the coffee was good. Fresh, too. He'd been to too many restaurants with wait staff from the Starbucks generation. They seemed to have trouble understanding that there was actually a time when people drank more than one cup at a sitting.

As if to back up this claim, his server strode over with a half-full pot in hand. "Top you off, hon?"

She was a curly-haired woman around his age. He checked her nametag for the first time: Sissy. "Why not." He was about to pass his quota, but this was a special day.

She finished pouring. "Still want to wait to order?"

Shaw glanced across the table at the empty side of the booth. "Yeah. I'm early."

"No hurry on my part."

After she strolled away, he glanced around. The restaurant was, in fact, half-empty. But that was a function of time, not quality. It was just past 9 a.m. on a Tuesday; he'd successfully dodged the morning rush.

The Silver Skillet always had one. Most of its menu items were staples at every diner from Charleston to Memphis. History, though, set this place apart. It had been around for over fifty years, with more celebrity visits than birthday candles. The restaurant remained one of downtown Atlanta's culinary must-sees, daily hosting an eclectic crowd of tourists, businessmen and Georgia Tech undergrads.

Shaw was about to turn back to his notes when his dining partner stepped through the front door. The man was in his early thirties, scanning the booths beneath a trimmed crown of dark hair. He stood an inch or two under six feet; neither overly handsome nor muscular, though enough of both, perhaps, to reward a closer look.

Shaw had only met Jeremy Kent twice. What he remembered was the man's confidence. It almost seemed like wisdom, as if he carried ten extra years of life experience in his back pocket. Right now, though, he looked nervous too.

Shaw took a sip of coffee as his counterpart spotted him and walked over. The older man stood and extended a hand. "Jeremy."

Kent accepted with a smile. "Mr. Shaw."

He winced. "John, please. Haven't I warned you about that?"

"Forgive me." They both sat down. "An old habit."

"There are far worse ones to have." Shaw slid his paperwork to the side. "Complements of your parents?"

"Mostly my mother."

He saluted with his mug. "She certainly left her mark."

Allison had relayed the story months before. Kent hailed from Winfield, a small town in Kansas. His dad was a plumber, still lived there; mom died of cancer just after her son graduated from Creighton. No brothers or sisters. Kent's degree was in finance, but he'd decided to join the army. Maybe looking for a fresh start.

It didn't take. He completed his required service, then found work with an accounting firm in Omaha. That was evidently his true calling. After a few promotions, he'd packed up and joined Kemper & Walls, one of D.C.'s sturdier firms.

Sissy appeared at the table with practiced timing. "Something to drink for you, sweetheart?" she asked Kent.

He pointed to Shaw's coffee. "Same, please."

"Black?"

"Yes ma'am."

She glanced across the table. "Another minute to order?"

Shaw nodded. Kent fingered one of the laminated menus as she stepped away. "I don't want to keep you."

"From work? Piles of files and a noisy courtroom?" He took another sip, then spread his arms. "This is my sanctuary."

"I can see why you suggested it."

"And I can see why you suggested this," he said, motioning back and forth between the two of them.

Kent stared back for a long moment, the slightest smile gracing the corners of his mouth. "Can't a guy take his girlfriend's father out to breakfast?"

"Not on a random Tuesday in early December. You and Ally have been dating for six months. What'd you expect me to think?"

"Six months isn't a very long time."

"I know. You're lucky I haven't thrown you out the door already."

They were both grinning by the time Sissy returned. Shaw handed her his menu. "Country ham breakfast, eggs over easy. I'm afraid I haven't given Junior here a chance to peruse."

"No need," said Kent. "I'll take the same."

Sissy turned back to Shaw. "He sucking up to you?"

"Like a pro."

She patted Kent on the shoulder. "What he won't mention is that it usually works. Especially when there's red-eye gravy involved."

"I've heard good things."

"You'll taste them, too. Just a few minutes."

Seconds later she was gone again. Silence returned, each man eagerly chewing on the quiet. Shaw had long forgotten his nervousness. This was infinitely better than tedious small talk.

Kent took his first drink of the strong caffeine. "I had a pretty good speech planned."

"I'm sure you did. Don't let me stop you, if you still want to give it." Shaw glanced toward his notes. "I know the value of good preparation."

"Nah, cat's out. Might as well roll with it." Kent took a breath, then stared directly back at Shaw. All of the sudden things weren't so silly. "You don't know me, John. You think you do. Allison gave you my history. You probably used your connections with law enforcement to run a background check on me." He took another drink. "But those are only statistics. They don't represent who I am."

Shaw sat back. "If this is your pitch, you've got a funny way of persuading."

"I just wanted to begin on an honest footing. That way, when I say I love your daughter, it might be easier to believe."

"It's easy already." Shaw studied his coffee. "You're right, Jeremy: I don't know you. But I know Allison. I can read her eyes when they light up as she talks about you. Or, if she happens to be over for dinner and you call, when she tries to hide a smile before excusing herself.

"This isn't some school-girl crush; she's almost thirty-years-old. She's got a good job and a stable of friends. Marriage might be the missing piece, but she's not emotionally desperate." He drained his mug. "What I'm trying to say is she's a grown woman who wouldn't risk her heart if she didn't truly mean it."

Kent paused. "And my heart?"

"That's where the 'risk' comes in. But I've seen enough to know its genuine."

"I thought you said you didn't know me."

"I know you're here. No one schedules this meeting for a cheap fling. And you've made the trip multiple times over the past six months. It's certainly not for money. Kemper & Walls pays as much as Allison's salary, and my 401(k) isn't worth the trouble." He set his empty cup aside. "'Love' is the only real explanation."

"Reasoned like a true attorney." A sheen of stress seemed to fall from Kent's gaze.

Shaw felt the same. "An old habit."

At that moment Sissy walked up with a fresh pot of coffee and two steaming plates. She spread them on the table and filled their mugs. "Can I get you boys anything else?"

Shaw kept his eyes trained on Kent. "No thanks. I think we're good."

5

A maternity ward was the only part of a hospital in which smiles and laughter were relatively common. That was why Allison Shaw still believed in what she did for a living. It was the constant presence of new life—loud, slick with sweat and blood, but still a miracle.

Maybe that's what made her linger at the edge of the room as one of her patients, surrounded by flowers and family, cradled her second child. Everyone crowding the bed seemed so happy. Such a scene only validated the post-labor maxim that the smallest arrivals made the largest impact.

Things weren't always so sunny. Too often, even in a modern day, state-of-the-art facility, there was no new life to celebrate. Stillborn deliveries, babies too premature to survive—these were also part of the job. Not to mention numerous new mothers who lacked the benefit of a single visitor. Few experiences were more pathetic than walking out of a hospital on your own.

The tricky part was balancing the comfort you offered to those who needed it with the professionalism necessary to maintain objectivity. How close was too close?

Such services, at any rate, were wasted on the reunion in view. Everyone still wore a grin; they hardly noticed her straddling the doorway. As she scanned their faces one last time, though, she couldn't help wondering if they knew the cost of such peace and happiness. Those benefits stemmed from a sense of safety, which almost always had to be earned by men and women in fatigues half a world away.

Some of them didn't even wear uniforms.

Allison stepped out of the room, unable to escape her thoughts. The flashbacks of Europe had continued with regularity: crashing into a cold river, held hostage at gunpoint, racing from assassins—none were images easily forgotten. She could still feel the fear. It had ceased to be debilitating; the nightmares ended long ago. But she'd awoken with a sobering, and rare, appreciation for everyday life. Most people didn't know how lucky they were to simply leave home and come back in one piece.

"Ally?"

She'd been shuffling down the corridor and turned to the nurse's station. The charge nurse stood behind one of the computers, holding a clipboard. "Yeah, Regina. Sorry. What's up?"

"I know you're due for a break, but I left my cell phone in 209. Would you mind grabbing it?"

"No problem."

She brushed a strand of brown curls from her face and continued down the hall. It reminded her more of a hotel than a hospital. Piedmont wasn't the newest such medical facility in Atlanta, but had kept up with its competition thanks to expansion and renovations over the years. Which made coaxing new mothers who didn't want to leave all the more challenging.

Room 209. She walked in. No lights were on, but the space was plenty bright from swaths of late-morning sunshine streaming through the window. Allison checked on a table near the door, even the bathroom; this wasn't the first time she'd retrieved Regina's cell, and her boss usually lost it on her way out. No phone.

She stepped farther in. The back half of the room was obscured by a drawn curtain; she brushed it aside. And screamed.

She immediately brought a hand up to cover the sound as her brain, first recognizing the presence of a man standing before her, identified him as Jeremy Kent. Allison felt the corners of her mouth rising even as the shock inside flooded her head. For a second, she couldn't move, her feet held in place by such conflicting emotions.

Then Kent pulled a small bouquet of roses from behind his back. "Payment for the surprise. I hope it's enough."

Allison took another second, heart slowly calming. Then she moved forward and wrapped her arms around Kent. He reciprocated. They'd been dating for six months, but hadn't seen one another for three weeks. Phone conversations only went so far to bridge the distance.

After a moment they released slightly, and kissed. Allison felt Kent holding her and allowed herself to forget, at least for a moment, that they were in one of the most sterile, unromantic settings imaginable.

They released once more and she looked up into his eyes. "You're enough."

"You're going to let me off that easy?"

She swiped the flowers and slapped him across the chest. "Don't ever scare me like that again!"

"That's more like it."

Allison glanced around reflexively for Regina's phone, then put two-and-two together. "Since when is it fair to use my boss for smoke and mirrors?"

"Since it was her idea. I was just going to meet you in the lobby"

They both took a breath, the initial rush of surprise subsiding. "What are you even doing here?" asked Allison. "You didn't call to say you were coming down."

"It was only for a single meeting this morning. I got in late last night, have to fly out in a few hours. I was going to call and see if you had time for coffee, then thought, 'why not in-person?'"

Allison smelled the roses. "They're lovely, thank you."

"How's it been this morning?"

"Fine. One successful delivery, and one happy family."

Kent brushed a curl from her cheek. "In a perfect world they'd always go together."

She held up the flowers. "Need to put these in some water. I was about to go on break, if you still want that coffee."

"Absolutely."

But Kent didn't move. For the first time, too, Allison realized he looked slightly nervous. A patch of anxiety sprouted in the pit of her stomach. "What is it?"

"What is what?"

She stared back at him, narrowing her eyes.

"I just…need to ask you a question."

She noticed Kent's hand hovering around his jacket pocket. Suddenly her anxiety changed character, from dread to expectation. Was that a bulge she saw—made by a small, velvet box?

"Have you ever read a short book that felt fuller than others twice as long?"

Not the question she'd been anticipating. But she recovered, nodding.

"It may not have had as many words, but each of them meant more. They had purpose, and power, beyond ordinary prose."

"Jeremy, I don't see—"

"That's us," said Kent. "That's why six months feels like ten years. I *know* you, Allison. And you've seen me as no one else has. We've risked our lives together. Every day I wish I hadn't pulled you into my world. But every time I thank God that it happened."

The ensuing silence caressed her shoulders like a warm blanket. Inside she felt a tug-of-war between prolonging this moment and embracing the next. Finally, Kent began reaching toward his jacket. Allison held her breath.

Buzz. It was his phone, and it pierced the still air like a five-alarm bell. A single ring, which meant a text. Kent redirected his arm toward the other side of his shirt. She thought about telling him to wait, but knew that wasn't an option for someone in his position.

He fingered his cell, glancing at the screen. Two seconds later this moment they'd created—the charged silence—crumbled to the linoleum floor. When he looked up, a shadow had crossed over his face. "I have to go."

The words were no surprise, but still cut like a knife. She tried one last, paltry stall. "No, you don't. Not yet." She gripped his hands. "What were you going to say?"

This earned her a sad smile, then a gentle kiss on the forehead. "I'll call soon about Jacksonville."

Half a minute later Kent was gone. Allison chose not to walk him out into the hall. She needed a moment to process what'd just failed to happen. Over her shoulder, yellow rays continued to split the clouds. It was going to be a beautiful day.

6

Ten minutes later Kent was back behind the wheel of his rented Camry, coursing too fast down I-85.

HARTSFIELD-JACKSON. 12:05 PM, DELTA. MEET YOUR PARTY AT THE GATE.

He'd already deleted the text, but the words lingered. More than anything, because they were practically his own. He'd chosen the CIA, even still believed in what it did. Conducting foreign surveillance, brokering friendships among allies—occasionally he even got to save someone's life. There were few things on earth more gratifying.

Such rewards, naturally, required sacrifice. Stunted moments like today could be par-for-the-course with Allison. But that's not what bothered him. In truth, she was right: he didn't have to go. Instead of still burning a hole in his pocket, the diamond ring he'd picked out could be on her finger. The whole wonderful, beautiful process might've taken five minutes. He'd have still arrived early for his flight.

It wasn't about time. It also wasn't merely about protecting Allison. She'd long ago made the choice to follow him into this life, and, thanks to Europe, knew the cost. He'd seen the fire of conviction still burning in her eyes.; there was no doubt in his mind she would've said 'yes.' Yet, something had stopped him.

By the time the airport came into view he still hadn't found what it was.

* * *

Atlanta may have been the metropolitan jewel of the South, but it could hardly be mistaken for New York, London or Tokyo. Yet its airport easily outstripped each of theirs. In fact, Hartsfield-Jackson International was the world's busiest hub, hosting 275,000 passengers a day. Many of them were traveling domestic, as the city's geographic location made it a mere two-hour flight from eighty percent of the U.S. population.

Into this commercial maelstrom Kent quietly slipped. After dropping the Camry between a pair of four-level rental-car parking garages, he'd crossed over I-85 on an elevated train and was now rolling his carryon through the domestic terminal's atrium. A sea of Delta counters came soon after and he joined the shortest line.

Five patient minutes brought him face-to-face with a perky brunette. Kent mustered up a benign smile and handed over his ID. She passed it back a moment later, along with a boarding pass. "Have a nice flight, Mr. Kent."

"Thanks."

He stepped from the counter and eyed the ticket: *Baton Rouge*, one-way. Hardly the destination he'd been expecting. TSA screening came next, then an escalator down to a second train that took him to the bowels of Concourse C. The airport's heavy foot traffic typically lay within these letter-designated corridors. He reached C's main level to find it no exception; a steady stream of humanity flowed shoulder-to-shoulder in both directions. He stepped into the fray, soon passing an infinite string of newsstands, restaurants and fashion boutiques.

Part of Kent's brain had already set Allison aside. He was now in the field—senses heightened, skills on standby. The crowd, as a matter of course, made him wary. This was a secure, domestic terminal, but threats could materialize anywhere. They didn't have to come from terrorists.

Or at all, in this case. He made it to gate C12 and claimed one of several empty chairs. Keeping half an eye on the scenery, he pulled out his phone and made a show of checking Twitter. A ratty paperback would've worked just as well, but he couldn't quite stomach the far-flung exploits of yet another macho spy. If nothing else, he'd just play tired—that was easy.

Five minutes passed before a figure approached from his left peripheral. A black man around Kent's age, slightly taller. "My text said something about a party," said the man. "Where are the cocktails?"

Kent looked up. "How long have you had that one in the chamber?"

"Since around Greensboro. Flight from D.C. was pretty quiet."

"One of these days I'll teach you how to read. It'll open worlds."

This earned a smile from James Baker, a fellow field officer. The CIA didn't use "partners" like law enforcement, but Kent and Baker were about as close to the concept as possible. They'd known each other long before recruitment; this wouldn't be their first rodeo.

"So," said Baker, sitting down, "what's in Louisiana?"

"Exactly." Kent scanned the concourse. "I suppose it's too much to hope this'll blow over in a few hours."

Baker took a moment, eyebrows eventually rising. "Your cruise."

Kent was set to meet Allison in Florida tomorrow. The ship—brand new—was called the *Empress Blue*. She'd sail for the Bahamas, then farther south. They were going with two other couples. It was a chance to leave life behind for a week.

Baker soon reconsidered. "Forget the boat. What about this trip—did you get a 'yes?'"

Kent nodded. "Allison's dad—breakfast—was the easy part."

"What other part was there?"

He looked at Baker. "I had the ring on me. Her hospital was less than two miles away."

"I thought you were going to wait for the Caribbean?"

"I should have. But then, look where we're sitting. I'd have lost the chance completely." Kent took a breath. "I still can't tell if getting halfway is worse than nowhere at all."

"Halfway? What do you mean—she said 'no?'"

"No. I was about to ask when…"

The light bulb clicked in Baker's mind. "When you received an urgent text from your superior." He checked his watch. "But we're not up against it. You had plenty of time to ask her."

"I know."

"So…why not?"

"I'm still working on that one."

7

"It's going to be fine." Leila Hassan placed a strategic hand on her husband's shoulder. Immediately he began to relax. His wife always seemed to know when to intervene. This time, though, she had help from the view. Through a large window, about a thousand feet distant, he watched the evening sun kiss the shores of the Mediterranean.

Keying in on the blue water, Michael Hassan—mid-forties, loving father, Prime Minister of Israel—matched his breathing with the surf's gentle roll. He'd long been afflicted by a strong temper, emotion rising uncontrollably within his chest. The dirty little secret was that it affected his mind as much as the rest of his body. Coming down from such anger stung with a special brand of mental fatigue.

He turned to his wife. "Must you always be so optimistic?"

"Yair Bachar is an understanding man. We had him and his wife over for dinner last month. Remember?"

"How could I forget? You made your ghanoush." Hassan took a deep breath and managed a smile. "Thank you."

She leaned in and gave him a peck on the cheek. "The table is being set."

"I won't be long."

Hassan watched his wife leave the room. *One more thing I don't deserve.* God surely was generous. Especially considering the way they met.

He'd been a fresh lieutenant in the Israeli Army. It was shortly after the peace treaty with Jordan, and the two nations were running exercises on both sides of the border. Pairing battalions, training together. On his first go-round, Hassan and a young Jordanian officer were tasked with leading two platoons on stealth runs. They were in the hills outside Ajloun, fifty miles northwest of Amman, when Hassan tripped on a loose rock and broke his leg. The closest hospital was Al-Iman, in Ajloun. Leila had just started as a nurse's assistant the week before.

Hassan brought his eyes back to the window. What if they had met twenty years earlier, when the two countries weren't so friendly? What would the Knesset have thought about him marrying a Jordanian? What if he'd had to choose between her and his current position? An easy answer. Even more fortunate, then, was he to be here. Today's evidence to the contrary, he still believed he was the right man for the job.

The problem was these gangs. Border skirmishes, near Gaza and along the West Bank, were nothing new. But this was different: young adults, many of them mere teens, using knives, homemade bombs, even sub-machine guns. Most of them, too, showed little or no regard for their surroundings. Just about every manner of building and bystander had served as collateral damage.

The tipping point had been this past Friday. A couple small explosives rocked an outdoor market in Ashkelon. A man had died, but also three children. Public outcry rose to a crescendo, and had yet to fall. But Hassan's hands were tied. Every rank of law enforcement was committed to the fight, even the Yasam. The PM had thought about employing the Home Front Command, but doubted their effectiveness. This danger was fast, mobile and faceless. He felt like the British traipsing through swamps in search of Colonials, or the U.S. military among his terrorist-harboring neighbors: what good was a cannon if you couldn't even find the mosquito?

Hassan's true concern lay in the source of the escalating violence. He had little doubt that Syria or Iran, or both, were behind such insidious attacks. They'd tried bullying Israel with broader strokes in the past; this was clearly a second wave, meant to test the mettle of a leader each nation considered too green—and yellow—to fight back.

For all his confidence, such a pointed threat had gotten to Hassan. He didn't notice his stress building until, at today's cabinet meeting, it was too late. Bachar, the Foreign Affairs Minister, had dared to question his strategy for dealing with the attacks. What resulted was a tirade unbecoming any head of state, particularly one who's responsibility was the protection of the most contested piece of land on the planet.

Embarrassment had gripped Hassan the moment he'd finished. He could feel every eye at the table crawling over his skin. His ministers, like Israel's citizens, needed their leader to project calm and control. Passion was fine, but such rampant emotion could only be described as weakness.

Yet, Leila's words still echoed in his mind: Bachar *was* an understanding man. This might all be fixed with a simple apology.

After dinner. Hassan could already smell the lamb from the kitchen. He took a step in that direction when the house phone rang on a table to his right. He was standing in the living room of a family retreat that'd been built by his grandparents over fifty years ago. Only a handful of people had this number; even less knew he was here right now. Hassan only needed one guess.

He lifted the receiver. "Tzadok?"

A seasoned voice filled the line. "Have I become so predictable?"

"'Reliable' is the word I would use."

"Spoken like a true politician."

Hassan managed another smile. Tzadok Neri was more than just his Minister of Defense; he was his oldest, most-trusted advisor, and a valued friend. The man had begun his career with extended IDF service, then spent nearly four decades in the Knesset. At seventy-one, he was a legend in Israeli politics. Despite the recent cabinet post, though, Neri wasn't particularly ambitious. He seemed content to offer wisdom from the sidelines, whether or not it was always heeded.

Hassan sank into a nearby chair. "What can I do for you?"

"Perhaps it's what you can do for yourself." There was a short pause. "Take an extra day off, Michael. Spend it there on the coast. Recharge the batteries."

Hassan felt his knuckles whitening around the phone. "Is that what the ministers are saying?"

"That's what I'm saying. Every man and woman sitting with you in that room today is still standing behind you tonight. They understand the stress you're under; they're under it too."

"Yes, but they didn't allow theirs to bubble over into a juvenile scene."

"I think the argument could be made that the pressure you're under is a bit more potent. What is that phrase the U.S. presidents like to use— 'the buck stops here.'"

"Harry Truman." As if any Israeli could forget that name.

"'That's right. 'Give 'Em Hell Harry.' The Americans love their nicknames. Maybe we should find you one."

"I shudder to think." But, Hassan realized, he was enjoying himself. Neri had worked his magic.

"By the way, don't worry about Bachar. He's already forgotten this afternoon."

"I plan to remind him by way of apology. My wife says he's a patient man."

"And you thought *I* was your closest advisor."

Hassan stood. "Okay Tzadok, you win. An extra day it is. I'll expect to find you've stolen my job when I return."

"If I were ever that stupid, my wife would kill me before you ever had the chance."

"Give her my love."

"Likewise to Leila."

They both hung up. Hassan turned to the window and stole one more glance at the Mediterranean, then stepped toward the kitchen. He was interrupted again, this time by a culprit three feet high and five years old. His daughter Talya ran forward and leapt into his arms. "Time to eat, daddy."

"If you say so, sweetheart." Hassan twirled her around, her long hair waving in the makeshift breeze. For over a decade he and Leila had tried for children, then finally given up. Three years later, Talya arrived. The greatest surprise of his life.

"How'd you get to be so pretty?" he asked. Her face made it easy to let the world go.

"I don't know," she giggled.

He carried her toward the doorway. "Let's go ask mommy. I have a feeling she had something to do with it."

8

Baton Rouge's Ryan Field was a far simpler affair than Hartsfield-Jackson. Their plane touching down just after 2 p.m. local time, Kent and Baker strode anonymously through the modest terminal. A second text had come mid-air: AVIS. 623 REDFIELD 70729. The zip code matched Erwinville, fifteen miles outside of town.

They collected a gray Chevy Malibu, under Kent's name, and were soon buzzing west on Highway 190. Bright sunlight washed the road from above; it was warmer here than Atlanta. A bank of thunderclouds, though, threatened in the distance. As dormant crops and live oaks rolled by, Kent let his mind go blank. Despite the mysterious summons, he'd long ago learned not to guess what may or may not lie ahead. *Ours not to reason why...*

Technically, the address was just outside Erwinville. Tracing a worn asphalt road, they finally saw a rusted mailbox with the proper address. Beyond, a gravel drive fed into a dense knot of foliage. Baker, behind the wheel, made the turn.

The driveway wasn't long, but curved from sight. Ideal seclusion. Both men scanned the trees mechanically. "Who'd they have to kick out of this place?" said Kent.

"It might be vacant. Prepare for spiders."

"I'm never prepared for spiders."

They'd developed the banter over time. It came easily, a natural catharsis against such a draining, and dangerous, occupation. Yet, there was always a moment when comedy deferred to the gravity of what lay before them. Kent could feel it happening now.

Continuing forward, they spotted a pair of vehicles tucked below a canopy of dying leaves. A Honda Civic, it's red paint fading, paled beside the shiny black of a neighboring GMC Yukon. Around a final hedge, fifty feet from the cars, lay the house. It was a simple ranch: wood siding, shingled roof, even a chimney. Baker pulled the Malibu off to the side and both men alighted. Their eyes took time adjusting to the darkened enclosure, its branched roof effectively blotting out the sun.

They walked side-by-side, boots crunching over a floor of rocks and dirt. Ahead, a man in a black suit descended a covered porch. Kent expected, and saw, the bulge at his right side and wire behind his ear. They'd met before.

The man stopped at the bottom of the steps. "Afternoon, gentlemen."

Kent nodded. "Craig. Any idea what this is about?"

"Above my pay-grade, I'm afraid."

"Can we join you?" Baker was only half-joking as he and Kent ascended the porch, soon pulling open a rickety front door. A small foyer lay ahead, giving way to the worn carpet of a living room. Natural wood and faux leather filled much of the surroundings; to the right, a kitchen's stark light beckoned. The space was old, but cleaner than expected. Nary a spider in sight.

A pair of men stood in the center of the living room to greet them. The one on the left was Peter McCoy, a veteran Agency officer and Kent and Baker's de facto handler. Ten years ago, he'd been a field agent himself; now, at forty-five, he could still fill out a suit.

They had no idea about the man on the right.

"Jeremy, Jim," said McCoy. "Thanks for getting here so fast. I know this isn't a typical briefing room; you'll understand why shortly." He motioned to the stranger. "This is Will Limon, Professor of American History at LSU."

Limon looked the part: fifties, salt-and-pepper hair, even a cardigan. His presence was also highly irregular, but, they assumed, would soon be explained.

He nodded toward Kent and Baker before McCoy signaled for them all to take a seat. The two newcomers straddled a maroon sofa as their senior, in a chair across, pulled out a folder. "Six days ago, a standoff took place between New Orleans police and an armed suspect in St. Louis Cemetery. Two detectives were able to subdue the threat and rescue the only hostage. The whole thing got about five seconds of coverage on the national news." McCoy leaned forward. "As you're surely aware, that cemetery—like most in the city—is unique. Its graves are above ground.

"One of the detectives, in a tussle with the kidnapper, crashed into the side of a grave. They were both large men; the impact knocked off some brick and mortar. Hours later, at the crime lab, writing was discovered on one of the broken slabs. Etched into the rock, on what would've been the inside of the tomb."

"Inside?" said Kent. "Isn't that cemetery centuries old?"

McCoy simply reached into the folder and handed each of them a sheet of paper. On it was a typed list:

April 15, 1865	Abraham Lincoln
July 2, 1881	James Garfield
September 6, 1901	William McKinley
June 28, 1914	Franz Ferdinand
August 22, 1922	Michael Collins
August 20, 1940	Leon Trotsky
January 30, 1948	Mahatma Gandhi
November 22, 1963	John F. Kennedy
April 4, 1968	Martin Luther King Jr.
March 24, 1980	Oscar Romero
October 6, 1981	Anwar Sadat
November 4, 1995	Yitzhak Rabin
December 27, 2007	Benazir Bhutto
December 19, 2023	
July 31, 2026	
February 5, 2046	

March 10, 2060

September 22, 2069

December 30, 2075

June 15, 2093

October 12, 2106

January 31, 2108

July 17, 2129

August 17, 2145

November 20, 2159

Baker looked up. "This was scrawled on the tomb?"

"Just dates," said McCoy. "We added the names."

"So…it's an assassination list."

"One that hasn't been completed," said Kent.

McCoy took a breath. "Our Directorate of Science and Technology brought in a pair of archaeology professors from Johns Hopkins to study the slab. Neither was shone a complete picture, for security purposes, but each dated the etchings on the rock at one hundred years old. Minimum."

A long silenced followed. "Do you realize what you're saying?" asked Baker.

Kent didn't wait for a response. "How confident were these men in their findings?"

"As confident as they could be. Our time constraints left little choice. But, either way, the margin of error would've been small."

"Then," said Baker, "a portion of these dates were carved before they actually occurred."

"Yes," said McCoy. A pall of gravity descended upon the room. They'd expected a briefing, and a threat. But this was different.

"Too many questions to ask just one," said Kent. "Where does this take us?"

"Back in time."

"As agent McCoy said, I teach American History." They were in the kitchen now, Limon cradling a glass of sweet tea. No one else was thirsty. "Specifically, antebellum history."

McCoy sat beside the professor at a small table. Kent, like Baker, preferred to stand. They could see Craig's partner sniffing foliage on the other side of a screened back door. Kent had folded the paper list in his hands; it still felt like a time-bomb.

Limon took a pull from his liquid sugar and set the glass down. "I don't suppose either of you have ever heard the name 'Emile Delacroix?'"

Two head shakes.

"He was born in Marseilles in 1830, the son of a wealthy merchant. In his teens, at a family reunion of sorts, he met and became fast friends with a second cousin, Matthieu Delacroix. Matthieu was part of a prominent Creole family and heir to a plantation about sixty miles downriver from where we currently sit.

"The two of them exchanged several letters while progressing through school. They corresponded in English, the better to sharpen skills with a language that still seemed like something of a secret code among their relations.

"Emile's father wanted him to be a lawyer. It's unclear whether this was Emile's preference, but, either way, he convinced his father to accept a trade: his pursuit of the law for permission to accompany Matthieu on his Grand Tour through Europe, after which some extended sailing was planned."

Limon spoke with practiced calm and authority. After another drink, he continued. "That's all that's documented for the next fifteen years. It's assumed their trip was taken, but no correspondence exists to provide certainty. Then, as Sherman was torching his way through Georgia, Emile wrote to his cousins, requesting a stay at their plantation for a 'much needed respite.' Odd timing, but they accepted.

"By then New Orleans was under Union control. But Emile, a mere civilian, slipped through the blockade. He arrived at the mansion shortly after landfall. For five full days he did manage to rest. By the sixth, he was dead."

Kent and Baker perked up.

"This is where fact ends and theory begins," said Limon. "Several years ago, I was at a bookstore in the French Quarter and spotted a dusty hardcover. Inside was a letter, dated just after the turn of the century. It was written by Marie Delacroix, Emile's younger sister, and addressed to her daughter. She communicated her misgivings over her brother's death. The event had always held an air of dread and mystery, and had haunted her forever."

Limon exhaled. "I don't believe in destiny, but this was pushing it. It was my first encounter with the Delacroix family, and evolved into nearly two decades of private research."

McCoy shifted in his seat. "The tomb in question, inside St. Louis Cemetery, was owned for over a century by the Delacroix family." He pointed to Baker's copy of the list, laid out on the table. "We checked the burial records. The specific vault from which the slab was loosed was the final resting place of Emile Delacroix."

Baker stood in silence. Kent was starting to wonder if Limon had anything stronger than sweet tea. He held up the folded sheet. "Are you suggesting Emile Delacroix etched these dates?"

McCoy nodded.

"That would mean," said Baker, "that he was buried alive."

"Indeed," said Limon, taking back the reins.

"But…what does he have to do with these assassinations?" pursued Baker. "And why carve the dates at all? He would've been sealed in with fresh cement. He could have kicked his way out."

"Not if he was poisoned."

Kent and Baker stole a glance at one another.

"Emile didn't sail to America to visit his cousins," said Limon. "He was running from something. *Someone.*"

Kent's eyed narrowed. "You have proof of this?"

"Like I said, a theory. After discovering Marie Delacroix's letter, I made arrangements to visit her estate in Paris. It took two years of polite pleading, but I was granted access to her collected correspondence. My guise was as a common researcher, wanting to shed light on an overlooked pocket of history."

Limon's eyes glazed slightly. "Not altogether false, really. Afterword I tried publishing my findings. Professional journals, magazines—I was laughed out of every one. I'm something of a pariah in the academic community. Thank goodness for tenure."

He refocused. "But after seeing Marie's papers, I had no doubt: Emile was in fear for his life. Letters to Marie and Matthieu, diary entries from servants who'd overheard him in corridors. He was conscious of some kind of threat, veiled but acute. There were even a few pages from his own diary with cryptic terms like 'them' and 'our group'. It was as if he were attempting to extricate himself from some nefarious entity."

Limon straightened. "In point of fact, I believe that was exactly the case." He gestured to the folded sheet in Kent's hand. "All those dates, together, are more than a coincidence; someone is responsible for creating and carrying out that list. A cabal that's managed to remain intact and undetected for the past century and a half.

"I believe, too, that Emile Delacroix was a charter member. But before the first kill was arranged, he wanted out. Maybe it was a change of heart or cold feet. This wasn't, though, the kind of club you simply left. They followed him across an ocean, completely tying off the loose end."

"Except they didn't." Kent was beginning to see the picture, even if he didn't believe it. "You said poison?"

Limon nodded. "Hemlock, curare—impossible to know for sure. Among Marie's records there is the journal of a chambermaid at the Delacroix Plantation. It speaks of Emile, one night, falling unconscious. A short time later he stopped breathing."

"How would the poison have been administered?" asked Baker.

"There's no record of any foreign substance or drug in the notes and letters I've come across. While this could mean everyone chose to stay quiet on the subject, the more likely scenario is that none of them knew. I'm not a murder expert, but Emile's enemies clearly were. They could have infiltrated the plantation at night, or stalked him on the grounds. He may not have even known when he was poisoned."

"But then," said Baker, "how was he alive to carve the stone?"

"Every immune system is different. Toxins can have varying effects depending on the victim. There are accounts of a full burial ceremony for Emile, including his internment in the cemetery. I believe he was alive through it all and awoke inside the darkened vault."

Kent noticed McCoy had stayed quiet through all this, letting he and Baker judge the information themselves. He turned to Limon with a grin in his eyes. "You're about half a breath from a full-fledged ghost story, professor."

Limon, to his credit, returned the gesture. "I know. But, as incredible as it sounds, it's the most legitimate explanation. Imagine Emile breathing after he faints, but to such a slight degree that no one notices. He wakes after the burial and, feeling the poison inside him, knows he has minutes to live. With that precious time, he chooses to leave a message. The greatest miracle is that someone actually received it."

10

"So, Emile scrawls this message in the hopes of exposing his enemy." Kent, along with Baker, had now joined the other two at the table. "Where do we go from here?"

McCoy nodded toward each man's paper. "Flip your sheets over."

Both did so. There was more typed writing, but it wasn't a list. The words, instead, formed what looked like a short poem. The first line was set apart:

The End of the World

Baker looked up. "A riddle?"

"Yes," said McCoy. "Also carved on the inside of the tomb.

"Have you solved it?" asked Kent.

He turned to Limon. The professor cleared his throat. "I managed to gather a few leads from Marie Delacroix's collection. References to other individuals who might have had their own notes and letters. All were dead ends, save one: Ines Bonfils. She was still alive, in Toulouse. Her great-great-grandfather, Patrice Bonfils, was Emile Delacroix's personal valet.

"Ines's grandmother—Patrice's granddaughter—recorded a deathbed message he'd uttered. He said it was a secret, one he couldn't take to his grave.

"Evidently, soon after his arrival in Louisiana, Emile held a private conference with Patrice. He handed his servant a small, square stone and leather satchel. Carved on the stone was a message which Patrice was not to look at, for his own safety. Inside the satchel was a generous combination of gold coins, francs and stock certificates.

"Patrice was instructed to take the stone and hide it in a specific location, far away. Then, to use the money and vanish—start his own life wherever he wanted. And never think of his employer again."

Silence returned as Limon sat back and finished off his sweet tea. Kent could see more pieces falling into place. "So," he said, "Emile knew his time was short. They were coming for him."

"What was on the stone?" asked Baker.

Limon frowned. "Only an educated guess, but the most likely answer seems to be the name, or names, of his enemies. At the very least, a sure way to identify them."

Kent was skeptical. "Patrice didn't steal a peek at the stone? Even with his employer's cryptic behavior?"

"If so, he didn't say. Nor did he divulge its location. I guess his conscious was clear enough."

"Then this is a dead end," said Baker.

"Not quite." Beyond his façade of dry academia, Limon had a talent for narration. "It's my contention that Emile, as you said, knew his days were numbered. He wanted to pass the information he had on to Matthieu, the one person he trusted who also possessed enough influence to make a difference. But he couldn't simply tell him.

"His enemies were professionals with a long reach. If his life was already forfeit, relating the secret verbally would only endanger Matthieu's. The solution was to wait—three weeks, six months—whatever length of time necessary to draw away suspicion. By then he would be dead, but Matthieu could freely retrieve the stone and announce the truth.

"All that remained was to describe for his cousin the stone and its location. To accomplish this, he printed two notes: the first held the one-line riddle, the second a longer, more specific clue."

"Wait," said Baker. "Two different notes? And why riddles?"

"Because," said Limon, "once again, his enemies were powerful. They, too, had a vested interest in locating the stone. A simple note could be scanned or stolen. But what if it were presented in a language only one other person could understand?"

"You mean a riddle written specifically for Matthieu?"

Limon nodded. "They sailed the world together; that had to be good for an inside joke or two. The clues could lead Matthieu anywhere."

"Makes sense," said Kent. "But we're here talking to you today, so I can only assume he never found the stone."

"He never left New Orleans," said Limon. "The day before Emile died upriver, Matthieu was run down by a carriage in the center of Royal Street. It was dark; police deemed it an accident, despite the carriage driver insisting Matthieu had been pushed by someone in the shadows."

"So," said Baker, "Matthieu was tracked down and murdered by Emile's enemies."

Limon nodded. "Upon arriving, Emile received word that Matthieu was staying at the family's townhouse in the Quarter. To safeguard his cousin, he didn't contact him, instead proceeding directly to the plantation. It seems his pursuers, nevertheless, made the connection between the two of them."

"What about the notes?" said Kent.

At this the corners of Limon's mouth formed the slightest grin. "The cabal's one mistake. Minutes before his death, Matthieu had collected an envelope sent by courier from the plantation. This, ostensibly, is the reason he was killed; the letter was not found on his person after the incident."

"They suspected it was from Emile," said Kent.

"And they were right. But it was only the first clue: 'The End of the world.'

The second, longer description was sealed back at the plantation, awaiting Matthieu's arrival."

"What gave Emile the foresight to print two different notes?" asked Baker.

"Simple: he was a lawyer. Contingencies were his specialty."

"And both of those notes contained riddles that, together, point to the stone's location." Kent eyed the professor. "How?"

Limon nodded toward the sheet once more. "See for yourself."

Below the initial line lay a stanza of sorts:

Open your eyes

To a chapel alone

The Right Hand gives way

To crimson and stone

"I found it hidden in plain sight among Marie Delacroix's collection. Without the other note it's mere gibberish."

"Explain," said Baker.

McCoy fingered the paper. "The short clue refers to a general area; its longer counterpart pinpoints the exact location of the stone. They must be used together."

"You're saying," said Kent, "that 'The End of the World' is a place, not a time?"

"Actually, it's both," said Limon. "Five-hundred years ago, Europe comprised the bulk of western civilization. Such a concept had its terminus at a geographical point in southern Portugal. You can guess what the locals called it."

"*The end of the world*," whispered Baker.

"Today," said McCoy, "the site still holds a structure—Sagres Fortress—built by Henry the Navigator. It's an open-air museum, bounded on three sides by sixty-meter cliffs. With a small chapel at its center."

"How long did it take you to put all of this together?" asked Kent.

"Too long," said McCoy. "But we had no choice. And now we know: if the stone really exists, it's there."

"What makes you so sure?" asked Baker.

"Two dead cops."

"Portuguese?" said Kent after a moment.

McCoy nodded. "We couldn't afford to commit our own resources unless it was a legitimate threat. Instead, our station in Madrid made a request to police in Lagos, the nearest large town to the site. They were given minimal information—just the wording of the second riddle, enough to find the stone.

"A pair of officers visited the museum after-hours. Never came back." McCoy paused. "One of their bodies was found yesterday by a fishing boat along the coast. A male, his throat slit before hitting the water."

"Are you saying he was killed at the fort?" asked Baker. "And dumped over the cliff?"

"That's the most likely scenario."

"Who did the deed?"

"The same enemy that dispatched Emile and Matthieu a century and a half ago." Neither of his officers found the words to respond. McCoy continued. "Follow me for a minute: whoever this group is, they stole the note Matthieu was carrying, 'The End of the World.' Assuming they deciphered its meaning, they know the general location of the stone. But they never retrieved the second clue. And the one is worthless without the other. They could search forever and not even think to look in the chapel."

By now Baker had gathered himself. "So, our 'cabal' has been watching this spot—through the decades—just in case someone comes along searching for the stone?"

"They might only patrol the area in the days leading up to each assassination. Either way, this group's anonymity is its existence; the stone would wreck that. It's certainly a secret worth preserving."

Silence enveloped the room. "We're less than a week from the next assassination date," said McCoy. He flipped the sheet over, nodding toward its group of murdered leaders. "The world isn't any more stable than it was a hundred years ago; this list proves the power of a single bullet. We need you to follow the path meant for Matthieu Delacroix. Recover the stone, uncover this group."

"What about Portuguese intelligence?" said Kent. "Or Interpol?"

McCoy pointed down once more. "Have you noticed something about that list? There's no failure. Every date corresponds with a successful kill. We're not dealing with amateurs here. And we don't have time for more dead bodies."

McCoy stood, signaling the end of the meeting. Baker held up a hand. "One thing I don't understand: why didn't Emile just carve the name of this group on the tomb? It seems to follow that the only reason he wrote anything was because he knew of Matthieu's death and that his plan had backfired. What difference do clues make at that point?"

"It probably wasn't his decision," offered Limon. "The poison would have disoriented him to such a degree that he was unable to pivot cognitively. Writing in code was likely the last thing he'd thought of before losing consciousness the first time, and the only thing on his mind when he reawakened."

A moment later they were all standing. Kent folded his sheet back up and slid it in his pocket. "Two dead cops are a pair too many. But am I insensitive if I say this all still feels like a fairy tale?"

McCoy shook his head. "But the stakes are the same. We've only got one shot at a happy ending."

11

Twenty minutes later Kent and Baker were on the road back to Baton Rouge. McCoy stepped onto Limon's front porch, the surrounding humidity holding out against the shade and season. He stopped at the edge of the steps and lit a cigarette.

Craig met him from the bottom. "I thought you quit."

"So did I." McCoy blew out a puff of white. "What do they say, 'a drag a day keeps the ulcer away?'"

"Yeah, I think I heard that one from my gynecologist." Craig took a swig from a half-empty water bottle. "Feds call yet?"

"Just. They're on their way."

Limon was the only civilian with full knowledge of the threat. Fortunately, he understood his 'word' didn't constitute adequate assurance of his silence. A team of FBI agents were driving up from New Orleans. They'd disable his internet and phones, then babysit him until this whole thing was over. Easier than shipping him off to Guam or Alaska.

"I was starting to worry." Craig nodded back toward the house. "You were in there a while."

McCoy shook his head, exhaling a cloud of stress. "This whole thing's a field of cotton."

"I'm sorry?"

"A serious threat dressed up as a harmless game—and all the deadlier for it." He turned to Craig. "My granddad used to tell stories of when he was a boy. Dirt poor, picking cotton in Mississippi. You'd get out in the field and start pulling the stuff by hand. At first it was soft, white, almost pretty. But before you knew it, your hands were bleeding."

Baker kept the Malibu just below the speed limit, cruising down Highway 190 through the gathering twilight. Baton Rouge was ten miles away. From there they'd fly back to Hartsfield-Jackson, then nonstop to Lisbon. McCoy had supplied care packages of cash, encrypted phones and passports.

Kent fingered the navy leather enclosing his new identity: Evan Graves, junior executive with a shipping firm out of Vancouver. After visiting a client in Atlanta, it was off to Europe. He decided this would be Evan's first overseas business trip and readied a mask of nervousness. Baker, as a South African tourist, had just finished scouring the American South and snagged a great deal on the flight to Portugal. Earbuds and Bob Marley rounded out a convincing picture.

"You going to call her?" asked the Cape Town stand-in.

Kent nodded, but kept his phone limp in his hand. "Sometimes I wish I had your life: a different girl every night, nothing serious." His eyes glazed distantly. "No one to let down when the sun comes up."

"Is that how you think it is?" Baker produced a weary smile. "You're right—at first the freedom is fun. Soon, though, it starts to wear. Independence becomes anonymity, which becomes invisibility. You start to feel lonely in crowded rooms. Nobody wants to come home to an empty house, but after a while even it beats bringing back a stranger." He glanced at Kent. "You and Allison have something. What we do isn't for everyone, but she can handle it. I was in Europe too, remember?"

Kent slowly exhaled. "Yeah, I remember." He dialed Allison and brought the phone to his ear. Four rings later it went to voicemail. He forgot she was in the middle of a twelve-hour shift. Honestly, voicemail might be easier.

Her cheery voice made its way through the recorded greeting. *"...missed your call, but leave a message and I'll get back to you."*

Beep. "Hey, it's me. You've probably guessed by now, but...I'm not going to make the cruise. You'll have to make my excuses. Just use the story we rehearsed." He paused. "Words aren't good enough, I know, but right now they're all I have. If you get this in the next few hours, call me back. If not, it might be a while before we can talk.

"You know how this works, Ally; I can't tell you where I'm headed. But I promise, you'll be there with me. I love you."

12

Upon exiting Lisbon's Portela Airport, Kent squinted through the morning Portuguese sun and six hours of jet lag. Extra legroom might've helped with the latter, but first-class was too much exposure for he and Baker to spare. As it was, Evan Graves spent the flight jotting presentation notes in a folder and staring out at the Atlantic. Eight rows back, a certain African tourist had stayed busy charming his exchange-student neighbors.

Kent rolled his suitcase through the rank to a waiting taxi. "Carvalho Batista." His Portuguese was a bit rusty, which would do swimmingly for a timid Canadian. The driver took a moment to decipher the near-gibberish, then shifted his dated Mercedes into gear.

'Carvalho Batista' was a hardware store near Lisbon's downtown corridor. Portela lay a few miles to the north. The Benz, freeing itself from the airport's surrounding web of asphalt, gained Avenida Gago Coutinho and turned south. Kent rolled down his window to admit a soft breeze whistling in from the Tagus River. The day's temperature was set to reach sixty-five degrees—not bad for mid-December.

Allison had called back just after they'd landed in Atlanta. The conversation hadn't been easy. Per Baker's prediction, she'd taken the schedule change in stride. The tremor in her voice, though, was unmistakable. This amounted to more than an alteration of vacation plans. Kent knew, and could do nothing about it. She might've canceled the trip altogether if it hadn't been for the other two couples. As it was, Allison deserved the rest and might still find some. It felt like the faintest of silver-linings.

They finally turned right, then made another quick left. One more intersection put the Mercedes on Rua de Dona Estefania. Kent readied himself as the store came up on his right. The cabbie hadn't tried to gouge him on price, so he tipped well and was out the door a moment later.

Carvalho Batista was an average-sized European business, which meant it might've filled the paint department at Lowe's or Home Depot. Kent walked in, practiced some more Portuguese, and exited carrying a hand tiller, some rope, a hammer and a pair of flashlights.

He hadn't taken two steps when a forgettable gray hatchback braked against the curb. In stride, he tucked his belongings in the back, took a look around and slid up front beside Baker.

They were twisting their way north again when his new chauffeur glanced behind. "Garden utensils for a grappling hook." He shook his head. "Why do I feel like Abbot and Costello about to steal the crown jewels?"

"Life's a toolbox, Lou."

Twenty minutes later they'd crossed over the Vasco da Gamma Bridge—at ten and a half miles, Europe's longest span—and merged onto route E1. This time their destination was the Algarve, Portugal's southernmost region. It was a three-hour drive. Kent settled in.

Or tried to. A single question continued to gnaw at his psyche: who composed an assassination list without any victims? He kept coming back to one word: *power*. Regardless of the eventual targets, the dates themselves told the real story. Kent had a theory that each day had been chosen at random. He couldn't help picturing a room full of secret men, rolling dice from the shadows. What better way to declare authority over time and circumstance?

None of this, of course, addressed the greatest puzzle: why? He convinced himself there was little to be gained by searching for an answer. Looking madness in the eyes never led to clarity.

13

They reached Lagos just after 2 p.m. Sagres, the fortress's namesake, lay in prime position twenty miles west. But its population barely measured two thousand people. Lagos was ten times larger, the easier within which to disappear.

Baker dropped Kent a handful of blocks short of their destination, then pulled forward for another fifteen minutes of diversionary driving. The breeze had increased with the ocean just a few hundred feet away; to the left, the city's Old Town beckoned like a fresh postcard. Kent rolled his luggage north with the casual gait of a contented tourist. Lagos, a summer escape for many, retained a portion of its vibrancy even as winter closed in.

Ten minutes beneath the blue sky brought Kent to a building whose tiled roof seemed to reflect the matching sun. The Tivoli Hotel blended suitably with the rest of town, save a system of maze-like hallways that gave it the impression of three separate structures pressed into one. Technically a four-star, it was old enough to avoid anything more than a cursory glance from most passersby.

He checked in and used the elevator, which stopped at the second floor. From there a mini stairwell brought him to his room. Baker would shortly follow suit, in a different wing of the building. There was little else either of them could do until nightfall. It was almost like being back in the army. *Hurry up and wait.*

* * *

Ten o'clock had nearly struck by the time Baker exited the lobby, his stomach still digesting the remnants of room-service risotto. Above, the sun had given way to a star-filled sky, its crescent moon a mere ornament amidst the constellations. A pair of acoustic guitars could be heard around the corner as Lagos mustered up its best off-season nightlife.

He kept his gait casual, zipping a jacket against the growing breeze. Fifty yards later the hatchback materialized through the gloom. Baker pressed the fob and slid in behind the wheel. He started the engine, then waited, its modest cylinders eventually warming to the task. Finally, the passenger door opened and Kent, after another glance around, climbed in.

Soon they'd slipped Lagos's glow and were heading west along a pitch-black stretch of N125. Neither man said a word. Baker stole a look across at Kent, knowing he was thinking the same thing: could this actually be real? They were closing in on what amounted to the moment of truth.

The town of Vilo do Bispo came first, then a left turn onto N268 toward Sagres. The latter was just tucking itself in as they threaded its quaint streets, soon emerging onto a lonely roundabout that, even now, seemed to signal the end of civilization. Beyond lay a humble peninsula, draped in shadow and bracketed by a vast, growling Atlantic.

The wind gained bite. Baker fought to keep the hatchback steady through the dim. He'd already cut his headlights and now slowed as their target came into focus. The northern edge of *Fortaleza de Sagres* presented itself by way of a twenty-foot-high stone wall, complete with a walkway along its top edge. The fortification linked one cliff ledge to another. With the water so far below, defenders of the ancient stronghold needed only to fortify the land side. It may have been past its prime, but the barrier showed no signs of crumbling.

The road ended by curving left and back up the way it'd come. Baker traced the asphalt, drifting about a hundred meters away from the wall before pulling to the shoulder. He shut off the engine. All they heard was the wind, howling through the door seams like a banshee on patrol.

They both exited. Baker gripped a flashlight, feeling naked without his gun; Kent removed the tools they'd purchased that afternoon from a small pack slung over his shoulder. He'd spent the drive from Lagos hammering the metal prongs of the tiller farther apart and fastening the rope to its handle. Mountaineering equipment would've been better, but a Lisbon shop owner was less likely to remember a casual green thumb than someone gearing up for the Pyrenees.

They reached the end of the road and stepped onto a footpath leading toward the center of the wall. It terminated at an entryway barred by a large door. Too heavy to force open, with a lock too thick to pick.

They broke off toward the wall. For the tenth time Baker checked behind, again finding no tail. Wading through a mixture of dirt and tall grass, they stopped mere feet from the barricade. The cloudless sky above provided just enough illumination to forego the flashlight.

Kent began swinging the rope. Despite himself, Baker suppressed a laugh. Had it really come to this?

Only has to work once.

Releasing the strand on its upswing, Kent watched the metal claw scale the stone expanse like a bird chasing freedom. It disappeared over the ledge, clattering to the floor high above. Then a gentle pull on the rope. Too much give. They heard the spiked head scrape against stone, a second later toppling over the wall. They had to step aside as it thudded into the ground, releasing a cloud of dirt.

Both men glanced at one another. *Go again.* It seemed they had all night. Kent retrieved the tiller and started swinging. Baker glanced around: still deserted, the soft glow of Sagres lining the horizon. The only other sign of life was a lighthouse on a neighboring cape three miles distant.

He heard the claw hit again and spun back. This time there was only a second of scraping before the prongs caught on one of the ramparts. Kent gave it several tugs, making sure. There was no give.

He began to climb. The spikes held. Soon he was a silhouette against the navy sky, shrinking with each tug upward. The wind attacked again, its chilled bursts slowing his progress. But then he was over.

After a quick look around, he waved Baker up. The latter began ascending. He kept a tight grip on the hemp, legs squeezing from below. It was a little awkward, but smooth enough. Baker resisted the urge to spy over the cliff edge toward the midnight waves below. Instead, nearly at the top, he focused on placing one hand over the oth—

Snap.

Kent was over the wall in the same instant, gripping Baker's forearm just as the claw—one of its spikes clearly severed—clattered past the rampart and disappeared into the night below. Baker felt his heart swell into his throat.

"I've got you," grunted Kent.

Perspiration came all at once, wetting his back, threatening his grip. Baker swallowed the pounding down and planted his feet against the sheer face of the wall. One big pull from both of them and he was hooking his leg over the ledge. They collapsed onto the stone floor, panting. Eventually Baker spotted the severed spike and held it up. A clean break.

"No more risotto for you," said Kent.

Baker grinned, handing over the steel remnant. "A memento."

Kent stuffed the tool piece in his jacket and they stood. Part of the walkway sloped down the other side of the wall. Beyond lay several acres of open ground. Interrupting the shrub-covered expanse was a sparse collection of man-made structures: a pair of modern exhibit halls, an auditorium, another lighthouse in the distance. And a chapel.

Kent led the way. They were descending the ramp when Baker shook his head. "One thing I still don't get: why kill the cops? If you don't have the specific location of the stone, wouldn't the goal be to let them find it first, then move in?"

"Maybe that's what happened, and we're already too late," said Kent. "Then again, circumstances dictate action. Maybe the environment wasn't right to let the cops make the discovery. If they do, and some accident keeps you from intercepting, they go free and your secret is out. Forever."

They neared the chapel, *Nossa Senhora da Graca*—Our Lady of Grace. Its whitewashed sides paired well with the salt they tasted on the stiff breeze. The front door was unlocked—no reason for a latch with a twenty-foot wall standing guard. It creaked open and they strode inside.

'Simple' was an overstatement. Benches ran across the entire width of the church, which couldn't have been more than thirty feet. Faint patches of moonlight wafted through windows on either side. The building's stucco walls led, inevitably, to a carved archway and the altar beyond. Sitting atop the latter's tile base, nearly filling the space, was a gilded retable.

Kent pulled out his own flashlight and both men trained beams on the far end. *The Right Hand gives way / To crimson and stone.* With their subject in view, each word held a new ring.

They started forward. "Think the altar's the focal point?" asked Baker

"Has to be," said Kent, looking around. "There's nothing else here."

They reached the retable. "'The Right Hand,'" said Baker. "It's capitalized. Jesus?"

Kent was nodding.

"But what does that tell us? Just what we already know—that the altar is the target?" Baker studied the floor and walls. "I don't see much crimson. Or stone, for that matter."

"The *Right* Hand," said Kent, turning to Baker. "What if it's a double meaning?"

"You mean literally to the right?"

"Yes." Kent arced his flashlight toward the base of the back wall, just to the side of the retable. After a step forward, he stopped. The only thing there was white stucco. This brought the church to a whisper, each second of silence threatening to erase what little momentum they'd built.

"Wait," said Baker, taking the lead. "What if it's *in* the wall?"

"You mean behind the stucco?" Kent ran his hand across the smooth surface. "I think that might be giving the valet a little too much credit."

"It's the only logical explanation. Maybe he realized the best way to keep the stone safe was to conceal it, paid a local for help with the masonry."

Kent was silent, processing Baker's theory. Suddenly he spun around and walked back through the archway.

"What are you doing?"

"Getting help." Seconds later he returned, hefting a two-foot statue of St. Francis of Assisi.

"You know how old that thing is?"

They both bent down. "I know if Frankie were alive," said Kent, "he'd want to be put to good use."

Baker moved a small chair out of the way. Kent wasted no time, ramming the statue—crown first—into the wall. It hit with a dense thud. Francis emerged intact, but the stucco sustained a large crack at the point of impact. Kent swung again, then a third time. Each collision sounded with the baritone of an avalanche. Baker reminded himself that there wasn't another soul for half a mile.

By now the gap in the wall had widened and caved. In fact, there seemed to be some clearance between the stucco and whatever lay behind. Kent hit it again, then again. He leaned back, grunting out short breaths.

"You want me to take over?" asked Baker, feeling inadequate with a mere flashlight in his hands.

Kent shrugged it off and continued a moment later. Two more minutes did the trick. After the smoke cleared, St. Francis sported a hairline fracture, but had easily won the battle. A rough rectangle, about the size of a serving tray, had been carved from the white surface. Kent retrieved his own flashlight and they both lit the void beyond.

It looked like...*stone*. Old, but intact. A second later Baker leaned forward. One of the rocks—maybe six inches square—wore the fleeting remnants of red paint. He reached toward it, heart back to pounding.

It wouldn't move. Kent quickly grabbed a candlestick from the retable and handed it down. Baker wedged the new tool into a crevice between the crimson stone and its neighbor. Flipping his flashlight around, he began hammering the butt down on the candlestick. The stone slowly began to shift, then finally slid free.

It fell at their feet, rock smacking tile and echoing through the deserted space. Each man shone his beam on the sound. Instead of a solid stone they found a hollow pocket—an ancient safety-deposit box—with a smaller tablet resting inside. Baker carefully, almost reverently, fished it out.

Before looking, both men mechanically strobed the chapel. Still empty. They turned their illumination back to the prize and…stared, confusion tickling their eyebrows. Kent glanced across at Baker, who flipped the rock over. Same result.

Black thunder rumbled in Baker's stomach. "You don't think…?"

"I don't know," said Kent.

It wasn't the answer either of them wanted. Forcing himself to take a deep breath, Baker slowly moved his eyes from the high ceiling down the walls. For the first time he noticed the windows had no glass. Just openings, relatively small, set deep within the thick façade. He turned back to the stone.

A loud thud to the left instantly diverted his attention. Something small and hard—maybe a rock—had hit one of the pews. Baker felt himself stiffen and sensed Kent do the same.

It was too late, and not nearly enough.

In the half-second each of them was locked on the left side of the chapel, a large figure leapt through the near window. Baker had never seen someone so big move so easily. The intruder—every bit of six-and-a-half feet—lunged toward the two of them. Both men only had time to react.

Kent pushed Baker back. The blade was out already, glinting bright in the entrant's right hand. He arced it toward Kent's exposed throat. Everything happened at lightspeed. The man's reach was too long. Steel split epidermis like butter, spraying red across the chapel floor. Kent toppled limply to the ground.

Baker froze, then realized he was about to join him. The only move was retreat. His attacker thrust forward, feigning a jab with the red-stained blade before countering with a left hook to the kidney.

Contact was solid. Baker's side blazed in pain, but he managed to minimize it by sliding with the momentum of the punch. This provided enough of an angle to strip the knife from the man's hand and, in the same motion, jam it into his thigh. His opponent merely grunted, left the knife in his leg and swung forward with a heavy fist. Baker, off-balance from his own futile attack, took it in the same throbbing kidney. He doubled over, then was thrown back to the wall by an uppercut.

His vision blurred, fresh blood pooling from both nostrils. He somehow managed to parry the next blow, but was tripped up a second later. The floor came fast. So did a boot to his ribcage, then another. He felt several cracks, even heard one. The knife was still in place, a forgotten nuisance.

The man brought his other leg up and stomped on Baker's exposed torso. Once, twice, a third time. Now he did remove the knife, its tainted steel glinting in the moonlight that shone through the windows. He flipped the hilt down, the better to finish the job.

Baker thought he might pass out before the dagger entered his chest. Just as darkness edged his vision, he saw a shadow flutter behind the intruder. An instant later a figure pushed off from one of the pews and rammed something sharp through the assailant's right temple.

Then everything went black.

14

Kent watched the giant fall, the broken tiller prong still protruding from the man's skull. He half-expected him to jump back up for Round Two. No dice. By the time the body hit the ground, it was a corpse.

Kent felt his neck: wet, and still leaking. But not heavily. Both carotid arteries were safe, which meant he'd stretched back just enough at the slash.

Five feet away, Baker had faded into unconsciousness. Kent leapt across and slapped him in the face. "Jim!" No response. He jabbed a finger into his friend's neck. After five seconds of despair, a faint pulse materialized. It seemed to match Baker's bloodied face, though the bleeding Kent couldn't see was what worried him most.

No one would be here for hours, yet the countdown in his head still chimed zero. Time to go. Before moving, he tore a strip of fabric from his undershirt and tied it around his neck. Then he tucked the stone, and their flashlights, into the pack he'd brought. This prompted thoughts about removing the knife. But what did it matter when a dead man lay in the center of the space? Francis's head and the hole in the wall could be explained by vandalism. Everything else, right now, was beyond his control.

Kent turned toward Baker when he noticed a flash on the tile to his right. Stepping closer revealed a phone, which could only belong to their attacker. He gripped the device and keyed its 'home' button. A bright screen flashed, then reverted to a password request. After a second's deliberation, he gave up and stowed it as well.

Each second grew louder as it slipped by. He bent toward Baker, hearing breaths that had become strained. Kent quickly angled his arms under the limp legs and torso, then lifted. He managed to muscle the dead weight into midair, slinging it over his right shoulder.

Kent felt the strain on his quads, his own breathing little better than Baker's. Soon, though, he steadied and began trudging toward the door of the chapel. Without a look back he stepped outside, the plane's telltale breeze mercifully cool on his skin.

He grunted his cargo across fifty yards of open landscape. There was still a possibility of more attackers, but Kent doubted it. They'd have been close enough to lend the first man aid if his ambush had gone awry. As it was, all that stood between him and a chance to save Baker's life was a twenty-foot-high stone wall.

They weren't leaving the same way they came in. Bypassing the stone ramp, he instead veered toward a heavy wooden door cut into the rock. Kent softly laid Baker down, careful to shield both of their faces from a surveillance camera mounted above the entryway. He then tried the handle. Locked. The wind continued to attack in furious bursts, chilling the fresh sweat on his skin.

Every option of egress raced through his mind, but was just as quickly dismissed. This was their only plausible exit. He was about to kick the door when he realized his boot would be no match for the thick wood. He needed…help.

He darted back to the chapel and retrieved St. Francis. The return trip took a bit longer cradling the dense statue. Upon arrival, Kent thought Baker had stopped breathing. It took leaning in close to hear each labored wheeze.

Bang. Francis held steady, but so did the door. Kent felt his arms burning and set the statue down. For thirty seconds there was nothing to do but breathe himself, mind splitting time between expectations of hope and failure.

He swung again. Same result. This barrier seemed ten times more solid than the chapel wall they'd just broken through. But he continued. Three blows, then six, then a dozen more. Kent dropped to his knees again, lungs heaving in the dry air. Two minutes of solid hammering had netted him dents and cracks in the wood, but no hole. He was trying to picture how thick the door really was when he realized he didn't actually have to break through, only bust the lock behind.

Lugging the statue off the ground, Kent attacked the partition again, this time focusing his efforts just above the handle. Francis, God love him, held together, headbutting the wood with penitent gusto.

At last, the barrier croaked and slid back an inch. Kent, his clothes now drenched in sweat, sent one last fusillade of energy toward his target. There was a muffled crack, then the door swung inward, revealing a pitch-black interior. He wasted no time, whispering thanks to a power much higher than Francis before dropping the statue and reaching for Baker.

He soon had the body over his shoulder and a flashlight at his hip. The artificial beam cut through the gloom in a conical arc, revealing a spare reception area and hallway to the left. He followed it, the weight on his frame tempered by a fresh boost of adrenaline. At the end of the hallway another door loomed. It was just as large, but they were inside: all Kent had to do was turn its lock.

He did, and stepped onto the pathway at the front of the fort. The moon-lit expanse before him was a shade lighter than the hallway, and in the distance, he could just make out the hatchback. There was still no one else around; their enemy had clearly been alone.

He concentrated on putting one foot in front of the other, wanting to break into a jog even as his shoulder started going numb. The car gained greater definition until, finally, they reached its back bumper. Kent leaned Baker against the passenger side, opened the door and dropped him into the front seat. Then he tossed the pack in the back and raced around to the steering wheel. Seconds later they were speeding into the night.

15

They'd just passed north of Sagres when Kent caught his breath enough to make a call. McCoy answered after one ring. "Do you have it?"

"The stone, yes. An address, no. Jim is injured, badly."

"You had company?"

"A plus-sized ninja. Six-six, two-thirty, at least. Jim's unconscious. I can't revive him. Could be internal bleeding."

There was a short pause. Kent could almost hear McCoy's brain juggling each incoming piece of data. "Has the threat been neutralized?"

"Completely. But the scene needs cleaning."

"You can't?"

"Not with that corpse. I had a hard-enough time dragging Jim to the car. Besides, I don't think he has much time."

Another pause. "Tell me about the stone."

"It seems to detail another location, probably for the next stone."

"The *next* stone? That's not possible."

"Well, then, I've got impossible weighing down my jacket pocket. General clue on one side, specific on the other."

"That means…the valet hid multiple stones."

"Or Delacroix enlisted multiple couriers."

"I don't like either scenario."

"Join the club. The next date on the list is in four days; if these clues create too long of a trail, we'll never reach the end in time."

"Why more than one stone?" asked McCoy, thinking out loud.

Kent held concern for the fragile life beside him, but the mystery in question mattered just as much. "It could be another of Emile's contingencies. If both initial notes were stolen by his enemies, they might decipher the first location…"

"But several would be a stretch," finished McCoy. "The first location, though, is all you'd need. Remove the stone from Portugal and the path dries up. Their secret would be safe."

"Unless Emile provided a back door for Matthieu to pick up the scent."

"A door we don't have. How much of a stretch are we talking about?"

Kent had already memorized the stone in his pocket. "Marry Jack Home."

"*Marry Jack Home*," repeated McCoy, surely transcribing the general clue. "Any ideas?"

"Not a one. I wish I could say the second half helps, but I don't see it."

"Give it to me."

"Hero of the Sea, long deceased, bow at the top, where north meets east."

McCoy paused for a third time. Kent wondered if it was to finish writing, or to fully digest the mountain they were now facing. Finally, he continued his impromptu debriefing. "What about the identity of your attacker?"

"A no-go. Pockets were empty. Caucasian, late twenties to early thirties, blonde hair. Beyond that, there's only his phone. The screen is password protected."

"Understood. Where are you right now?"

"Heading north on N268, just short of Vila do Bispo." Another village asleep for the night. Kent pushed the hatchback as fast as discretion would allow. "We've got one more day on the books at the Tivoli in Lagos, but no ID in the rooms."

"Good. Stay on your current track. I'll call back in ten with more direction."

"Right."

"And Jeremy?"

"Yeah?"

"Well done."

Kent glanced across at Baker. "Keep reminding me, will you?"

Nearly ten minutes later, the hatchback pierced the approaching darkness north of Carrapateira. Kent considered trading his two-lane track for the speed of an open freeway, but the A2 lay a full twenty miles east. It would also have a greater police presence. The last thing he needed was some eager patrolman catching a glimpse of the passenger seat, even if Baker—in the right light— might pass for merely plastered.

The asphalt tributary he occupied was shrouded, mostly, in a tunnel of foliage. Branches from separate trees kissed one another through the gloom above. There were, however, occasional breaks in the undergrowth. Open fields stretched the horizon beyond, their normally-brown expanse tinged a weak silver beneath the cloudless sky.

For the first time he allowed his mind to wander back to the fort. McCoy had been right in Louisiana: they weren't up against amateurs. All that check- ing for a tail—how had he and Baker missed the threat? Whatever the answer, their intruder's combat skills matched his stealth. He'd clearly had training in both—if not state-sponsored, then some lethal approximation.

Kent now pressed the pedal to the floor. There was little chance of detec- tion in the rural space between the last town and the next village. He hadn't seen another pair of headlights in ten miles.

Why, then, was he still gripping the steering wheel with ivory knuckles? Perhaps for the same reason he found it harder and harder to glance toward the body in the passenger seat. As if each turn of the head would capture the moment it became a corpse.

It shouldn't have mattered that much. He and Baker were professionals. You respected one another, even formed a bond, but never allowed such attachment to compromise an operation.

That, though, was on paper. Reality wrote a different story. The two of them were friends—brothers. They could cut up with the best, but many were the nights they'd also gone late discussing everything from politics to philosophy. In the rare moments he'd dreamed of a future wedding, Kent hadn't, until recently, had a particular bride in mind. He'd always known who the best man would be.

His cell buzzed. "Yes."

"We're tracking your phone," said McCoy. "Keep heading north. There's a safe house an hour beyond Lisbon. I'll text you the address. Station Chief in Madrid will meet you there. He'll have equipment and a doctor."

Kent finally stole another look at Baker. "It'll be long after midnight before we arrive. He may not make it."

"It's the best we can do."

Kent knew better than to protest. There weren't many options here. A hospital might be closer, but, even if their passports held up, meant an unacceptable level of scrutiny. Baker would either survive the next three hours or he wouldn't.

McCoy exhaled over the line, as if to offer some reassurance. None came. This wasn't the realm of pep talks. Kent, himself, could only find the simplest of phrases. "Thank you, Pete."

"Just call me when you get there."

They both hung up. All that was left to do now was drive. And pray.

16

Almost there. The past three hours had felt like as many days. But Baker was still breathing.

Kent could no longer see the lights of Lisbon in his rearview, and was glad to be free of them. Avoiding the city's relative congestion would've been preferable, but detouring to the east might've added another hour onto the trip. Time his friend didn't have. As it was, they'd managed to evade notice and were now jostling down a dirt path, its narrow width hugged on both sides by barren fig trees.

Curving to the right seconds later, Kent found a break through the bark and spotted a distant house. Its worn tile roof gleamed in the faint starlight. He maintained his speed. Meters fell by, the structure beginning to take shape.

It was a humble ranch—maybe a thousand square feet—wrapped in a weathered mixture of stucco and cement. Now Kent did slow, just slightly, as the car neared a short gravel drive. The details of his and Baker's trip had been set; McCoy was aware of their vehicle's make and model and had surely passed the information on. Still, Kent knew a gun or two would be watching from the shadows.

He pulled off the road and into what was actually more of a miniature parking lot than a driveway. An SUV and van rested near the front of the house, a dusty Citroen off to the side. The moment Kent rolled to a stop a man exited the front door and strode toward the hatchback.

He was short, young—mid-twenties—with curly hair and the skin of a local. Kent had cut the engine and met the newcomer around the passenger side. "You must be Jeremy Kent," said the man, offering a curt hand. Kent accepted with a nod. "Jose Santos." He reached for Baker's door. "Any update on his condition?"

Kent reached past to remove the seatbelt. "His breathing's weakened, but still constant."

The man reached for Baker's legs. "Doc's inside."

Kent slipped his arms beneath his friend's shoulders and lifted the dead weight. The entrance wasn't far. They shuffled across the rock beneath the glow of a modest porchlight. A trio of concrete steps led to the door. Kent took the first with a grunt. "You the resident?"

Santos nodded. "The past six months. It's been quiet until tonight."

In the next moment they crossed the threshold, held open by another stranger. Caucasian, jacket and slacks, pistol hidden along his waist. Kent heard the door close behind as they moved into a tiled living room. Beyond, beside a small kitchen, what had probably been a dining room glowed bright and clean under white lights. A middle-aged man in a white button-down shirt, sleeves rolled up, waited beside an apparent assistant, similarly dressed. Behind them lay a cot and array of medical machinery.

They needed no direction. He and Santos crossed to the bed and set Baker down on its soft linen. Without a word the man up front nodded and turned toward his new patient. His protégé then closed a curtain rigged to the ceiling, effectively sealing off the makeshift operating room. Kent wondered why an unconscious patient needed such a barrier, then realized it wasn't for the patient.

The room was sparsely furnished: a leather sofa, pair of wicker chairs, floral sketches hanging in sanded cork frames. Kent stepped around a glass coffee table and locked eyes with the man by the door. Should he introduce himself? *This isn't exactly a cocktail party.* Just as the silence was beginning to turn awkward, footsteps echoed down a hallway to the left.

The figure dragging them was an immediate presence; Kent easily pegged him as the station chief. He was black, built like a linebacker, but wearing a pristine blazer. He extended a thick hand. "Perry Briggs, COS Madrid."

Kent accepted and introduced himself.

"I was sent the details through e-mail," said Briggs. "You look just like your photo, minus the blood and stubble."

"Thank Pete McCoy. I hope his call didn't wake you."

"McCoy? Try Vanning. I was in the middle of a nice cabernet. No one at the Agency outranks a glass of wine, but the Director's an exception." He gazed directly at Kent. "Why did I just send two good officers down to Sagres to remove a body?"

"If Vanning didn't say, you know I can't."

"Good. Because if this whole thing isn't Top Secret, it's too much trouble." Briggs gestured toward the curtain. "What are his chances?"

"Better than they were five minutes ago. Thanks for setting up so quick."

"It was easier than I expected. Doc's a friend; he can keep a secret. The equipment was simple with his help."

"What about his assistant?"

"One of my guys, came from the Army. Three tours as a medic in Afghanistan."

Kent gazed at the curtain. Low voices drifted through, but weren't clear enough to understand. He could hear clothes rustling on the other side. Fast, controlled movements. He was reminded that this might be the critical moment: in the next few gulps of silence, Baker's fate could be sealed, one way or another.

"*Okay…nasty…cleaned…*"

He turned back to Briggs. "What?"

"I was asking if you were okay." The COS nodded toward Kent's throat. "That's a nasty cut. We'll get it cleaned."

Kent reached up involuntarily for his jugular. He'd removed the strip of fabric on the drive over to find the wound had clotted dry. Now all his fingers felt was a crusted ridge, maroon—maybe black—against his hairy neck. "It was a knife…looks worse than it is. I honestly don't know how it missed an artery."

"Life's a game of millimeters, right?" Briggs paused as the front door swung open. A new face stepped through. From the look of him, another officer.

"We're clear outside," said the entrant.

"Luis posted?" asked the COS.

A nod.

"Thanks Jack." Briggs turned back to Kent. "This gets me nervous. We've just given that dirt track more traffic than it sees in a week."

"How long are you staying?"

"A few more hours, at least. Boss's orders." Briggs clamped a mitt onto Kent's shoulder. It would've felt trite from someone with less inherent authority. "Forget how that sounds, though. We're happy to be here."

Kent nodded in understanding. "That makes one of us."

Briggs grinned slightly, then straightened. "I was told to retrieve a phone from you."

Kent reached inside his jacket and pulled out their assailant's cell. "It going all the way to Langley?"

"Yep, and fast. Diplomatic pouch. Courier will pick it up from the embassy in Lisbon the moment I get it there." Briggs fingered the device. "Guess they're not after pictures of the Portuguese countryside."

"For all we know that could be it. Worth a shot, though."

The COS stowed the phone and pointed toward the curtain. "This could be a while. You want some sleep? There's a spare bedroom."

Kent shook his head. "I'd never make it that far. Not while he's still under."

"Fair enough. How about something to eat?"

"You got any coffee?"

Briggs nodded to Santos, who was already walking toward the kitchen.

Despite the caffeine, time made a liar out of Kent. He lounged asleep at the end of the sofa, head back, feet on the coffee table. Stress and fatigue had hijacked his consciousness the moment he closed his eyes. Now, though, he jolted awake as the curtain snapped open.

How long had he been out? He checked his watch: an hour. The house was quiet. Briggs, he remembered, had gone down the hall; he could hear typing on a laptop. Santos sat forward on the far side of the couch, flipping idly through a magazine as if this really were some kind of waiting room. Across, in one of the wicker chairs, sat a man he didn't recognize. *Luis.* Jack must've taken the next shift outside. Beside him sat the doorman, who'd earlier introduced himself as Bruce.

The doctor stepped forward and they all stood. Kent spotted the medic behind him, too, but focused most of his attention on Baker: still prone on the cot, eyes closed. The telemetry near his head continued to blink, its hollow, forlorn beeps sounding off the tile like the plea of some junkyard droid from *Star Wars.*

The other men deferred to Kent, who faced the doctor. The medical man's expression was inscrutable. Briggs strode from the hallway and split the crowd, stopping beside Kent.

For a second no one said anything. Then, finally, the doctor took a breath. "He's alive. We made a few incisions, managed to stop the bleeding. But he's lost a lot of blood, and…"

"And what?" asked Briggs.

"I can't induce consciousness."

More quiet. It didn't take long to understand. "A coma," said Kent.

The doctor nodded, empathy creasing his face. "I'm sorry. But he's stable. We've got him on an IV for fluids and nutrients. With proper rest, he'll have a chance."

Kent had seen the size of their attacker, heard the blows delivered to Baker's midsection; 'chance' was overwhelming victory, no matter how much he hated this moment. He forced his hand forward, grasping the doc's. "Thank you."

The man accepted with an eye toward Briggs. "I'm not quite finished. Need to clean up, run a few tests."

The COS nodded, and like that the conference ended. Each officer stepped back. Briggs turned to Kent. "You okay?"

Kent stole a glimpse at Baker. "We play the cards we're dealt. It's the job."

"It's the *life*. No halfway in this world."

Kent nodded, wishing the words weren't so easy to believe. The man on the cot, if nothing else, was a professional; he knew the game. What of the woman back in Atlanta—had she chosen this life? In a way, yes—she'd chosen him. Still, it didn't seem fair. What if it were her in that bed?

Kent reached into his pocket, forgetting the ring was no longer there. He'd left it with McCoy. It was too much of a risk to his cover. *You left the engagement ring with your agency handler.* If that didn't just say it.

17

Dawn came with a whisper. Kent didn't notice until shafts of orange light pierced the front door's glass cutout, grazing his vision and pulling him from a much more comfortable world. He'd been sleeping again, this time sprawled across the length of the sofa. The only sound came from the ticking of a nearby wall clock; his only immediate company was Baker, still unconscious.

He eyed the clock: 8:15. Sitting up, he rubbed his eyes, digesting the last few hours. Briggs had left with Jack and Luis around 4:30; there wasn't much more they could do. Bruce took the doctor home about an hour later. Better to avoid missing a hospital shift at the last minute, raising eyebrows. The medic, currently napping, would stay another full day to finish running tests on Baker.

That left Santos, who came striding in from the kitchen carrying two steaming mugs of coffee. He set one of them on the table in front of Kent and claimed a chair opposite. He paused from drinking his own cup to answer the look in Kent's eyes. "I heard you stir. The pot's fresh."

Kent was on the ragged edge, his additional sleep a mere blink of relief. Yet he took an indulgent whiff of the beans before diving into the hot liquid. "Was that part of your agency training—to know who needed coffee?"

Santos finished another sip and looked around. "Sometimes I might as well be an intern here. I wasn't kidding about the inactivity."

Kent nodded, still groggy. "Sorry, this is where I'm supposed to say something about staying the course, that you're important. Give me a few minutes."

Santos waved him off. "I'll make it worth my while. Maybe start running coke out of this place. Hide it in the coffee grounds."

"Now you're thinking. Shows initiative. Langley'd be impressed." Kent took another drink. Outside, a wren's serenade made the morning official. He chose not to dwell on the maddening absurdity of easing into such a beautiful day while his closest friend clung to life twelve feet away. "So," he said, searching instead for a question, "you from down the road or across the globe?"

Santos exhaled. "A bit of both, I guess. Parents were born in Sao Paulo, moved north just after getting married to help my great uncle run a café in the Bronx. Five years later they bought the place from him."

Kent managed a grin. "Which means our intrepid agent-to-be cut his teeth waiting tables."

"And pouring coffee."

"Some skills never die."

Santos paused. "What about you?"

"I'm about as bland as they come."

"Not based on last night."

Last night. It was already history. Kent absently fingered the fresh stitches on his neck. Santos pointed to the spot. "Doc did a nice job. You can hardly see them."

"I still feel a bit like Frankenstein."

"At least you're not seven feet tall."

"Never thought I'd have that going for me."

Santos drained the rest of his mug. "Does that mean you'll be leaving here in broad daylight?"

"If only I knew." Kent had rolled the clues around in his head every free second and come up empty. A few hours back he'd checked in with McCoy, who'd already consulted Limon: same result.

He heard the wall clock, each tick of its second-hand feeling like an hour off their schedule. An extended delay simply wasn't possible. They needed help.

He eyed Santos, preparing to violate several decades worth of carefully cultivated security protocol. "Jose?"

Santos had been studying Baker, but now looked back. "Yes?"

"What if I told you I had to solve a riddle, written by a Frenchman over one hundred and fifty years ago, referring to a specific location somewhere in the world."

"I'd say the CIA isn't quite what I thought it was."

Kent didn't laugh. "Marry Jack Home."

Santos cleared his throat, sobering. "That's the riddle—Marry Jack Home?"

Kent nodded.

"'Mary' as in the name, or the ceremony?"

"Ceremony." Kent stared into his mug, the remaining liquid offering up a bitter aroma. "I've racked my brain for a prodigal 'Jack.' Still don't know what it means to marry someone home."

Santos hesitated. "Is this some kind of game?"

Kent shook his head. "As real as it gets."

Santos went quiet, started to speak, then stopped. He leaned back in his chair, defeat already starting to play at the corner of his eyes. Kent knew the look, and the feeling. There was just so little to go on.

This isn't supposed to be easy. Right. For anyone other than Matthieu Delacroix, the entire line of code was actually designed to be uncrackable. It felt like trying to follow a trail of breadcrumbs that'd disintegrated ages ago.

They sat in silence. Ten minutes ticked by. Twenty. The wren continued its song, cadence now mocking the notion of a quick solution. They could be here for weeks—longer—and not get any further than they were right now.

Santos stood, raising his mug. "You want another? My brain needs a jolt."

Kent shook his head.

The younger man began shuffling toward the kitchen, then flashed a sour smile. "At least we're failing together. The sad unity of brilliant minds."

Something tickled the back of Kent's brain. "What did you say?"

"Well, I was being generous with the word 'brilliant.' I certainly wouldn't put myself—"

"No," said Kent, moving to the edge of the sofa. "Before that. *Right* before that."

Santos mentally recycled the phrase. "A sad unity?"

"*Unity*," repeated Kent. "Like 'union.' A word for coming together, maybe even during a ceremony." He looked up. "Marry Jack."

Santos completed the puzzle. "*Union* Jack."

Kent stood up, traces of adrenaline beginning to oil his tired bones. "The UK." He substituted this into the rest of the riddle. "United Kingdom Home." It was like a devilish form of algebra.

Santos stepped forward. "You said this riddle was written a hundred and fifty years ago. I'm a little rusty on my nineteenth-century British history—are we sure the phrase 'union jack' existed then?"

It was a good question. Kent didn't know either, and pulled out his phone. A moment later he was nodding. "We're clear by at least a century." He rolled the new words around in his head again. *United Kingdom Home.* Pangs of elation continued to fire, but already a looming wave of fear threatened to douse them. They'd had a breakthrough—now what? The phrase was still a mystery.

"What does 'home' mean, then?" asked Santos, forgetting his refill and sitting back down. "The home of the UK? That would have to be the capital. London."

It made sense, but didn't fit. "No," said Kent, before he really knew why he was saying it. He felt like he had enough of a handle on what the answer wasn't. Something about London would've been too direct. He sat down too.

This stage was more complex than the first. 'The End of the World' had been a simple phrase; its elusiveness lay in the misdirection, and mundane nature, of its wording. No proper nouns, but once you realized it referred to a place instead of a time you were nearly there.

'Marry Jack Home' was completely different, a true cypher. He saw now that the words were never meant to run together. At least, not the original words. 'Jack' had only worked when 'Marry' changed to 'Union,' and even then, they were simply a gateway to 'United Kingdom.' Every code had a key; for the text before them, it was substitution. "'Home' doesn't refer to England," he said. "It's something else."

But what? An actual house? Some figurative finish line or representative building? Kent couldn't tell if taking each word separately was any easier than attacking the phrase as a whole.

More minutes passed. The wren, and wall clock, were on the verge of further fraying his nerves when Santos's gaze suddenly widened. "France."

Kent looked up. "What?"

"You said the riddle's author was French. What if he was just referring to himself—*his* home?" He paused. "Too simple?"

"No," said Kent. "It's perfect." *United Kingdom France.* He could have stretched across the table and planted Santos with a kiss.

"But what does it mean—something they have in common?"

"That'd be a long list. Wars, royalty, customs." Kent thought a moment. "It does, though, need to ultimately point to a specific location."

"So, *land* they've shared."

"Or fought over." Kent no longer minded the surrounding ambience. Their answer was close; he could feel it.

Soon Santos raised his eyes hopefully. "What about the Channel Islands? They're geographically closer to France, but administered by the UK."

"Maybe," said Kent, trying to recall whether Guernsey or Jersey was larger.

"Or Normandy," said Santos, gaining momentum. "Part of France, but at one point ruled by England."

Kent began to nod, then stopped, shaking his head instead. "The location has to be definitive. This author would have left nothing to chance." He felt like a marathoner fighting a steep grade on the twenty-sixth mile.

The room went quiet once again, each of them bracing against the encroaching silence. It was a living, breathing thief, there to negate the precious progress they'd made. Kent cycled through regions, countries, continents—whatever thin scenarios his frayed mind could muster. Santos appeared to be doing the same, eyes boring through the coffee table as if it were a crystal ball.

Finally, the younger man shook his head. "I don't know." The words cut even sharper than Kent expected. "It doesn't make any sense. Geographically, Britain and France are neighbors, but they've been at each other's throats for the better part of the past millennium. No place in the world was big enough for both of them."

Big enough. Kent tilted his head in realization. "What about Canada?"

Santos clearly knew his history and straightened in understanding. "A British territory with a French-speaking province." Just as quickly, the spell of excitement faded. "But it's still not definitive, and an even larger area of possible locations."

Each word true. Something inside, though, wouldn't let Kent dismiss the idea. There had to be another key, one more secret to unloc—

He stood up, heart pounding, eyes distant. "Oh, aren't you a clever one." Santos seemed to sense the words weren't for him, but still looked confused. Kent's gaze cleared. "Montreal." He repeated himself, as if to keep the information from sinking back into obscurity. "Montreal, Canada."

This time *he* knew the history, acquired a lifetime ago, glowing in the corner of his memory like a stubborn beacon. He focused across the table. "Before it was renamed, Montreal was known as Ville-Marie—City of Mary." He exhaled. "*Marry* Jack Home."

Santos stood once more. "Are you sure?"

"I don't have time to be sure. But it's enough." He glanced at Baker, then stepped toward the hallway. "I've got to make a phone call."

Before he was out of sight, Kent turned, nodding directly at Santos. "That's good coffee, Jose."

18

The clouds parted in seeming deference to the Rolls-Royce Phantom, its silver carriage glinting beneath a shy sun. The sedan moved with engineered grace, navigating a winding driveway of snow-capped gravel. Pristine lawns, themselves coated white, hugged either side of the path like frozen rivers. A bare hedgerow and cluster of oaks donated doses of austere beauty, while a glass pond silently cried out for the companionship of departed fowl.

Even in the desirable enclave of Het Gooi, ten miles southeast of Amsterdam, the scene bordered on ostentatious. Yet no one seemed to notice. Neighbors, old and new, readily embraced an attitude of natural acceptance. Tourists were even more distant, most never venturing this far inland, the rest passing by with obliging disinterest. The grounds and car were a practical museum, to be admired and forgotten in the same glance.

This was the result their owner, Edmund van Leer, had striven years to perfect. Right now, though, ensconced in the Phantom's cavernous backseat, he felt incapable of enjoying the fruits of his labor. Instead, he'd folded his copy of *De Telegraaf* and was staring vacantly out the right-hand window.

It wasn't worry that seized his thoughts—it was intelligence. Only a fool ignored his adversaries. And Van Leer had just been introduced to one of particular note.

The Phantom rounded a bend as if it were on air; he decided it was worth the five-hundred thousand euros he'd paid for it. Up ahead, just entering his window's frame, was a house to match. Its red brick seemed to go on forever, elegantly wrapping three neoclassical stories. From the time she'd been built, nearly two centuries earlier, only minor repairs had been necessary to keep her the envy of every structure within a hundred miles.

The gravel forked into two paths. Edmund signaled his driver, who wordlessly forsook the ample rear garage for a crescent-shaped entry at the front of the house. The British sedan soon eased to a halt and Van Leer alighted. He gulped in a shock of icy air and climbed a stone walkway toward the front door.

Just as he was reaching for its handle, the aged wooden barrier swung inward without a creak. A tall, muscular figure nearly filled the threshold: Max, the head butler. The man was a third-generation servant who'd inherited the lead post two years back from a cancer-stricken father. Well before, though, he'd been known to perform the odd errand for his employer, regardless of legality. The scar above his left eye was proof of such determination—a trait eclipsed only by his loyalty to the Van Leer name.

Edmund stepped through and allowed Max to remove his coat. Even as the door swung shut, a faint chill lingered in the expansive foyer. The space's granite tile led to a distant solarium. Floor-to-ceiling windows framed the entire back wall and increased the disparity between inner gloom and the bright day outside.

Shadow and sunlight—evil versus good. It wasn't the first time Edmund's mind had keyed on such a metaphor. For someone in his position, there was always the temptation to label yourself the 'light.' Bringing balance—correction—to a less fortunate world.

Rubbish. Such sentiment amounted to little more than childish posturing. The real solution was simply to revel in the darkness. There was a certain transcendent satisfaction in knowing you'd planted fear and helplessness in so many others. Watching it play out always felt like a bonus.

"A drink, sir?"

Max only spoke when necessary. The baritone query brought his employer back into the room. "I'll get one myself," said Edmund. "Tell my brother I'd like to see him, in the library."

Max offered the slightest of nods and turned away. His movements were efficient, back straight. Discipline that came naturally after three years in the Royal Netherlands Army. His current domestic duties lacked such physical benefits, but the basement beneath their feet housed a spacious gym of which he took constant advantage. The man had no trouble filling out his charcoal uniform. For his part, neither did Edmund. At fifty-two, he was ten years older than his servant, but in proportionately excellent condition.

He broke off toward the left, gaining a wide hallway before slipping into a two-story room lined with books, and more books. Generous swaths of mahogany and leather melded with the staid crackle of a stone fireplace against the far wall. Van Leer strode across the carpeted floor to a shelf of glass decanters.

He chose the nearest, Dutch gin, its clear liquid perfectly still within the thick crystal. A mere ribbon inside the first glass wasn't quite enough, so he poured himself another. Then, for the thousandth time, he raised his gaze, admiring the space. But there was no need; he had every corner memorized. You never forgot the room in which your life completely changed.

It was over thirty years ago now, an overcast patch of December. He'd just returned from university, on his first full day of holiday break, when his father, Maarten, called him into the library. He was instructed to close the door, which was unusual. But Edmund obeyed. The next moment both men were sitting in stuffed leather chairs, facing the fire.

No preamble. Maarten pulled out an old sheet of paper, browned at the edges and sealed between two glass plates. Closer inspection revealed a letter, addressed to one of their ancestors, Sigmund van Leer, dated 1865. The bulk of prose, as his father pointed out, came second; the note's initial import lay with its salutation: *your humble servant, J. Wilkes Boothe.*

Edmund's first impression was one of confusion. It was a deserving historical relic—especially considering the familial connection—but hardly worth such measures of secrecy. Then his father did highlight the body of the message. Edmund could still feel the adrenaline electrifying his veins as he read each word: *my anger compels me…accept your proposition…this plan for death marks new life…will not fail…*

And so it began—two hours of radical explanation and enlightenment. With rapt, hungry attention, Edmund processed the revelation that the last ten generations of his family had anchored a continuous society of assassins. His father spoke with little emotion, but rare and irresistible pride.

Sigmund and his siblings had already chosen a list of dates stretching two centuries into the future. The specific targets were merely the personal whim of each successive group. Who they were wasn't as important, so long as their death made a significant impact. Lincoln became the first casualty in an invisible war for pure control.

Edmund might've thought he was being led on, but his father came prepared. For each assassination, tangible evidence—printed correspondence, photography—linked the House of Van Leer to the killer. Booth was the first recruit, and became something of a template: young, angry, only needing a final push. Such motivation could come in the form of money, weapons—on more than one occasion, simple words of empowerment.

Finding these soldiers was a relatively simple task. The Van Leers had entered the banking sphere in the mid-seventeenth century, at the height of their nation's golden age. Since then, and up to the present day, they had quietly presided over one of the world's most successful investment empires. Information, and influence, could be stockpiled at a rapid rate and disseminated across the globe.

Sometimes, however, there was no viable recruit; sometimes an operation had to be carried out by the family itself. Or, in other cases, assistance provided. Oswald had turned out to be a shaky choice for Dallas in '63; if it hadn't been for Edmund's great-grandfather on that "grassy knoll," their streak of successful kills might've been broken.

For this reason, those members of every upcoming generation of Van Leers with knowledge of the scheme undertook a program of physical training that went well beyond mere fitness. Gun handling and accuracy, martial arts, wilderness survival—each was stressed to the point of perfection. The latter two were common enough to avoid suspicion, and, with the buffer of wealth and privilege to circumvent Holland's strict gun laws, the first was also possible. Superior results could be achieved quietly. Much like the operation as a whole.

For, despite its profound implications, the agenda of assassination was easy to conceal. Each target date stood years apart, with plenty of time to plan and often no direct involvement necessary. A man could easily fulfill his duties as banker, husband and father without anyone knowing the truth. It wasn't a double life so much as a hobby.

And yet, no man lived forever. This plan of action was always meant to be larger than any single individual; sooner or later you had to pass the knowledge on. The trick, Edmund's father had said, was knowing where—and when—to send it. The recipient had to possess a particular mettle; loyalty and secrecy were critical. First-born had been passed over for younger siblings, size and strength traded for intelligence and emotional detachment. Edmund swelled at the certainty in his father's eyes. *You're ready, son.*

Before they were finished, though, the most important question had to be answered. *Why?* The answer was simple, and had been proven correct within Edmund over the past three decades.

What was there beyond wealth? What horizon of achievement lay past a purchase price? Truth was, the Van Leer family had claimed a place among Europe's financial elite for the past three-hundred-and-fifty years. Gold and silver had long ago lost their luster. Only one prize could now satisfy such an exalted thirst.

Power. Over people, events, nations. To know that lives were forever altered, the course of history changed as a result of your actions was an intoxicating high that only increased with use. For this reason, Edmund admired those leaders—Alexander the Great, Napoleon, Hitler—with the strength and will to subdue their enemies.

He also considered them idiots. Their objective was to control the world with their hands, and they each, eventually, failed. Better to bind your target with an invisible rope. As his grandfather liked to say: 'why rule the world on a stage when you can change it from the shadows?'

Edmund was in the center of the library now, interrupting a shaft of pale light streaming through one of the room's high windows. He glanced toward a leather sofa on the right. Like the fireplace, it held its own memories, branded within his psyche for the past ten years.

He'd decided to tell his wife. This was typically forbidden—not on principle, but predisposition: women tended to possess weaker resolve, missing the ultimate goal for a field of sympathy and emotion. But he was convinced Rianne was different. She'd raised their twin boys with a stern hand and reasoned like an actuary. What an effective partner she would make, working with him to fulfill the next date on the list.

Once he'd told her, though, he knew he was wrong. He'd closed the library door, just like his father; it'd been a quiet summer evening up to that point. She absorbed the news with requisite confusion, then incredulity, then anger and fear which melted into silence. Edmund could hear the crickets chirping outside.

It was not meant to be. He should have seen it coming: Rianne possessed the raw material for such an endeavor, but lacked the vision and courage to see it through. She started breathing heavily, voice rising, on the verge of hysterics. They needed to tell someone, expose the truth. Surely the authorities wouldn't hold them culpable for the sins of past generations.

Edmund managed to calm her and, after displaying some reluctance, voiced his agreement. But not tonight. They both needed rest. In the morning they could present their case with a clear head. She nodded, already looking haggard. Shortly thereafter she bid him goodnight and left to lie down.

The next morning came, but she never awoke. After running some tests, their physician, on retainer, called it a heart attack. Which was strange as her family had no history of heart disease. The doctor found some cotton fibers in her throat, which may have matched the material of the pillowcases. But surely that was just coincidental. No need to conduct an autopsy. The Van Leer family had endured enough sorrow.

Edmund pulled his eyes away from the fire, as if the memory might burn him. Then the door shut. He spun to find a man who could've been his twin. The entrant was a hair younger, a touch thinner, but otherwise identical. It'd been that way since childhood. "Gin before lunch," said Jakob van Leer. "Must've been quite a meeting."

Edmund thought about the file he'd received just over an hour ago, from an MI6 friend working out of the British embassy in The Hague. He'd memorized its contents, and would likely never forget. "Forgive me if I'm not in the mood for banter," he said, finishing his drink.

Jakob poured his own. "And thus, my point."

Edmund made his way across the room. His brother's tone—playful, bordering on passive-aggressive—was merely a mask for rage boiling underneath. It was a natural response, considering the death of his son twelve hours earlier. But Bram hadn't just been killed; he'd failed. Six-six, with his speed and strength—such a waste. Edmund reminded himself that their current adversary was a slight step up from Portuguese police.

At least Bram had had the presence of mind to record the attack with his phone and simultaneously transmit the video. It seemed a drastic fail-safe, especially considering the device spent most of the time in a dark pocket. But it paid off. The resulting playback arrived on Edmund and Jakob's phones instantly, including a quick shot of a man's face just before the screen went black.

They met at a simple table flanked by matching chairs. Neither sat down. "Where's Kai?" asked Edmund, resting his empty glass on the cherry wood.

"Upstairs, sleeping off the shock of Bram." Edmund nodded. Mistakes like last night weren't supposed to happen.

Kai was now Jakob's only child, the surviving sibling of a dual adoption that took place over twenty years ago. Such artificial means of augmenting a family had long been implemented by past generations of Van Leers. Continuing the lineage—and thus, stewardship of the assassination list—was paramount. Marriage might've been a simpler solution, but Jakob had failed to find a woman with the right combination of subservience, apathy and fertility.

The better for her not to have heard of Bram's death, anyway. It was violent, and they couldn't afford the inevitable depression and panic. Edmund himself had received news of the event through a law enforcement connection in Lisbon. It'd happened at a small chapel within the fort grounds. *One hundred-fifty years of waiting and it was in the church the whole time.*

There was blood on the floor and walls, probably from more than one person. He was meeting his lawyer this afternoon to begin damage control. The family kept a low profile, but their wealth still made waves. By default, Bram was something of a local celebrity whose absence would be felt. Perhaps he was a good Samaritan who noticed potential vandals and tried to stop them, with tragic results. Slain, as it were, by his own virtue.

Jakob cleared his throat, breaking up the headlines forming in Edmund's mind. The older brother pulled an envelope from his jacket and slid it across the table. Jakob removed its contents. "A single sheet?"

"We're lucky to get that much. This man's a ghost."

In the upper-left corner was a photo matching the face sent to each of their phones. "Jeremy Kent," began Jakob. "Officer within the CIA's Special Activities Division." He mumbled through a few details, then scanned further. "Decorated soldier…Special Forces." A moment later he set the paper down. "Finally, a man worth killing."

The words were weighted with confidence, anticipation. As much as he tried to ignore it, Edmund felt the same conviction coursing through his veins. When you'd conquered everything else, a fresh challenge was what you lived for. In a sense, Kent was no different than Lincoln or Kennedy—an assignment, a gift. *A drug.*

"Are the twins still in position?" asked Jakob.

Edmund nodded. "I've forwarded them Kent's photo."

"Then he'll get no farther than the second stage. Assuming he's even found it."

Edmund felt a twinge of jealousy toward his own sons. It was their fortune to fulfill, but part of him ached to pull the trigger himself.

Edmund folded the paper back into the envelope, returning it to his jacket. Jakob finished his drink. "We should consider informing Henrik. I know he's just a cousin, but he's been loyal. He deserves an opportunity."

"I've already told him."

"Oh?"

"He's on a special assignment."

Jakob nearly laughed. "Moreso than this?"

"Trust me."

19

Less than four days remained until the next date on the list. Despite his recent discovery, Kent felt the weight of every ticking second—primarily because more than a single life hung in the balance. Assassinations were never isolated.

Sometimes the collateral damage came quickly: in the week following Oscar Romero's murder, a massacre at his funeral claimed thirty more lives. In other instances, the carnage took its time. Four years after the death of Franz Ferdinand, they still hadn't finished stacking the bodies.

Once the smoke from World War I finally did settle, one bullet had killed ten million men. Such runaway power was almost unimaginable. Especially when you were the last chance to stop it. Kent peered outside from his window seat, never having felt more alone than he did right now.

Montreal, he knew, was down there, somewhere below a thick layer of stratus clouds. The Airbus had left Lisbon over seven hours ago and made good time. Part of him, ironically, was in no particular rush to arrive. Assuming this was the right location, someone else was on the ground, waiting to slit his throat all over again.

The plane banked north, preparing its approach. Kent's mind drifted with it, back to the safe house in Portugal. Before leaving he'd walked up to Baker, still unconscious on the cot. The two of them had been through too much for inane platitudes. Kent simply grasped his friend's limp hand, closed his eyes and prayed once more. God didn't keep off-hours.

The unmistakable feeling of descent brought him back inside the plane's cabin. Thick fog caked his window, but seconds later they were through the clouds. Ahead, Pierre-Elliot Trudeau International Airport spread its arms like a welcoming diplomat. The maze of runways and hangars lay in a suburb twelve miles west of downtown. Off to the left, Kent could just make out a bundle of skyscrapers hugging the St. Lawrence River.

They landed at 1 p.m. on the dot, ten minutes ahead of schedule. A minor victory for Air France, as if Kent cared. He was waiting for nightfall, dinnertime. If the stone was here, he was confident of its location. But the cover of darkness and pedestrians would be necessary in such an open space.

As the jetliner taxied toward an open gate, Kent pondered the specific clue yet again. Pinpointing the city had made deciphering the exact site an elementary exercise:

Hero of the sea

Long deceased

Bow at the top

Where north meets east

The 'hero of the sea' could only be Horatio Nelson. Kent had had the entire flight to discover that the city's French-Canadians were no more enamored with Napoleon than their British neighbors. Shortly after the Battle of Trafalgar, both groups financed a monument to the admiral. Nelson's Column rose sixty-two feet above Place Jacques-Cartier, a city square within Old Montreal.

'North' and 'east' clearly denoted a corner of the column. He thought he had a handle on 'bow at the top' as well. *Only one way to find out.*

The Airbus eased to a stop. Kent waited in his window seat while most of his fellow passengers pounced for their carry-ons and began edging down the aisle. As if the plane were in greater danger of crashing now that its wheels were on the ground. Most of them would be stuck waiting together at baggage claim, anyway.

Once the stampede thinned, he reached up for his own pack. It was simple canvas, bought at the airport in Lisbon and stuffed with some hastily selected clothing and toiletries. Briggs had sent a man to the Tivoli to retrieve his and Baker's effects, but they wouldn't see them again. Nothing raised a red flag like traveling without luggage.

Before long he was off the plane and following the herd toward customs. More important than the sack on his shoulder was the passport still in his pocket. There was no evidence that he was being tracked electronically, and thus no need to change documentation. Evan Graves, his junior shipping executive, was just packing a little lighter.

When Kent's turn to enter the country came, he stepped toward a man who's premature balding did little to dampen a pair of energetic eyes. They glowed with typical Canadian friendliness. 'Evan' handed over his papers and the man started shuffled through the booklet. Kent had memorized the room the moment he'd entered, but glanced around once more.

If everything else held true, his adversaries still only had access to the general location. And this was different than Portugal. Sagres had a population of two thousand; Montreal was four million, the second-largest city in Canada. They couldn't possibly guess his destination in town. Their only hope was tracking him to it.

He'd have started right here, with international arrivals. Plenty of time to spy your prey snaking lazily through the customs line. There was no reason to think they knew what he looked like, but he couldn't take any chances. Especially if the degree of expertise was similar to what it was in Sagres. At that level, you knew how to tail a ghost. And become one yourself.

Finishing his tour without spotting a threat, Kent spun back to the window just as the man was returning his passport. "Welcome home, Mr. Graves."

Kent nodded. He tightened his grip on his bag and began to edge toward the main concourse. Technically, the attendant's words were true. Vancouver may have been another two thousand miles away, but this was still Canada. He tried to look satisfied.

Angling past a café, Kent masked his heightened senses with a façade of nonchalance. A few figures nevertheless caught his radar—the man in the corner wearing sunglasses, a pair of stern-looking travelers elbowing through the center. These, though, were quickly dismissed as false alarms.

He walked another few yards before finally laying eyes on his target. The man wore a hunter green cap and maroon vest, just as McCoy had said. He turned his head and made the slightest eye contact with Kent. Then he was moving, inward, around a cluster of tourists. The two men quickly closed the gap separating them. No one noticed the stranger brush past Kent and drop a set of keys into his palm. Neither did Kent pause to give them a second chance, but instead pressed farther ahead, eventually gaining an escalator. Soon the main entrance loomed before him, its bank of windows lit by swaths of bleak sunshine.

He abruptly slowed, feeling the hairs on the back of his neck stiffen. One more look around: *nothing*. A rare swing and miss for his body's alert system. He chalked it up to fatigue and continued toward the automatic doors.

An instant later he was outside, dodging traffic beneath a covered walkway. As if to officially welcome him to Canada, an icy gust swirled around a bus and nearly knocked him off his feet. Five more seconds of like punishment earned him access to an enclosed skyway. Immediately the airport cacophony faded. The skyway forded a busy street and led directly into a covered parking garage.

He walked in silence, smiling to an elderly couple heading in the opposite direction. He'd deleted the text from his phone, but the words still hung fresh in his mind. *Blue Sentra, third level.*

He exited the skyway into the shadow of the garage. Its thick concrete diluted the sunlight, but also the wind. The air swept along the corners and walls, howling in protest against such rigid environs. He made his way to the third level. It was nearly full of vehicles, and empty of people. He pulled the key fob from his pocket and tapped the 'unlock' button. Fifty feet ahead, a pair of brake lights flashed in greeting.

Kent reached the Sentra seconds later and popped the trunk. He still had cash, and a passport, but they were no longer enough. This was a different situation than Sagres; the threat was now real. After one last look around, he lifted the carpeted floorboard. Beneath lay the spare tire—and a Glock 19, its black polymer gleaming in the gloom beside two spare magazines.

The rest was academic: Sentras were common and unremarkable; he soon blended into the A-20 traffic heading northeast toward downtown. Along the way, he stopped at a Home Depot for a few supplies, then made for his hotel of choice: *La Tour Belvedere*, a midtown high-rise with just enough anonymity.

Kent parked a block up the street, lugged his bag from the trunk and backtracked toward the lobby. Inside it was stylish, spartan and void of other guests, save a pair of women speaking rapid French in the corner. They appeared completely oblivious to the surrounding crawl of life. Kent made his way to the front desk where a young female attendant, flashing a plastic smile, exuded a welcome level of disinterest.

It was the middle of the day, but did they happen to have a room ready? What luck. It was on the fifth floor? That would be fine. And how would monsieur be paying? Yes, cash was always acceptable. Did monsieur require anything else? Perhaps assistance with additional luggage? Indeed, traveling light *was* a talent these days.

Her grin was a touch more genuine as he walked away. Still, Kent was confident she'd forget him in minutes. That was his real talent.

Soon he was riding the elevator to the fifth floor. It slid open onto a deserted hallway. He found his room, pulled out the key and entered a simple space. Polished hardwood floors gave way to fresh black and white linens; a large window did its best to catch every remaining sliver of gray light.

Kent laid his bag on the minimalist bed and stepped to the glass. He parted the shades and looked down. The street below, Boulevard de Maisonneuve West, was covered in afternoon traffic. Beyond, a row of stone townhomes shared space with nondescript apartment buildings. He glanced along the thoroughfare and its side streets, but found nothing out of the ordinary.

Back on the interstate, he thought he'd had a tail. Six car-lengths behind, in the left lane. A white Ford sedan. But it had turned off long before the Home Depot came in sight. He closed the shades, questioning further his internal threat detection.

Kent moved his bag to the floor. The mattress looked soft, but would it bring sleep? He'd settle for mere rest, and could do little else right now anyway. Easing himself onto the comforter—and the Glock below his pillow—he clasped his hands behind his head and studied the ceiling. The distant ring of activity outside joined the room's muffled heating system to create a tolerable symphony of calm. Eventually, he closed both eyes, letting his mind settle on the first peaceful thought to come along.

20

In this case, about four months ago, along the shores of Lake Anna, Virginia. Allison had flown up to D.C. for the weekend, and they'd made the two-hour drive south to spend a day in the sun. It was mid-August—hot, but with enough whisper of the coming fall to keep things pleasant.

They'd made their way to a state park where a beach hugged the water. Plenty of others had the same idea and were already crowding the sand. So the two of them settled for a grassy slope set back from the shore. Allison began laying out sandwiches and fruit; Kent uncorked the wine. No actual picnic basket, but they did have a blanket to soften the grass.

What he remembered most was the silence. He lay propped on an elbow; she sat upright, floral skirt draped over her pretty knees. Lunch passed without a word, each of them comfortable with the quiet. They really hadn't been dating long enough for such intimacy, but the process tended to speed up once you'd dodged the same bullets.

Finally, Allison set her glass of chardonnay down and scanned the crowd. "Do you think you could ever be like these people?"

"You mean…"

"Oblivious. Unaware of your surroundings."

Kent smiled. "You mean relaxed."

"I didn't say that."

He sat up straighter, following her gaze down to the shore. "Never completely. This job, it seeps into your bones." She was nodding. "Does that bother you?"

"I suppose it should. But then, we all have to find our own version of normal."

"'Normal' is overrated."

She laughed. "Spoken like a true original."

Kent, though, knew the thoughts that lay behind those sky-blue irises: could this really work? Were they just kidding themselves these past few months? The same questions continued to echo in his own mind.

He'd been told by many in his profession that settling down, in anything resembling the traditional sense, was a fantasy. At the time, he hadn't cared. Yet, he now realized, he'd never quite closed the door. Part of him always felt that it might only take the right girl to make the impossible work.

Allison was as right as they came; the fact that she'd made it through the dangers of Europe and remained with him today was proof enough. But she was still a woman, aching for assurance that she wasn't destined to become a widow. Assurance he could never give. Who wanted that kind of 'normal?'

"Do you ever think about kids?" she asked.

My, we're checking everything off the list today. Weeks ago, Kent had stuffed a diplomatic answer to this in his pocket, but the question so caught him off-guard he forgot to pull it out. Instead, she got the unvarnished truth. "Yes, probably more than I should."

He didn't need to look to see the combination of timidity and hope flash in her eyes. They'd yet to personally broach this subject, but Kent had seen her come alive when speaking of her sister Amy's twins. It was one thing to play aunt, quite another to be a mother.

Allison took a sip of vine-ripened courage. This was clearly a conversation she'd planned ahead of time. "I've had friends say they wouldn't want to be responsible for bringing a kid into this crazy world."

"Do you agree?"

She took a breath. "No. I think that's more excuse than reason. Ask the right person and the world's always been crazy."

"Then where does that leave us, boss?"

"Depends—why shouldn't you think about kids?"

"Because I'm not sure there's room for them in the life I'm living."

"Kind of like a girlfriend?"

"Children are a tad more fragile."

"And yet…"

Kent sighed. "They still feel like a bit of a miracle. Something so small and helpless, yet alive. I've always thought that loving a child, feeling them love you back, was a window onto something higher. Like…"

"How Jesus loves us." Allison smiled. She'd long ago abandoned the faith of her own childhood, but encountering Kent's zeal had rekindled something within. She'd found a church in Atlanta and decided to give it a chance. There were still plenty of questions, but, for the first time in years, she was interested in the answers. "Does that mean you'd ever consider a family?"

He was silent for a long moment. "In a way, I think I always have. I just…could never see how the pieces would fit."

The sun was setting by the time they made it back to Kent's Honda. He held Allison's door for her, then slid behind the wheel himself. And didn't move. After a few seconds she placed her hand on his. "You okay?"

"Yeah," he said, staring vacantly through the windshield. "I was just thinking, today was the closest I came to a vacation in over a decade. The last time, I was still in college. My folks and I camped with some cousins in the Missouri Ozarks. It was Memorial Day weekend—dirt cheap, but boy did it buy some memories."

A sudden tear wet the corner of his eye. "That was the summer before my mom found her lump. Guess you never quite know how life's going to turn."

He spun her way. "What about you—"

She'd started to cry too, tears of empathy rolling down her cheeks. Then, in the same motion, she cupped his face and brought her lips to his. They'd kissed plenty of times before, but this was different.

It went far beyond the mere physical. For the first time, someone was willing—and able—to share the burden of his pain. Because of that, perhaps, he noticed his arms snaking around Allison, pulling her close. It would be so easy to go all the way.

And took all of his willpower to pull back instead. Continuing now, as right as it felt, was wrong for too many reasons, including endangering this woman he was beginning to love.

Diving into his world was a one-way ticket. He wasn't quite ready to subject her to that. Eventually, though, she'd have the freedom to decide. In the end, the question wouldn't be whether she loved him back; it would be whether that was enough.

21

"How late do you think you'll be?"

Hassan pressed the phone to his ear, as if it might help bridge the distance between him and his wife. He'd been told more than once that which he already knew: he loved his family a little too much. It'd always seemed like a good problem to have. But then he'd heard about a friend from college who'd been walking down a Tel Aviv street with his wife one evening. A pack of drunk teens passed by; one of them had slurred a few unrepeatable words in her direction.

The man turned around, threw the youth to the pavement and started pummeling his face. A pair of bystanders reached in just before it turned to murder. Even so, his friend was quickly convicted and now in the middle of serving a fifteen-year sentence. Separated from his wife and children, all in the name of *love*.

"Just another hour or so," Hassan said.

"Then I'll wait up."

"You don't have to do that."

"Of course I do. It's our half-anniversary."

"*Half-anniversary*. Now you're just teasing me."

"Only one way to find out."

He smiled. "I love you too."

The line went dead and Hassan set his cell phone down beside a sea of scribbled notepaper. It was unfair to have to concentrate now, but the contents of the words brought him focus. They represented a true chance to secure lasting peace for his nation. Such a scenario would guarantee his family a greater level of safety than he ever could on his own.

A distant car horn sounded outside the bullet-resistant window behind him. He hardly noticed; the noise had become part of his daily routine. So had the view, whether tonight's inky veil or the scorch of an average day. His office, several stories up, provided near complete insulation—and protection—from Jerusalem's relentless commotion below.

Hassan had resumed his work, crossing out a string of superfluous adjectives, when he was stopped once more by a knock at the door. A half-breath of frustration. "Come in."

The partition swung open, and Tzadok Neri stepped through. He closed the door softly. "My apologies. I know it's late."

Hassan stood and nearly scurried around the front of his desk. He couldn't help it. Over the phone was one thing, but Neri's physical presence commanded authority—even if he didn't seek it. Sometimes the Prime Minister had to remind himself who was actually in charge.

"Tzadok." Hassan extended a smooth palm. "What are you still doing here?"

"A defense minister has plenty of his own work. I had one last thing on my mind." He exhaled. "Thought it could wait until tomorrow, but…"

"But you're standing, when you should be sitting." Hassan waved to a pair of leather chairs. "Can I get you something to drink?"

"No, thank you. I won't take too much of your time." Neri slid into a leather pocket. "Does Leila mind your late hours?"

Hassan claimed the other chair himself. "Yes. I suppose that's a good thing. The day she stops caring is the day I shouldn't bother coming home."

"A beautiful irony."

"What about Sarah?"

Neri shifted his weight in the seat. "When you've been married as long as I have, your wife either understands or she's already gone crazy."

Hassan chuckled, but said nothing. It was Neri's cue to continue. He didn't speak right away, instead sobering into a weathered shell of experience. Finally, he nodded toward the papers on the desk without taking his eyes off his boss. "Don't do this."

Hassan matched Neri's silence, and his stare. "You're a little late, Tzadok. We're days away."

"Yes, and I know others have peppered you with the same request for the past three weeks. Consider me your last line of reason."

The PM noticed the glint of aggression in Neri's eye, one of the subtle traits of strength that'd allowed the man to survive in politics for over forty years. Yet Hassan was a fighter, too. You didn't rise to this office—and certainly wouldn't keep it—without standing your ground. "I can't stop now. We're too close."

"I know you think you are." Neri sat back, relaxing slightly. "I'm sure the words on that paper are honest, and probably quite good. But they represent a fantasy. In the real world, the leader of Israel never occupies a public stage beside the leader of Palestine. It's not tradition; it's self-preservation."

"I'm willing to sacrifice my career over this."

"I wasn't talking about your career."

Hassan paused. "It worked in Oslo in '93."

"Yes, for about five minutes. But Rabin and Arafat signed the agreement in Washington. Six thousand miles away from an army of nationalists who'd have gladly blown each of their heads off for stooping to such a compromise." He took a breath. "Forgive the verbiage. I was here in the nineties; I know how these things turn out. If not in war, then the illusion of peace."

Hassan's face tightened into a new shade of resolve. "I appreciate your passion, Tzadok. Not least of all for my own safety. But I've made up my mind. You've seen the process—the phone calls, sample reports. Khalidi is a good man. He and I will never agree fully, but we've found enough common ground to build a future. We just need a spark. Something for our people to grab hold of and remember. A symbol."

"And you think you'll find it in East Jerusalem?"

"Yes. The two of us on a platform, speaking of peace, shaking hands. Not across an ocean, but in the center of this nation's most contested piece of land. It's not easy to forget something you've never seen before."

Neri didn't move for a long moment. He continued staring across at Hassan, until it was almost uncomfortable. "Alright," he finally said. "I suppose every leader of this country deserves a chance to try for the improbable."

"You don't believe in me?"

"You're the only part in all of this that I do believe in." Neri stood. Hassan followed, as if he were the guest. "Though I never pegged you for an idealist."

"I'm whatever suits the moment. Ideas only get you so far, but sometimes there's nowhere else to begin."

Neri nodded. They started inching toward the door. "And your security detail?"

"I can't imagine they're excited. This is a difficult assignment."

"You don't seem very worried."

"It's Shin Bet. Failure isn't in their DNA."

22

Kent woke to a cold, dark room. He'd managed sleep after all, but had left the warmth of a near-perfect memory far behind. Hostile air seeped through the window to his left, its vapors joined by stark, artificial light skirting the curtains. The rest of the space's minimalist charm had shifted to a sort of offensive neutrality; everything from the TV to the alarm clock seemed to be leveling the same question he'd long asked himself: *why are you doing this?*

Who in his right mind would consistently travel, with little information and less notice, across the globe to endure myriad threats against his own life in hopes of saving those of others he'd never met? It'd always made him think of soldiers in the 101st Airborne during World War II. In the early hours of D-Day, dawn still a whisper on the French horizon, they'd parachuted through a lethal shower of anti-aircraft fire and landed behind German lines. But before accomplishing any of this, they chose *to jump out of a perfectly good airplane.*

Why then…why now? The only answer that ever made sense was another question: who else was going to do it?

In the end, it always boiled down to belief. Kent believed in God, which meant human beings weren't meaningless raw material; they were intentional creations worth protecting. There would always be threats to strip life away. Jesus had been willing to die to preserve such life. Kent figured there were worse examples to follow.

And so he rose, through the fatigue and isolation, out the door and down to his car.

* * *

The wind bit into his neck and down his spine as he stowed his duffel bag inside the Sentra's trunk. He'd almost left it in the room, but didn't want a repeat of Portugal. In any way. At least the traffic was cooperating; brake lights stretched up and down Maisonneuve. Not quite bumper-to-bumper, but thick enough to provide some cover. It lasted the entire drive downtown.

Still, he thought he spotted another tail: a gray Toyota Highlander, hugging the shoulder about fifty feet behind. Yet, once again, it turned off well before he'd reached his destination. Twice was stretching the limits of credulity, but each time he'd been heading downtown amidst heavy traffic. He was bound to share the road for stretches. Overall, the odds still gave the edge to coincidence. Even if he didn't like it.

Each building grew larger as Kent threaded the city center. Five-star restaurants and trendy jazz clubs fell by without notice; such was his focus this close to the task at hand. As always, his heart had begun to race. An old habit. It wasn't nervousness; more like a pump, filling him with a reservoir of adrenaline, just in case.

Maybe tonight he wouldn't need it. Things could go smoothly—he'd find the stone and quietly escape without anyone trying to kill him.

Maybe.

Five minutes later he slipped into a parking spot along Rue Notre-Dame, two blocks north of the statue. Outside, the crowded sidewalks gave him hope for a busy square. Never let it be said Canadians allowed the cold to keep them from a good time.

Kent opened his door and stepped to the rear of the Sentra. Waiting for a young couple on his side of the street to pass—politely smiling their way as they did so—he popped the trunk. A last look around: he had a few seconds before anyone would be close enough to see clearly. He reached inside, pulled out an orange hard-hat and put it on. Next came a matching vest and pair of safety cones. The final pieces were a small flashlight, splitting wedge and sledgehammer.

He dropped the wedge and light in his pocket and started walking south, the hammer dangling surreptitiously at his side. A random gust whipped across his face, as if willing him to turn back. He trudged through it, lowering his head like a street worker who'd decided the overtime wasn't worth the chill.

Even so, he had to marvel at the protection such an identity afforded. Wear plainclothes while walking down a city street at night, with a sledgehammer, and police would be on the scene within minutes; slap on some neon cloth and suddenly you were just part of the scenery. Perception, assumption, social norms—as a field officer, these were part of his arsenal, just as potent as a knife or gun.

Kent waited for a car to pass, then crossed Rue Saint-Claude. One block to go. To his right, Montreal City Hall loomed with clear pride of its European ancestry. Second Empire limestone rose toward a copper roof, which, in turn, yielded to a twinkling sky. Kent lingered on the stars for the slightest moment, wondering if they were the same Emile and Matthieu might've seen two-hundred years ago.

Then he turned ahead, the details of the present rushing back into his mind: the make and model of each car that passed, the clothing and hair of every person within eyesight. The practice had become second nature, a permanent appendage. He could no more turn it off than change his eye color or blood type. Now, like nearly every time, he saw no threat.

That included Place Jacques Cartier, which spread before him as he reached the end of the block. Sloping down toward the St. Lawrence River at a slight angle, the square's stone floor was a good fifty feet wide and hugged on either side by several canopied restaurants. The column itself stood at the top beside Rue Notre-Dame, Nelson barely visible against the black night.

Kent's pulse had settled to the speed limit as he stepped forward and joined a scattered but sizeable crowd admiring dual rows of miniature Christmas trees sprouting from an equal number of oversized containers. This was where his uniform backfired. The façade was necessary, but drew greater attention in such a relatively confined space. It would work, though. He only needed ten minutes.

Already receiving looks of confusion from a few in the crowd, Kent quickly edged toward the northeast corner of the monument. Its original foundation consisted of several large stones cemented together. They lasted just a few feet before giving way to a more modern level of slabs. These, in turn, supported an iron rail that encircled the inner base of the column.

Within those few feet of original stone is where he would look. *Bow at the top.* This had to mean the layer just below the slabs, where the slope of the ground didn't interfere. Kent eyed a square stone directly on the corner. Emile's courier might've enlisted more masonry help to force the tablet inside such a solid wall. Either way, Kent had to believe it was there.

A man standing near the corner stepped away. Kent wasted no time placing the cones in the vacated space. This cleared the immediate area further. He glanced around one more time, then stepped forward and swung the hammer down toward the target area. It hit with a dull thud—fairly quiet, but enough people noticed the movement. He didn't stop. A second swing, then a third. Bits of rock flew free, but the stone didn't budge.

Gathering himself with a quick breath, Kent pulled out the wedge, turned it sideways and began chipping into the concrete beside the stone. By now, most of those within earshot were looking his way. He could feel their gaze piercing his back. *Does he work for the city? Why would they send just one man, and at this hour?*

Kent continued chipping. He stole brief glances toward the road ahead, still spotting no danger. The nearby crowd was his rear cover. He'd have liked to supplement this with his own eyes, but that meant pausing his work and spinning around. Right now, he couldn't afford to stop, or even slow. The quicker he finished the better.

Concrete hardened with age, which complicated his task. Eventually, though, the wedge bore deep enough to catch in the rock. He could now swing the sledge more freely and stood up to do so. This time he did sneak a peek at the crowd and paid for it with the sight of a woman advancing. She was young, mid-twenties, but carried herself with activist bravura.

"Excuse me," she said in French, her tone combative. "What are you doing?"

It was a perfectly reasonable question. "Sorry for the inconvenience, Miss," said Kent, also in French. "City comptroller's office filled out the order. Minor statue refurbishment."

She paused, digesting the BS. "Minor?"

Kent nodded. "Just the base. Evidently there are some structural irregularities."

She looked up at the column. "What are you going to do?"

"Just switch out a few stones. Most of the work will be done tomorrow."

"Why are you here tonight?"

"Head start." Kent paused, aware of the precious seconds ticking by. He bit his tongue; if she bought this it'd be worth the effort. "We've got a full slate of work this week, need the extra time."

It was a flimsy reason, but just credible enough. After an uneasy silence, she nodded and stepped away. Kent was about to turn back himself when he spotted an older man near the rear of the crowd, a cell phone pressed to his ear. Each word he spoke seemed to further tighten the scowl on his face. Kent couldn't hear, but saw the man's lips form *officier* and *patrouille*. So not everyone liked his story.

Three minutes. It was a guess, but this was a busy part of town. Any self-respecting metropolis kept its law enforcement stationed accordingly.

He spun back immediately, hammer already swinging down toward the awaiting wedge. Metal met metal with a sharp ping that seemed to reverberate throughout the square. More heads turned. But the corner stone moved—a centimeter, maybe two.

Kent swung again; again, there was movement. Not much, but the wedge drove deeper into the concrete, awaiting its next push. He gave it, then another, his arms starting to feel a slight burn. But he could see an inch of daylight within the concrete now. It wasn't so much a complete gap as a deep crevice.

For a fleeting second, as if a mandatory tonic to his mounting excitement, he had the sinking fear he was wrong. Not a CIA field officer, but an overzealous fool, banging away on some anonymous rock, unaware of the surrounding looks of confusion and pity stripping his tangerine hide.

A man on a cot kept him swinging. *One minute.* Most of the crowd, having heard the old man's call, remained close. Such was the pull of a possible arrest. At the very least they'd know whether the man before them was truly a city employee. Potent ammunition for the water cooler tomorrow morning.

Outside of the occasional furtive glance, Kent kept his head down. The helmet and vest continued to serve as a small force-field, their presence lending just enough legitimacy to keep the nearest buzzed patriot from trying to pull him off their sacred monument.

The stone above was massive, its weight making the work difficult. Kent could feel the seconds slipping away, the promise of flashing lights starting to flirt with his peripheral vision. The cap of the wedge was nearly flush with the stones, but still the concrete held. Just a few more—*there.*

Kent felt his chest flutter as the corner stone slid free. It was still squeezed by pressure from the slab above, but had turned enough for him to scan its backside. He quickly pulled the wedge out and removed the flashlight, shining its thin beam into the widened crevice.

The initial sight was a haze of dust and rock that likely hadn't breathed air for well over a century. Kent blew into the gap, closing his eyes as the particles brushed across his face. He opened them a second later, conscious of the crowd still keeping its distance on the left. To the right, flashing lights really had arrived. He ignored them and peered inward.

It shouldn't have been a surprise. He'd found the tablet in Portugal, just where the clue had said it would be. But looking inside—seeing the back of the stone hollowed-out, spotting the tablet resting within—easily took his breath away. This wasn't just a rock; it was a message, one that'd been waiting to be received for much longer than anticipated.

"*Bonsoir, Monsieur.*" The words were firm, cloaked in the thinnest sheen of obligatory courtesy. Kent was already reaching inside the stone. In one quick motion he pocketed the tablet and stood to face a young policeman. The man looked cold and tired, despite a thick coat and traces of coffee on his breath.

"*Bonsoir,*" answered Kent, his mind racing through options for a smooth escape. At the same time, he felt a presence to his right. The old man, stepping to the front of the line to claim his prize.

"I called, officer." He nodded toward Kent, the scowl still pronounced. "This man is destroying a historic statue. I don't believe his story is genuine."

The cop turned to Kent and exhaled wearily, as if preparing to resolve a trivial dispute between two teenagers. "And what is your story?"

Kent recited his lines once more, adding that the city council assigned the refurbishment 'priority' status. The policeman didn't seem impressed. Kent couldn't tell if it was the man's disinterest or a flaw in his own performance.

Finally, the cop looked down, studying the stone and tools. He might've taken Kent at his word, but the old man and surrounding crowd radiated too much pressure. It was his job, after all.

"Are you the foreman for this project?"

Kent shook his head. "Site manager will come tomorrow, with the rest of the crew."

The policeman stiffened. "Well then, I can't let you continue without a permit, or some sort of written authorization from the city council."

"Of course. Boss said I might need it." Kent began rifling through his pockets. "Thought I put it…"

Five more seconds until the next lie would be necessary. He was still dry on ideas. *Run?* He already had the stone, and they'd hardly order a city-wide manhunt for a rogue construction worker. But there had to be a better way, a quieter exit.

"I'm sorry, I must have left it in my truck. I can go get it."

The cop was about to respond when someone sneezed behind Kent. It was loud enough to cause the uniformed man to lean slightly to his left, curious of the source. In that moment Kent happened to glance across Rue Notre-Dame toward a small, deserted square that had been obscured by the policeman's head. He knew it to be Place Vauquelin, highlighted by a dormant fountain and statue of its namesake, another French naval hero.

Before he could focus back on the cop, he noticed a glint of light from the square across. It was just behind the statue, two-hundred feet away, but flared to the forefront of his brain. Kent immediately pulled the officer down and dove to his left just as a deafening crack pierced the cold.

23

The chunk of column just above Kent's head exploded in a spray of gravel. He tucked his legs against the corner of rock and saw the cop dive behind a metal post. Everyone else froze, realization turning to terror in their ghost-white faces. Then the screaming began.

Place Jacques Cartier became instant chaos as the crowd began running for cover. Kent, his Glock now out, heard another bullet ricochet off stone inches from his head. Such accuracy only confirmed what Portugal had already solidified: these were professionals. If not by sanction, then skill.

He waited. One second. Two. The crowd continued to shriek, its collective panic reverberating off the surrounding rock. For his part, Kent knew he was safe if he stayed put. The sniper had no angle and would be forced to leave as police arrived. He'd worry about his own escape once he made it that far.

Except, he wouldn't. Through the scattered throng, he spotted a man racing his way. The stranger gripped a Ruger and quickly aimed. Kent could only flatten himself against the ground. Two thunderclaps struck stone above. He was already rolling and fired back. The shots missed, but were enough to send the new foe diving behind a metal trash can. Kent took the half-second reprieve and leapt to his feet. The closest legitimate cover, a pub's glass façade, was fifty feet of open space away. He risked the gap, feeling the target on his back as his sluggish legs churned through the chill. There was no other way.

Initially, the surrounding chaos was a shield; his nearest pursuer couldn't find a sightline through the manic crowd. The sniper, though, was different.

It was hard to hit a moving target, especially from a distance. The man behind the scope would settle for one shot: grip his rifle firmly, exhale, pull the trigger.

Kent held his own breath, halfway home. A snake of alarm suddenly flashed up his spine. He turned without stopping, squeezing three rounds before his opponent could level the Ruger. Each hit closer than before, forcing the man back once again, giving Kent a final two seconds to reach the pub.

No time for doors. He planted both feet and dove toward the window.

The rifle's report came an instant before the glass around him shattered into a thousand pieces. Acute pain sliced through his abdomen as he tumbled over an empty table and onto the floor. Shards fell like rain. *No time.* He jumped up, adrenaline nearing its peak. The bullet had missed, shredding the edge of his jacket near the shoulder blades. But, below his stomach, a triangle of glass had lodged itself inches into the skin. A wave of pain rose, then crested as he pulled the shard free. Blood chased it through the puncture.

He ignored it and ran. The man with the Ruger would be closing in, the sniper angling for a closer shot. Kent darted through the pub toward the kitchen, seeing pockets of terrified patrons huddled beneath tables. He'd missed their screams amidst the flurry of glass.

Stainless steel flew past his vision, blurring with other diners who'd retreated further from the gunshots before crouching beside staff in temporary paralysis. Kent felt the sting of fear himself as a fresh wave of muffled shrieks amongst the tables announced his opponent's arrival.

He didn't have to look to know the circle of blood below was expanding, soaking his shirt and draining precious energy. Ahead, a few brave souls had made it to the rear entrance and fled. The door stood ajar, framing the dark, icy night like a gold exit sign. Kent trained his eyes forward, deciding for the last time not to offer verbal reassurance to the frightened faces before him, lest he give away his exact location. These people, like those in the square, would survive; he was the only true target.

True enough, it turned out, to send two killers. The realization hit him like a brick wall, even as he physically bowled through it. *Two* killers. That's why he hadn't found a tail in the airport, nor on the roads: one followed him part of the way, then peeled off; the second—different haircut and clothing, different make and model—resumed the hunt.

The cold air, though he'd just left it, stung his face and hands. He abandoned the doorway and immediately cursed the scene ahead: a narrow alley, completely cut off on the left by an extended garage. His only option was to the right, which meant his pursuer wouldn't even have to slow his stride to wonder.

Kent dashed ahead, each labored breath a visible cloud of white. He could see Rue Notre-Dame, its oblivious traffic a mere seventy-five feet away. He had to make it there before the Ruger behind him exited the building.

He tore off his vest, the helmet having fallen loose the moment he'd dived behind the column. An instant later, halfway to the street, he passed a parked car and thought about stopping to make a stand. He'd have the element of surprise. But the notion vanished—the sniper could still be close, even steps away. He'd be cornered.

Ten Feet. Half a second, passing in slow-motion. Kent saw a pair of gates at the entrance and thanked God they were open. He continued at full bore. All at once, though, he felt his pursuer's presence: at the other end of the alley, taking aim. No need to turn around. Kent lunged for the stone edge. The crack of the Ruger shook the night, its nickel-plated bullet taking a chunk out of the rock hairs above Kent's head.

He rolled to the ground, then sprang up, the sidewalk stamped with a patch of crimson. The pain in his stomach was getting stronger, sharper. He ran south, away from the column, holding his gut with one hand and the Glock in the other. A glance over his shoulder toward Place Vauquelin brought no sign of the sniper. He quickly reached Rue Saint Vincent and turned left.

The street was long, narrow—a gauntlet. Several cars lined its right side. He angled toward them, forcing each pained stride. No doubt the man with the Ruger was still coming fast; his partner could be lurking in any one of the surrounding shadows. The longer this chase went, the closer Kent felt the noose tighten around his neck.

He continued to suppress what was an overwhelming urge to look at the tablet. Did the words scrawled upon it signal another location or the end of the line? Did they make sense at all? None of it mattered if he didn't survive the next five minutes.

Nearly a hundred feet down, Kent came alongside a Toyota SUV. He ducked behind and glanced back up the street. The man with the Ruger was sprinting toward him, lethal focus dominating his young face.

Younger than Kent expected. Mid-twenties, sharp features—European, maybe west or north. There was no time to ask. Kent raised his gun, stepped out and fired two rounds.

The first missed the man's neck by inches; the second dug into his right shoulder, jerking that side of his torso back in a violent spasm. He didn't stop, though. Switching the Ruger to his left hand, he continued racing down the road, a machine programmed to terminate.

Kent was already sprinting himself, further down the street and away from the Ruger's sightlines. A spray of fresh bullets dented subsequent cars, the shots more than accurate from an off-hand. A final slug shattered the windshield of a Volkswagen directly beside Kent. He rushed into the next intersection and dove right, onto Rue Sainte Therese.

No more running. His abdomen felt like a meat grinder, churning his own flesh. Movement was becoming hard enough without eluding a pair of professional killers. His only chance was to be the last one standing, and walk out of here.

When Kent had leapt to safety on the new street, he'd almost cracked his skull on a car parked tight against the near curb. There were just a handful of seconds before the Ruger turned the corner. Strafing around to the other side of the vehicle—a Ford sedan—Kent crouched against the pavement and spied beneath the chassis.

Silence reigned, its only competition the muted whine of sirens finally arriving at the original scene. An icy gust poured in from nowhere, battering Kent's exposed frame like a beached schooner. He kept his balance and spotted the man's boots a second later, rounding the edge with more caution than before.

Kent crept toward the front rim of the car, Glock poised. One more look below. He froze: there were no feet. Just the instant, telltale note—from above—of weight denting metal. His chest surged into his throat as he sprang upward. At the same time the man slid over the roof of the car, leading with the Ruger.

Kent clutched the gun hand and bent the wrist inward. The man grunted in pain and discharged the pistol off-target, inches from Kent's left ear. All immediately went quiet, his eardrum ringing, starting to bleed. But he maintained his grip, pulling his adversary off the roof and slamming him onto the pavement. The Ruger clattered away.

Kent had his finger on the Glock's trigger but paused for the briefest second, the screeching in his head blurring his sight. The man took advantage and lifted a heavy boot toward Kent's stomach. Sole met slit and he howled in pain, doubling over. The Glock fell to the concrete.

The man scrambled to his feet; Kent forced himself to recover. There was nowhere to hide. They stood in the middle of the street, a pair of urban gladiators. The man winced from his bullet wound. Dark blood soaked his shoulder. But he quickly pulled out a small knife and circled around Kent. They were each crouched in defensive stances, forcing the dense air into their lungs.

Finally, the man lunged toward Kent's sternum. Kent parried the attack, chopping the knife from his foe's arm. But the man kept moving, spinning forward and sending his right elbow surging into Kent's exposed temple. Searing pain brought a darkness that threatened the edge of his vision. It seemed to stop, then continued its advance as the man wrapped his left arm around Kent's throat.

The assailant was no larger than Kent, but possessed the grip of a giant. Shadows turned to thunderclouds in Kent's eyes, slowly eliminating stubborn vestiges of light. A dozen methods of escape had already failed the checklist in his mind. Seconds remained; he was down to primal means of survival. Clawing, scratching, grabbing…nothing worked.

Then, with his view all but black, he found the man's right arm, wrapped slightly behind his back for protection. Kent pulled hard on it. No sound came first, just a trembling in both his adversary's shoulders. Then, suddenly, a scream of agony ripped the still air. He kept pulling, the force of his effort commensurate with the release of pressure on his neck.

It was soon too much; the man let go. Hazy forms began to redefine themselves in Kent's eyes. The man swung his left arm over to break Kent's grip, leaving himself defenseless to a counterattack. Kent drove his fist into the bullet wound once, then twice; another yell echoed down the street. Kent hooked his right leg behind his opponent and slung him to the ground. Immediately he turned, eyes scanning the pavement for the Glock. Its polymer gleamed ten feet away.

That's when he saw the car: rushing down the street directly toward him. Fifty feet, closing fast.

He didn't need to eye the windshield to know the man behind the wheel was the sniper. His partner must've had some kind of tracker on his phone or person. A detail that no longer mattered. It, like every other distraction, was simply noise that fell upon Kent's near-deaf ear. The only thing his good one heard was the angry growl of the vehicle's four-cylinder engine. Each tire gripped the lane like the claws of a predator. It was just a Civic, but at fifty miles per-hour any car was a deadly.

One chance. He lunged toward the Glock, knowing the man behind him would soon recover and go for his own gun. The car neared at greater speed now, the gap between its grille and Kent's face disintegrating.

He reached down, scraping his palm across the cement, grasping the pistol. In one motion he raised its barrel toward the front windshield.

There was no one there.

He spotted the sniper an instant later, rolling to the right twenty feet back. The man had jumped out early, realizing Kent would reach the Glock and take aim. The driver's-side door hung open like a limp wing.

Kent could feel the car's hot breath on his legs. He jumped up, planted one foot on the hood and dove right. Almost simultaneously, the Civic's door smashed into the Ford and broke off with a loud crunch.

Still airborne, Kent glanced behind. The other man had also rolled free of the car and was reaching for his gun. Kent tumbled to the ground beside the mangled door. A roar of metal and glass swallowed the thin lane as the Civic collided with a hotel facade on the far end.

Kent saw the sniper settle himself and take aim with a pistol. He thought about raising the Glock, but only had milliseconds—there was no time for accuracy. Instead, he tilted the door over his torso.

Two shots. Kent felt their impact, each round ricocheting off the metal barrier. A third did not come. His first instinct was to check the shooter, but instead he trained his gaze down the street. The man with the Ruger was collapsing to the ground, a fresh bullet hole staining his forehead.

Kent immediately turned back, reaching for his Glock with the door still splayed across half his body. The shooter, seeing the unexpected result of his attack, had frozen for a split-second. Kent grasped the polymer handle and swung it on target. His opponent's movements were a mirror.

Two more shots.

Both rounds from the Glock reached their destination—the left side of the man's chest—before he could completely pull the trigger on his own gun. The slugs did their work, burrowing deep beneath the flesh and knocking their victim off his feet.

Kent slowly slid the door off and crawled to his feet. The street had gone instantly, eerily quiet. He could hear no other sound than his own labored breathing. He started forward, left hand putting pressure on his throbbing abdomen, right pointing the Glock's barrel at what he knew was already a corpse.

Ten more feet eliminated all doubt. The man stared back with empty eyes, his mouth open, a trickle of blood draining toward the cold pavement. Kent noticed his jaw, cheekbones; he might've been the other's twin.

They were family. What did that mean?

No time to wonder. This street wasn't exactly a deserted chapel. He could still hear sirens a block away, police securing the square. Minutes from now they'd be swarming this area, along with employees and guests of the hotel. He'd already lost about as much blood as he could stand.

Jogging back to the first body, he pulled off the man's jacket, carefully holding it free from his bloody stomach. Inside was the wallet he also wanted. Turning, Kent stuffed his own coat—minus the stone—in a nearby trash can and dashed toward the shadows of Rue de Vaudreuil.

24

"You want a refill, Ally?"

The largest speakers were across the room, over seventy feet away, but Allison could still feel their heavy throb. "What?"

Becky Townsend held up her own empty glass with a raised eyebrow. Allison shook her head: two apple martinis were fine to get her going; a third would've had the opposite effect. "Suit yourself," Becky said with a smile.

She was already flagging down their waiter, a slick-haired beanpole who looked like he'd just finished ninth grade. Her boyfriend, Petr Arnold, was stationed beside her and waved the young man off. "My steak's finally settled." He nodded toward the dance floor. "Why don't we get some exercise?"

An extrovert like Becky needed no convincing. Two more excited nods came from the other side of the table. Sam and Erin Carter had been a little quiet at dinner, but were now starting to loosen up. Allison was glad. Inviting two couples who didn't know each other on a weeklong vacation was a risk that looked to be paying off.

Allison had crossed paths with Erin over a year ago at a medical conference in Atlanta; Sam worked IT for Coca Cola. The two of them—married a year now—seemed a glowing example of commitment. Allison found herself studying their interaction, admiring the clear traces of romance and friendship. They appeared to genuinely enjoy one another's company.

That was the challenge, of course—learning to savor time with your spouse, even when you had a great deal of it. Far rarer was the inverse: two people hoping to spend decades together, yet seemingly destined for mere days here and there.

Allison pushed her martini glass away, further distancing herself from the room's accoutrements. Was it possible to feel alone in the middle of a crowded room? *Yes.* Beyond an army of bass-notes, and the crush of several hundred short-term friends, lay the empty seat at her side. 'Alone' didn't limit itself to human geography; it seeped into your bones.

"*Ally?*" The voice sounded distant, but managed to bring Allison back into the room. She suddenly realized she was the only one sitting. Becky, leaning over the table, tried again. "Ally, you coming?"

Allison glanced around: for all its top-shelf alcohol and designer clothing, the club had the distinct feel of a rollercade. Flashing strobes relentlessly pierced every neon shadow; a thin layer of indistinct smoke softened the gloom; the pop beats were loud, fast, forgettable. She stood. "Actually, I think I'm going to sit this one out. I could use some fresh air."

A buzz of expected protest from the quartet flew across the table. Allison shook her head. "Thanks, but I'm fine. You guys go have fun. I'll catch up later." *Or tomorrow.*

There was a short silence. Insistence played in each of their eyes, but they seemed to see her mind was made up. Becky finally nodded. "Okay." She turned to the other three. "I'll catch up with you."

Petr put his hand on her arm. "Babe—"

"*Just* a minute," she said, reciprocating the movement. Becky may have loved to party, but every so often she reminded you she was an adult.

Like Allison, she was a nurse. The two had met through an overseas work program and hit it off. Becky used to live ten thousand miles away and still had the Australian accent to prove it. Now, though, with Petr's five-karat engagement rock weighing down her left hand, she'd moved across two oceans to his flat in Vienna. Taking a week off to cruise the Caribbean with her closest girlfriend was hardly a detour.

Petr, Sam and Erin stepped onto the tile floor as a fresh song hijacked the speakers. Allison couldn't tell the tune from its ten cousins that'd come before, and realized that was probably the point. Becky traced the outer edge of the table and sat down beside her friend. "Tell me this won't become a routine."

"What?" said Allison.

"You know what." She gestured in the general direction of the outer deck. "Jeremy wouldn't want you moping out there any more than I do."

Allison bristled at the last verb, even if it were true. "Why do you think—"

"I know you, Ally." Becky shifted her weight on a pair of suede heels. "For the record, I think your boyfriend's a great guy. But I certainly wouldn't have forgiven him as quickly as you did. What makes an accountant cancel at the last minute, anyway?"

"I told you," said Allison, hardly having to manufacture a defensive tone, "a billion-dollar client had an emergency. Jeremy wasn't the only one. A whole team of lawyers and CPAs got called in." She tried, in vain, to conceal the growing lump in her throat.

Becky's expression soured, as if she'd finally broken free from a daze. She reached forward and hugged Allison. "I'm sorry, sweetie. I'm not mad at you; I'm not even mad at Jeremy." She pulled back. "I'm just...frustrated with the circumstance, you know? I wanted this trip to be perfect."

Allison recovered enough to place a hand on her friend's shoulder. "It will be, I promise. We'll do so much in the next seven days even you'll be tired." This drew a small grin, enough for both of them to build upon. "Now go out there and rescue Petr."

Becky eyed the dance floor, its generous length lined with sweating bodies. "He's a great dancer."

"Only when he's got a partner."

"That's what I'm afraid of."

Allison lifted Becky's ring finger. "If she doesn't have one of these, she's just a substitute. Kick her out."

Becky gave Allison another hug and shuffled toward the throng. She turned back knowingly. "I'll see you tomorrow."

"Don't be so sure. I might surprise you tonight."

Becky shook her head. "You couldn't fool me if you tried."

25

Allison stepped outside and was immediately met by a warm breeze. She stole a look back at the club's entrance, realizing the space beyond could've been anywhere. Which made the fact that it was in the center of a cruise ship either a compliment or an insult, depending on perspective.

The *Blue Countess* was over a thousand feet long and hosted four times as many passengers. Six hours ago, she'd slipped out of Jacksonville with surprising grace and was now gliding toward Grand Bahama beneath a quilt of stars. There were five more ports of call ahead of them across the eastern Caribbean. Yet the *Countess* was an island to herself. In addition to a second nightclub along her stern, the boat held a casino, movie theatre and nearly a dozen restaurants. Allison wondered how many passengers would even bother to disembark.

Despite her size, the *Countess* possessed surprising touches of beauty. Blocks of glossy marble anchored a nearby pool bar; almost every window, including those wrapping the distant bridge, sparkled amidst crystal accents. Allison herself strode across a teak deck straight out of the White Star Line's luxury catalog.

She took a deep breath. Her escape wasn't all a lie; she really had needed some air. She thought she was the only one, too, until a slight figure emerged from around a corner. It was a man—a boy—just as young as their waiter and also part of the cruise staff. Maybe some kind of deckhand: he wore navy shorts and a white polo.

Head down, he didn't seem to notice her until they were about to pass.

Just in time, he looked up and tipped an imaginary cap above a mop of blonde hair. Allison nodded, managing an obligatory smile. As they stretched apart, she didn't look back but remained locked on his green eyes. They were lonely, which made sense; most crews were a mix of nationalities and isolated from mainstream society by large swaths of water and time.

Allison made a mental note to improve her smile during the next exchange. For now, she cleared her mind and stepped toward the railing. Beyond its waist-high metal gleam, darkness dominated the horizon. A few small dots of light—probably other cruise ships—peppered the void.

She reached the edge and looked down. The water, lapping against the hull several stories below, was invisible. She could hear it, though. This was the one place that made every ship—large and small, past or present—equal. It was a universal feeling, standing at the point where your vessel met the sea, staring into an expanse of possibility.

Alone. She tried to shut the word out again. This time, though, it meant something different. Something more.

More days wondering where Kent was, knowing she would never find out. More nights on her own, hoping for one phone call and dreading another. She glanced up, stars dancing around fresh patches of cloud. This wouldn't be the only trip Kent missed. The worry and disappointment she was experiencing now weren't instances, they were a lifestyle. Was she willing to work that hard? Was he worth it?

Already she'd felt the effects of such a relationship. Tonight wasn't the beginning. Only she'd known, when they'd gone out with friends, why Kent consistently claimed the outer seat of a booth. Only she'd caught his eyes scanning the exits, cataloguing every new person who walked in. Part of his secret would always be hers to bear.

And yet, she could almost imagine a world in which none of that mattered. Where mere fragments of time spent together added up to a complete life. Because when Kent held her, she felt invincible; when she looked into his eyes all she saw was…home.

"'Nice night' doesn't quite say it."

Allison nearly jumped out of her skin and over the railing. Three feet to her left stood a man—tall, handsome, already throwing his hands up in apology. "Sorry. I've got a bad habit of treading softly."

Between pounding heartbeats, she got a better look at him. His hair was dark, near shoulder-length. Tailored suit, unbuttoned at the collar—he looked like he'd just stepped off the set of a commercial for a high-end brand of vodka.

He offered a disarming smile. "Let me try this again." He reached out a hand. "Rick Samuels."

She hesitated, still catching her breath. "I'm sorry, do I know you?"

He chuckled. "Not yet. I saw you back in the club. Didn't get a chance to introduce myself before you walked out."

She'd suspected, and now she knew. But what was a little harmless flirting? This was a safe enough place—they were out in the open; a few other people had started strolling nearby. "Why would you want to do a thing like that?"

"Because there are hundreds of good-looking women on this boat and somehow you're in a different class."

Allison laughed. "Does that line work every time?"

"I don't know, it's my first attempt. But you seem like someone who appreciates honesty.

It was a cheesy excuse, but he'd used it with conviction. She decided to play along. "My name's Allison."

"Allison...?"

"I make a point of requiring at least two minutes of conversation before giving out my last name."

"Fair enough. I'm sorry to interrupt your solitude, Miss Allison. Were you enjoying yourself?"

She sobered slightly. "More or less." A pause. "How do you know I'm a 'miss?'"

He pointed to her left hand. "No ring, and, at the risk of sounding like a stalker, you didn't seem paired up with any of your friends."

She tilted her head. "You must've had a lot of time to observe."

"More like another old habit that won't die. I used to be a cop."

Her gaze widened, then fell on the suit. "Have you upgraded? That thing would've cost half a patrolman's pension."

"A perk of the job, though this trip's not much more than babysitting." He took a breath, leaning against the railing. "I work for a corporate security firm out of Las Vegas. Inside the club we just left are two CEO's from merging construction companies trying to convince themselves—and their wives—that they're still twenty-five."

"And you're here to protect them from…bartenders and pirates?"

"Whatever helps them sleep at night. Their peace is my paycheck."

"What about now, leaving your post? Aren't you worried about some break-dancing assassin?"

"I think they can spare me for one *Electric Slide*."

She studied him a bit more. He looked to be in his late-thirties, toned and tanned. Probably well-traveled, protecting clients across the globe. She pictured him doing this same thing on another ship in another sea, with another woman. "Is this how you seduce all your fellow passengers?"

"Only the ladies. Men aren't so patient." She chuckled. "How am I doing so far?"

"Just fine, though this is where we stop." She raised a palm to make the point. "Any more and it wouldn't be fair to you. Or my boyfriend."

His eyebrows rose, and then he grinned. "Now who's the one with the line? You want me to walk away, I'll walk away. But don't ask me to believe there's some guy out there who'll let a woman like you take a cruise on her own. No one's that stupid."

She looked down for a moment. "I'm flattered, Mr. Samuels."

"Rick, please."

"And my boyfriend can be an idiot. But he's also very real."

He paused. "Well then, he's quite a lucky guy. For me to miss this trip I'd have to be saving the world."

Allison was silent. Rick gazed out to sea, like a prized debater reconciling himself to unexpected defeat. "At least let me walk you to your stateroom"

She shook her head. "Going to enjoy this weather a bit more. But thanks for the offer."

"As you wish." He mustered a smile. "Goodnight."

With that he turned away, padding off as silently as he'd come. She watched him shrink against the extended deck, suit shimmering beneath the ship's bright lights. His broad shoulders seemed to have drooped slightly. She almost felt sorry for him.

But couldn't quite bring herself there. Even in rejection, the man had a smoothness to his gait, an air of unnerving confidence. Allison couldn't escape the feeling that she was being played.

26

Kent hadn't looked back at the two dead bodies. Hugging the new coat tight around his shoulders, fighting the urge to double over in agony, he walked south along Rue Saint Paul. Three blocks later he turned west, beginning a long detour around to his Nissan. The car should've remained unknown to authorities, and such a circuitous route was the only way to reach it undetected. The center was still a massive buzz of police activity, but they hadn't yet established a solid perimeter.

He'd kept to the shadows, just another native braving the sharp chill. Eventually—his new coat now spotted with a touch of crimson—he made it back to the car. Rue Notre-Dame was quiet; the area directly around the column had been roped off, but fell far short of the Sentra. The relative warmth of its cabin—the mere chance to sit back—were momentary heavens.

Kent's body pleaded with him to shut down. It would've only taken an instant, and lasted forever. His brain—stronger than every aching muscle—overruled the request. Instead, he brought the Sentra around in a U-turn and began searching for a deserted pharmacy.

It was the only task more immediate than leaving town. He'd long ago abandoned the thought of flying out. Even if police didn't yet know who or what they were looking for, their search would start at the airport. Train and bus stations came next. He was going to have to drive to safety. Roadblocks were a possibility, but took time to establish and had to cover myriad points of egress. The odds were good enough to test—as if he had a choice.

Ten minutes later he found what he was looking for off Rue Sainte Catherine, the blue cross above its doors framed by the moon's pale wash. Fifty feet overhead, steady traffic trundled across the western edge of Jacques Cartier Bridge. Kent pulled around to the rear of the building. It was dark, quiet. He gritted his teeth and exited the car; blood continued to trickle down his abdomen. The threat of unconsciousness returned. One way or another, this was his last stop.

He'd have given anything to just shoot the back door off its hinges. Instead, he searched the parking lot for a few small pieces of metal. Soon he'd dismantled the lock, then a simple alarm. He made straight for peroxide, bandages and a medical sewing kit. Then came water and pain medication.

Fifteen minutes passed. He stood in front of the store's bathroom mirror, eying the results of his do-it-yourself surgery. The stitches weren't perfect, but they'd hold. His left ear was a different story. The trickle of blood down the lobe had dried, and he'd cleaned it away. There was still pain, and almost no hearing. Any sounds he could catch were faint, as if miles away. It was impossible to know, right now, if the loss was permanent.

Kent wiped up the rest of the blood, wiped down his prints and stole a Canadiens t-shirt from a promotional rack. Two hundred dollars left on the counter for the damage and he was gone.

The next hour passed, blessedly, without incident. Fifty miles outside the city he'd pulled into a truck stop and traded the bloody clothing for a ballcap and jacket to cover his shirt. Twenty miles farther he'd exited onto a service road, curved to the shoulder and cut the Sentra's engine. Then, and only then, did he allow himself a look at the tablet that'd been burning a hole in his pocket.

For a moment, its cryptic words took his pain away. He was reminded that this was a tangible message from the distant past. It felt like a dream—something that shouldn't exist.

Then, just as quickly, the pain returned. The rock felt heavy in his hands, the etchings sharp. It was a message, yes, but not a benign one. More like a piece of cursed treasure. Words that didn't treat his wounds, but caused them.

Now, guiding the Sentra southwest along Highway 401, Ottawa's lights dimming in the distance, he had little idea what the new clues meant. Even more important, though, was whether they represented the final link to the assassins' identity. It was becoming clear that another step after this one simply wasn't possible. The kill date would be here in a mere seventy-two hours—and counting.

27

"Some kind of bird!"

The man standing in the middle of the living room had a knee raised and both arms out. At the sound of these words, he nodded excitedly and pointed to another man sitting beside McCoy. This second man was leaning forward, eyes gleaming in concentration. Some people loved games.

The first man gestured with each hand in a circular motion, as if to say more was needed. Six feet across a floor of soft carpet, gravity was transferring the few remaining grains of sand through a plastic hourglass. A spark of tension filled the warm room.

"A stork," said the sitting man. "A crane!"

The man on his feet made the same motion with his hands. The other opened his mouth, but couldn't find the right word. A brief patch of futile silence followed, then a quartet of women across the room shouted "time!"

The pressure immediately subsided. The actor lowered his limbs, crumpled up a small piece of paper and tossed it in a bowl near the hourglass. "It was a flamingo," he said to the three men before him. There was some quiet laughter and discussion of the clue as he joined his team's ranks. A few in the party reached for half-filled wine glasses.

The man who'd been guessing turned to McCoy in thinly-veiled frustration. "Where were you on that one, Pete? We're losing."

McCoy knew his brother-in-law meant well. The man had married

Susan, McCoy's younger sister, and was a good husband. As the vice-principal of a nearby private school, he brought a genial attitude home every evening. This, though, wasn't a hallway of timid teens. It was a group of peers, and his competitive side had won out. It was understandable. What else did the man have to care about right now?

McCoy might've thought the same thing for himself. His duties were certainly different—terrorists instead of teachers, countries for classrooms. But in a strange way, his world often felt normal. You simply got used to the carnage, if for no other reason than the fact it never stopped. There was always another threat over the horizon. Such a life, for the right kind of person, eventually became manageable.

But not tonight. An hour back he'd received a cryptic text from Kent: '*Alive, with stone. Leaving city, will contact soon.*' Fifteen minutes later clarification came as a surge of updates besieged his phone. The streets of Montreal had just witnessed a shootout and foot-chase; a dozen bullets, two dead bodies. The press would be all over it, especially considering the likelihood of a third gunman who'd yet to be identified.

"Sorry Dan," said McCoy, shaking an empty bottle of Budweiser. "Think I need some more liquid motivation." He stood and faced the entire group. "Anybody want a refill?"

One hand went up, on the far side of the room. It belonged to an attractive woman around McCoy's age, whom he'd just met tonight. "I'll take another bottle of Stella, please."

"You got it."

A second later he was striding toward the kitchen in exasperation. The woman's name was Kate Nichols, and she was all Susan's idea. McCoy's sister had made plenty of comments over the years about him meeting someone, but tonight words finally became action. Kate was new to the area and had recently begun working alongside Susan at the University of Maryland.

There were three couples at tonight's house party, and another pair of third wheels. This, evidently, was to be the meet-cute from which two lonely forty-somethings spread their wings as star-crossed lovers. McCoy was noti-fied of the arrangement in advance; Kate had been spared such a mortifying heads-up.

Instead, all she'd been told was that Susan's workaholic brother had miraculously agreed to join the dinner party and they needed one more person to even out the teams for games afterward. McCoy reached the refrigerator and found himself wondering whether Kate had seen through the ruse.

The rub of it all was he liked her. She was smart, successful and funny. If Susan had suggested a blind date, the two of them might've gone out together and had a great time; at least they'd have known what they were into. The thing McCoy hated most about tonight was its indirection. For her part, Kate remained upbeat. Maybe she was simply determined to make the best of an awkward situation.

Which brought him back to Montreal, though 'awkward' was far too kind a word. It would've been naïve to assume Kent wasn't somehow involved in the violence. Had he been shot? Bleeding out in a darkened alley? The word 'alive' rang through McCoy's head, reminding him that an officer of Kent's ability was trained in the art of self-assessment. *If he were dying, he would've said so.* If only that made the waiting easier.

The worst part was McCoy could do little to help. The CIA didn't exactly have an army of assets in eastern Canada. He had, though, made a few friends within CSIS, the country's primary intelligence wing, and knew the cultural attaché at the American Embassy in Ottawa. Shortly after news of the event came through, he'd excused himself to the bathroom and sent texts requesting information. Had the bodies been ID'd yet? Was there any further information on the mystery shooter? He'd yet to receive a response.

The simplest thing would've been to leave the party and drive to Langley. They were currently in Wheaton, Maryland—his office was only ten miles away. But the alcohol here had just started to flow; checking out now would've raised too many eyebrows. Even if everyone at the gathering, including his sister, thought he was a glorified pencil-pusher.

It didn't feel like a particularly noble sacrifice, but it was his part to play. So he clutched a beer in each hand and strode out of the kitchen with a forced grin. Rising laughter filled the living room at the other end of a short hallway. That's when his phone began to vibrate. Setting the bottles down on a thin table, McCoy looked at the screen with wide eyes.

He immediately ducked back through the kitchen toward a door leading to the rear patio. His answer came in a near-whisper even as he stepped outside into the chilly air. "McCoy."

"Am I the top story?" Kent's voice was tipped with the slight rasp of exhaustion, but came through clear.

"Not until the press slaps names onto your John Does. Were they the only two?"

"Yeah. Might as well have been an army, though. Just like Portugal."

McCoy could hear the grimace in Kent's words. "You're injured."

"Just a flesh wound."

"This isn't Hollywood, Jeremy. I need you operable."

"I'm fine," said Kent, a shade of defiance punctuating each word.

McCoy paused before asking the next question. "What's your location?"

"South of Ottawa, on the 401."

"Are the police onto you?"

"I spoke with a patrolman, up close, before the shots. He'd have raised the alarm once he saw I wasn't one of the corpses. There was also restaurant surveillance footage. Probably blurry, but I couldn't chance staying put. The noose would've tightened quickly."

"What direction are you headed?"

"West—Toronto. That should give me enough clearance to safely board a plane."

"Where to?"

"Island Melody."

"I'm sorry?"

"That's the clue: *Island Melody.*"

Silence enveloped the patio, McCoy's heart slowly sinking within his chest. *Island Melody.* That could mean…anywhere.

"From Toronto," continued Kent, "I can access the Caribbean and Atlantic. But there's no sense in moving until we know more. And no, the specific clue hardly helps."

"Text it to me anyway," said McCoy, still recovering.

"Already done, along with the ID info from one of the men I killed."

"You think it's legit?"

"The way these guys work, I'd almost be disappointed if it were. I'm guessing we struck out with the phone?"

"Langley's still trying to crack her. Mother of an encryption package. I don't know if that means what's concealed is worth it, or just a dead end."

"And the body?"

"You weren't kidding, a giant. Team had a killer time dragging it out of the chapel." McCoy paused, despair giving way to frustration. "Nothing on the prints. We'll have to wait a bit longer for DNA."

"Another wonderful day in the CIA." Kent let the sarcasm hang, then grew quiet. "How's Jim?"

"Same story. Santos checked in this afternoon. Breathing's normal, eyes still shut. For all that, he seems peaceful."

Quiet bit the other end. McCoy allowed himself an extra moment. "Jeremy, you know how this works. The longer he's out, the less chance…"

"I know."

McCoy believed him. Theirs was a business of human atrophy. Casualties had to be born, without a step lost. Even if they tore your heart out.

Suddenly there was nothing left to say. "I'll be in touch," said McCoy.

The line went dead a moment later. He gazed beyond the patio, eying the frost accumulating on his sister's dormant lawn. It always—

"Pete."

McCoy spun to find Dan standing in the doorway, confusion marring his face. "What are you doing out here?"

He held the phone up. "Sorry. Friend of mine had a rough day."

"Well, aren't you the good Samaritan."

McCoy stepped back inside. "I don't know. It's feeling more and more like work."

"You're willing. That's what counts." Dan closed the door. "All the more reason to get you back to the party."

"Oh?"

"For Kate." They started walking through the kitchen. "She deserves a nice guy in her life. Call me crazy, but I think you two'd really hit it off." He paused. "Have you ever thought of asking her out?"

McCoy put an arm around his brother-in-law. "You know, Dan, I just might have to."

28

Edmund van Leer thanked the heavens for such poor visibility. Anything that increased the challenge sharpened the challenger. In this case, fog had rolled in ahead of the dawn, smothering the landscape beneath a cloud of damp and cool. He could barely see fifty feet ahead.

Perspiration still came, heaviest on his forehead and lower back. Running two miles—the last hundred meters at a dead sprint—would do that to you. Now he'd traded the dirt track for a lawn between tall hedgerows. It was a fluid transition; this was all part of the same exercise. Accuracy only counted if you could maintain it through exhaustion.

The pistol lay on a nearby table. He gripped its cold steel, rolled ahead and fired two shots at the first target. Both slugs thudded near the center of the thick, wooden circle. Edmund dashed ahead, sliding on the wet grass and squeezing two more rounds toward a mark thirty feet ahead. Slightly less accurate, but still close.

One more station—another pinpoint burst—brought him to the final test. He rushed toward a second table, laid the handgun down and gripped a rifle. Kneeling, he rested the barrel on the table and stared down the hedgerow into the gloom. As if part of the exercise, the fog thinned just enough to reveal a final target one-hundred-fifty meters distant. Edmund focused in, let out a deep breath and squeezed the trigger.

The crack of the larger gun shook the still air. He traded the rifle for a nearby set of binoculars and surveyed the result. The .30 caliber bullet had burrowed deep into the wood three inches from dead-center. Tight enough for a kill, which was all that mattered. He flashed the scenery a rare grin and reached for a bottle of water on the table.

He heard a pair of approaching footsteps between swigs, but kept drinking. The gait was long, casual, their owner no mystery. Soon a tall, wiry man appeared through the mist. He moved easily in khakis and a worn leather vest. Trimmed white hairs hid beneath a brown shooting cap, though a matching mustache still announced his age. He stopped six feet short and tipped his bill. "Morning, Edmund."

"Morning." Van Leer reached out half-heartedly. "Won't you step close enough to shake a man's hand?"

The newcomer shook his head. "Not when his guns are active. 'Never crowd a shooter and his weapon.' That's the first rule here."

"Of course." Edmund stuffed the pistol away and cradled the rifle. He angled forward and gripped the man's hand. "Good to see you, Jesper. Fine day for a shoot."

The man looked around. "If you say so. I'm afraid not everyone shares your enthusiasm." He nodded at the nearest target. "Weather certainly hasn't slowed you down. Maybe you could show my students a few things."

"My words would fall on deaf ears." They started back toward the track. "You teach men to protect. I'll always be a hunter."

Jesper smiled, but had nothing to say. They continued walking, through the heart of what was known as "The Academy." Fifteen years ago, it'd been a neglected swath of green pasture. Today, over one-hundred acres of the best security-training money could buy.

Jesper Aarden was a retired colonel in the Royal Netherlands Army. His lack of relative wealth was balanced by lofty stature within the community. This secured him an invitation, years ago, to one of the parties the Van Leer's were forced to throw to project a sheen of local goodwill. Free food and booze were enough to fool the most seasoned skeptic, much less a gaggle of naïve, sycophantic neighbors.

But Jesper was a bit different; he at least lived in the real world. After a couple of Amstels, he'd cornered Edmund and mentioned an idea he had for, essentially, a bodyguard training site. These days, government officials weren't the only ones with security details. Athletes, movie stars, corporate executives—all had need of protection, and were willing to pay well for it. But while law enforcement and the military provided core experience, another step was needed to refine the skills and temperament of elite sentries.

The Academy was born shortly thereafter. Jesper started with himself and six "students." Now he led an army of lieutenants, and their specialized training ground was one of the most prestigious, if secretive, of its kind. Applicants came from all over the world, paying top dollar for such tactical expertise. Whether or not they joined legal enterprises after graduation was a separate issue. The Academy itself was a completely legitimate operation.

Government opposition had fallen beneath the weight of Edmund's influence. Soon the necessary permits were issued. The possibility of prestige, and the promise of tax revenue, didn't hurt such a cause.

Initially funded through a series of corporations devoid of the Van Leer name, the project was now a well-oiled, self-sustaining machine. Jesper was the sole owner and operator, but the family had free access to the facility whenever it wanted.

They reached the track and stopped. Thick fog continued to coat the air, but an orange glow now lit the horizon as the sun defiantly burned through the clouds. Jesper turned left, toward the camp's main lodge. "Probably still some breakfast on the table. Hungry?"

Edmund shook his head. "All business this time. I've got to get cleaned up for a board meeting in two hours."

"*Cleaned up*," echoed Jesper. "Draped in a designer suit, raking in profits from the comfort of an office." He paused. "Sometimes I wonder whether I chose the right profession."

"Don't wonder." Edmund took one more look at the course he'd just completed. "Fresh air, with a gun in your hands…no amount of money can buy this kind of freedom. It's the pinnacle."

Jesper was about to respond, but instead squinted ahead. Edmund followed his gaze, spotting a figure approaching through the mist. "A little early for the first exercise," said Jesper. "I don't think—"

"He's one of mine," said Edmund, turning to his companion. "It's been a pleasure, Jesper."

A spark of hesitation lit the man's eyes, but he recovered quickly. "Of course," he said, nearly bowing to the camp's real owner. Without another word Jesper spun and began marching back toward the lodge. Edmund exhaled, remembering when one man's fear was enough to satiate his addiction. There was simply no drug like power.

He remained still, watching Jakob close the distance between them. The younger man didn't speak until he was directly in front of his brother. "It's confirmed."

Edmund paused, briefly. "It's a forty-minute drive. You could've called."

"This isn't the kind of news you deliver over the phone."

"You think I care that my sons are dead?"

"I think you care that Kent is one step closer to completing the puzzle."

Edmund started the quarter-mile trek toward his parked Range Rover. "All the CIA did last night was pay us a compliment."

Jakob kept pace alongside. "By eliminating two of our best assets?"

"By sending their best to do so." Edmund stopped and turned toward his brother. "Montreal was a death trap. The twins were both trained to kill, and good at it. They had the element of surprise. It's not the kind of scenario you're supposed to survive."

"What are you saying?"

"I'm saying the agency is desperate, and no matter how skilled he is, their man's cashed in all his luck to get this far." Edmund started walking again. "I'm saying it's Kai's turn. Kent has handled our head-on threats, but he can't compete with misdirection."

29

The rain was moving out. Stubborn drops still danced upon the Chevy Tahoe's expansive windshield, but the rising sun claimed a growing swath down the middle of Pennsylvania Avenue. Gray and purple shadows tested the edges of an intense, orange center. It shone like a rare, two-toned rainbow.

McCoy was too nervous to notice. He'd met the President on two prior occasions, but both had been within social settings and lasted a grand total of about thirty seconds. *"Hello, sir. Have you tried the punch? Yes, I think I saw your wife talking to the French Ambassador."*

Today was different. He was here in an official capacity, summoned for his expertise, discussing a threat that had the power to spread fear and death to nearly every corner of the globe. Never mind that only a handful of people knew about it; that only made each man's slice of burden greater to bear.

The SUV slowed at a stoplight and McCoy stole a glance at the man beside him: five-foot-eight, pale, one-hundred forty pounds soaking wet. Thomas Vanning hardly looked like the director of a rotary club, much less the CIA. But he *wasn't* nervous. And it wasn't the first time. The man never seemed rattled in situations like these. McCoy often wondered whether such calm came from experience or a rare, innate confidence. Vanning did have an amazing intellect. If only they could think their way out of this one.

They passed 17th Street and flashed identification at the police barricade. Since the Oklahoma City bombing the stretch of Pennsylvania directly in front of the White House had been restricted to authorized vehicles. The Tahoe went from its confines of rush-hour traffic to the almost pampered isolation of an open road. It was too early for tourists; a few joggers were their only company.

They reached the north entry gate and turned right, once again providing ID. Then it was up the driveway, veering away from the actual House and toward the West Wing. Their driver swung the SUV around a circle of asphalt and eased to a halt on the far side of the entry portico. McCoy saw the Marine doorman as they passed; POTUS was already here.

The driver, and the additional guard beside him, stayed put as both of their passengers alighted. McCoy concealed a grin; no CIA officer would ever have a car door held open for him. It was one of Vanning's pet directives, a subtle bulwark against the continual threat of political entitlement. *"Never forget: you're more cop than congressman."*

There was nothing they could do about the front door. Upon approach, the white-gloved Marine—no eye-contact, no wasted motion—turned and pulled the partition open. They hardly had to break stride.

The tiled vestibule was probably the most ornate space in the entire complex. Most of the West Wing was merely functional, sporting the same drywall and carpet found in typical mid-level office buildings.

Ahead lay the lobby, a modest eight-hundred square feet since the Nixon administration but currently highlighted by an ornament-laden Douglas fir. The rest of the room balanced simple furniture with gilt-framed artwork and an eighteenth-century bookcase. To the right, a dark-wood desk anchored the near corner; behind it sat a security guard. McCoy guessed the receptionist wouldn't be in for another hour.

Vanning was in the process of giving their name when a man appeared from the left, looking for all the world like he'd just stepped off the set of an Aaron Sorkin drama. Around McCoy's age, he flashed a set of bright eyes beneath a crown of perfectly-groomed hair. He began walking forward, shifting a folder to his left hand and stretching out his right. "Morning, Tom."

Vanning accepted with customary restraint. "Scott." He turned. "This is Pete McCoy, part of my senior staff. He's running point on the op."

The man nodded and offered McCoy the same greeting. "Scott Foster. President's Chief of Staff."

Now McCoy remembered. He'd seen Foster a few times but never had the pleasure of an introduction. The man had graduated Yale law and become a lobbyist, then traded millions in fees for public service. This post was hardly pittance, but McCoy couldn't help wondering if, one day, Foster planned to switch places with his boss. He decided to give the guy a chance; ambition didn't always come with an angle. Some people just had too much energy.

Pleasantries over, Foster started back the way he'd come. "Follow me, gentlemen."

They did, and soon left the lobby for a quiet corridor. The Roosevelt Room slid by on their right, its center conference table dominating the surrounding space. Ahead, the hallway curved to the right. Entryways on either side led to various offices, most empty. An aide passed them in the opposite direction, leather briefcase slung over her shoulder. She nodded to Foster and maintained eye contact with his companions.

The Oval Office lay directly ahead; no fanfare or warning. There was little need to check in with the President's personal secretary, who'd yet to arrive anyway. They bypassed her office and entered off the corridor.

Immediately things grew brighter. Sunlight, now a golden yellow, spilled through large windows along the room's southeast wall and washed the plush carpet at their feet. A pair of sofas flanked a marble fireplace, across from which lay the iconic Resolute desk. With no one behind it.

Foster closed the door once they were all in. "President should be here shortly. He had a few irregular beats during his last heart check. Doc wants him to stay regimented with the exercise."

"I'm guessing that didn't make the evening news," said McCoy, gaining his footing enough to speak freely.

"'Fit as a fiddle,' I think was the headline. Press can't resist their clichés."

Vanning glanced around the room. "Alvin still in New York?"

They'd discussed it on the way over. Two months back, a rogue faction of the Pakistan Army had gotten its hands on a store of plutonium. It turned out to be nothing—the mix was tainted. For a short time, though, the threat had been real. Alvin Sanders, Director of National Intelligence, was set to present the U.S.'s analysis of the situation to the UN Security Council this morning. Not something that could be rescheduled.

Foster was nodding. "He flies back this afternoon. We'll brief him then."

"Let's hope we have some good news," said Vanning.

On cue, the door to the Rose Garden swung open and the President walked in. Matthew Billings cut a striking figure: Six-two, silver hair, broad shoulders. He *looked* like the leader of the free world. But his requisite charm was genuine. Everyone said when it came to personal settings, he was more peer than president. His clothing today—nylon pants and a Michigan State sweatshirt—proved the point.

The man behind him lacked the luxury of such a wardrobe. As National Security Advisor, Bill Dyson wore a suit and tie like everyone else. But unlike Foster, he never let it go to his head. A hair shorter than Billings, and a few pounds heavier, Dyson bore his position with stress and pride—what most Americans expected from a cabinet-level post. He and the President had been close since their days as junior Rust Belt congressmen over thirty years ago.

The President set a half-empty water bottle on his desk and led the way toward the group. Introductions were made. Billings released McCoy's hand with narrow eyes. "We've met before."

"It's hardly worth a thought, sir."

After a moment Billings' gaze widened. "General Steiner's retirement party. You liked the punch."

McCoy failed to hold back a smile. "That was over nine months ago."

"I never forget a face." The President walked back to his desk and the water bottle. "Which is why I called you out here at such an ugly hour. Good intel is valuable in any form, but sometimes you've got to hear it from the source." He took a swig. "You're as close as I can get to Jeremy Kent."

Seconds later a Navy steward walked in carrying a tray filled with mugs and a silver carafe. "Ah, TJ, right on time." The President pointed to a coffee table between the sofas. "Please."

The young man set the tray down with nary a rattle of ceramic and silently retraced his steps. "Good enough for the Waldorf," said Billings after the door was closed. "And I don't even have to tip."

This earned a few chuckles as Foster reached for the tray. "No," said the President. "My office, I'll be mother."

Soon each cup was filled with steaming caffeine, some blacker than others. Billings claimed a leather chair in front of the fireplace. The other four were already camped out on the sofas. "Alright," he said, "where are we?"

He was looking directly at McCoy. The younger man turned to Vanning, who gave the slightest nod of approval. McCoy cleared his throat. "Mr. President, I understand you've been briefed on last night's events in Montreal. I've confirmed, from Kent himself, that he retrieved the second stone. However, he's had little success deciphering its code. That's essentially what it comes down to. We can only take this one step at a time, and we're paralyzed until we know the next location."

Billings took a gulp of coffee. He kept his eyes on McCoy for a moment longer, then set his mug down on the table. "Last night is all over the news. I trust we're not exposed?"

"No, sir." This from Vanning. "Kent was working alone in Montreal and left no ID. Prints and DNA will lead to dead-ends. All the police have are sketches."

Dyson leaned forward. "How long until the next date on the list?"

"Less than thirty-six hours," said McCoy.

"And where is Kent now?"

"Toronto, awaiting a direction."

"How do we give him one?" asked Foster.

Vanning frowned. "We have limited resources for deciphering such threadbare clues. Excepting Kent and Sanders, the only help we have beyond this room is a history professor in Louisiana."

Foster checked his notes. "Will Limon?"

McCoy took this one with a nod. "His knowledge on the Delacroix family is extensive. Retaining him to help solve each successive riddle only made sense."

"Containment?" asked Dyson.

"He lives alone, no neighbors. We have a constant team in and around his house to ensure isolation. He's not the type to try anything."

"What about the university?" asked Foster.

"Sick leave." McCoy chanced the slightest grin. "Symptoms were sudden. I hear the flu's just as bad down south as it is up here."

There was a pause. "I've considered," said Vanning, "opening this up to a few of my staff with the right security clearance. But…"

"But you—we—can't afford a leak," finished the President. "Let's hear it, then decide. This round must be a doozy."

McCoy felt every eye in the room suddenly turn his way. This time he didn't need his boss to nod permission. He faced the President. "Sir, just to reiterate, each recovered stone has contained two riddles: one general and one specific. The general has referred to a city, the specific an exact location within that city for the next stone."

He had the words memorized, but read from his folder in the spirit of officiality. "'Island Melody.' According to Kent, that is the general clue."

This was met with an expected cloud of daunting silence. The words were damning every time he said them, an impossible mountain made of five syllables. McCoy continued. "This obviously means an island. Owing to the fact that each general clue has narrowed the search to a particular city, we've seen fit to eliminate larger bodies like Australia and Japan. But beyond that it gets tricky. Plenty of islands have only one principal town or port, to which the clue could easily be referring."

"I assume," said the President, "that you've considered the 'melody' angle? Some regions—the Caribbean comes to mind—are more known for their music than others."

Vanning was nodding. "We also cross-referenced the known history of Emile and Mathieu Delacroix with the parameters of this clue. In both instances, dozens of possibilities still exist."

"Might the specific clue shed light on the general location?" asked Foster.

McCoy was already scanning his folder.

"Make a stand

Cornering evidence

Cross beyond Portland

Toward your deliverance"

One word was easy to key on. "We've already looked into Maine and Oregon," said Vanning, anticipating. "The latter has several small islands off its coast, but none stand out."

"There's even a Portland Island off the UK's southern coast," said McCoy. "But it has no overt connection to music. And this clue shouldn't lead us there anyway. Based on the pattern, we should already know the island from the general riddle."

Silence returned. McCoy knew he was right, and could see in each man's eyes that they agreed. "What about 'cornering evidence?'" asked the President. "Could that suggest some kind of law enforcement? Another statue, perhaps?"

Vanning nodded. "We looked into it. But—and I hate to sound like a broken record—that's still not definitive enough. Even if we were to pinpoint a monument or statue, it's a bit of a wild goose chase. We need a high degree of certainty before moving forward."

Foster emptied his mug. "I say we go for the British island. It's our best chance."

"But that's the point," said McCoy. "We can't leave the location to chance. Guess wrong and we miss the deadline."

Foster immediately sprang to his feet. "I hate this!" He paced away from the sofa, scattering expletives across the rounded chamber. McCoy knew the feeling, especially in this room. They were the most powerful men in the world, and they were being held hostage by a game. It was as if Risk had become reality, and everyone was losing.

The President turned to Vanning. "Tell me you've got an ace up your sleeve, Tom."

Vanning was just starting to shake his head when Dyson tilted his own. McCoy caught the movement and zeroed in on the NSA. "What is it?"

Dyson looked up, thinking. "What if 'Portland' isn't a place?"

This was enough to pull Foster back. "What?"

"Portland cement." Dyson shifted forward on the sofa. "Follow me for a minute: my cousin's a building contractor. He uses stucco on exteriors all the time. One of the main components of stucco is Portland cement. You all know what stucco looks like. Where have you seen it before?"

Foster was already tapping through his phone. "Stucco…a chief feature of Palladian and Neoclassical Architecture." He continued, burrowing deeper into the device. "It looks like…*here*." He glanced around. "It looks like the White House."

The President reached for the phone, which was given. After a moment he glanced up from the screen. "So, what are we saying?"

"We're saying," offered Dyson, "that Portland cement—especially over a century-and-a-half ago—points to a specific type of building."

The President chuckled. "But guys, we're looking for an island. A small one. Stone columns are the last thing you'd find."

Vanning straightened abruptly. "Unless it was a colony."

McCoy turned his way, feeling his heart skip within his chest. "A British colony."

Vanning was nodding and looked to the President. "Sir, you know your history. The British Empire stretched around the world. And they brought their buildings with them."

The President took a breath. He eyed each man in turn, finally coming back to Vanning and narrowing his gaze. "You think the word 'Portland,' in this riddle, denotes British colonial architecture?"

"It follows."

"But it's still not definite. Why are you sold on this theory instead of the others?"

"Not sold, sir, but confident. This gives us an exact structure that houses the stone, which the specific clue is designed to do."

"Although," said McCoy, "we don't know which exact structure."

"And I don't mean to blow the party dead," said the President, "but we also still don't know the island. You're right, Tom: I do know my history. The British Empire had more outposts and territories than it could count. Which means there are still too many possibilities.

"It's a start, sir," said Dyson.

"And it's good work." The President rose. Each man followed. "But I can't bet our national security on confidence." He faced Vanning. "Brief your staff, Tom. If we don't solve this soon, a security leak will be the least of our worries."

The asphalt was nearly dry as the Tahoe retraced its tracks down Pennsylvania. Their driver maintained his usual reticence. Vanning was on his cell with the deputy director, arranging a meeting for 10 a.m. It wouldn't be the last. McCoy imagined a room full of senior officers and young savants, all racking their brains for a thread that'd worn thin over a century ago. He needed to call Limon again.

A bump in the pavement jostled him free from his thoughts. The SUV slowed to a stop for a red light at 21st Street. For a moment everything stilled. McCoy could hear the V8 idling in line with the rest of traffic. He sank back into the upholstered seat, shielded from the biting wind and impatient horns outside. Vanning's soft cadence began slipping into the background collage. His own thoughts threatened to wander once more.

Then, across the street, he happened to notice a bus shelter. One of its side panels advertised a rock concert coming in the spring. It was colorful, but…*did those things ever work?* Half a second later, still staring at the ad, his synapses ignited and he froze.

It couldn't be that simple.

But the more he thought about it, the more everything fit. It wasn't just too much of a coincidence; it was the answer.

He turned to his left. "Tom, get off the phone."

Vanning gave him a sideways glance. They were close, but McCoy had never before referred to him as anything other than 'Director' or 'sir.' "Excuse me?"

The Tahoe was moving again. McCoy watched the bus shelter fall by as he looked his boss directly in the eyes. "*Now.*"

30

If O'Hare and LAX were cities in themselves, Toronto's Pearson Airport wasn't far behind. Seven square miles of runway and terminals, it touched more than one municipality and served the fourth-largest metropolis in North America. All in all, a good place in which to disappear.

But not until rush hour. Kent had reached the city limits just after 4 a.m. and pulled into an all-night diner. While at best the police had grainy surveillance video and rough sketches, the men on the other end of this puzzle knew exactly who he was. Or at least what he looked like. And airports were likely destinations. They'd been waiting at Montreal; it was reasonable to assume they'd be waiting here. He needed the cover of a crowd.

So he'd spent two hours in a corner booth, drinking cheap coffee and burying his face in the day's *Toronto Star*. The city had enough of its own news, but—such was the relationship between shootouts and circulation—Montreal's busy night still managed to claim a spot below the fold. It wasn't the first time Kent had read about himself on the front page. He couldn't help imagining the next batch of headlines: 'German Chancellor assassinated.' Or worse, 'A Member of the Saudi Royal Family.' *The Pope*? There was no best-case scenario.

Before leaving, he'd locked himself in the bathroom and lifted his shirt. Through the mirror's haze of grease, he could see the bandages were holding well. There was some crimson visible, but no saturation. He was also starting to regain some hearing in his left ear. He swallowed a few more pain reliever and climbed back into the Sentra.

It'd nearly been seven by the time he turned into an eight-story parking garage across from the airport. He'd left the Glock in the trunk and notified McCoy. It was painful, like parting with a child. But lugging a pistol on an international flight brought the kind of attention he couldn't afford.

Outside, there was no sun, but the slate gray ceiling did little to insulate the December chill. Collar up, Kent shouldered his duffel and made his way into terminal one.

Three more hours brought him up to the present moment, slouched against a bank of chairs along the far wall of the concourse. He'd pulled his cap low over his face and was practicing the art of sleeping with one eye open. Assuming the proper application of skill and experience, it wasn't quite as impossible as it seemed.

The thought had crossed his mind to wait somewhere off-site, but he needed to be able to select a gate and leave quickly. Besides, his current view offered ideal countersurveillance against anyone who might've picked up his trail. As it was, he'd seen no suspicious faces.

And a million benign ones. There was no lull in an airport this large. Business travelers mixed with tourists in wave after wave of headlong humanity. Many were looking at or talking on cell phones, others studied tickets and checked baggage. Some were secure, others frazzled, but Kent couldn't help envying each and every one of them. At least they knew where they were going.

He was about to pull out his newspaper from the diner when a man—late thirties, average height and build—broke from the stream of travelers toward the seats. He held a history magazine in his left hand. A moment later he chose a chair two spots to Kent's right and sank into it with a sigh. For a few seconds he was still, staring at the crowd with mild interest, almost zoning out. Then he sat back and opened the magazine.

But he didn't look at it. Instead, he turned to Kent. "You waiting too?"

Kent hesitated, then realized any reticence on his part would only draw a brighter spotlight. He lifted his bill and met the man's gaze. "How'd you know?"

"What else can a guy do in these seats? Sure ain't lounging for comfort." He flipped a page idly, then leaned in closer. "Is it a woman?"

This earned a near-genuine smile from Kent. "Not that lucky."

"Wrong word, pal. My wife and I were in here last month. To see some friends off, y'know. She spots a handbag for sale that she likes. So now, today, we come all the way back just so she can snoop around the stores. *In an airport.* Who does that?" He turned another page, shaking his head. "She buys me this magazine, tells me to read it while I wait. I don't even like history."

Kent eyed the man's worn boots and jeans, and could already see the matching pickup truck outside. Right now, his better half would be caressing a black leather purse, convincing herself it was worth the extra credit card debt. Kent managed a shrug. "You know what they say: happy wife, happy life."

The man snorted. "Yeah, well, pinch me when we get there."

One-sided conversations were work for both parties, and silence soon took over. The man continued to flip through the magazine, never spending more than a few seconds on any page. Kent's mind retreated back to square one, rolling the most recent riddle around for the thousandth time. But the more the words tumbled through his psyche, the more they receded into oblivion. It was as if he'd been studying the same scene for too long, and needed a fresh set of eyes to notice the obvious.

Ten minutes had slipped by when a short woman in knock-off designer boots broke free from the streaming foot traffic and waved toward the seats. Kent turned to his neighbor. "I think that's your cue."

The man looked his way, then straight ahead. A frown crept onto his face. "I'm worse than our dog. Don't even need a leash." He stood and tossed the magazine on the empty chair between them. "Enjoy that for me, will you?"

Kent thought about offering a vague line of encouragement, but instead simply nodded. The man began walking away, then spun back. "You know," he said, pointing to the magazine, "there is one good-looking article in there. Page fifty-six. It's on that famous American western feud. The Hatfields and the…"

He snapped his fingers, trying to recall.

"McCoys."

"That's it."

All at once, Kent knew. The only question was why it'd taken him so long. Had to be the fatigue.

Casually, he reached for the magazine. McCoy must've had his reasons for not simply sending a text. Inside, at the designated page, was an envelope. Kent opened it and removed a single slip of paper. An airline ticket, to…He read the destination, then read it again. *Of course.* Every ounce of exhaustion immediately melted away.

Singapore.

After the complexity of Montreal's riddle, it was almost cruel to make this one so basic. *Sing*-apore. Island *melody*. But it fit. The puzzle had finally come together. Kent, though, had little time to marvel at such antique ingenuity. The clock was still ticking.

He stood, slowly, forcing an air of nonchalance into his reenergized bones. The duffel bag felt lighter in his hands as he began heading toward the gate notated on the ticket. It was a long walk. It'd be an even longer flight.

31

Everyone in the ballroom was underdressed. Par for the course on a cruise ship. Nobody had stuffed tails and gowns into their carryon. Most women wore some form of skirt or sundress, the men polos and khakis. But Allison, reclining at one of several round tables, found herself surprised by how well-appointed the room itself was.

Said stands were draped in silk tablecloths and surrounded a gleaming hardwood dance floor. Large paintings graced all four walls, their golden frames bright beneath the glow of half a dozen chandeliers. Further above, numerous skylights peaked into the starlit darkness. The scene was just as striking as her time in a similar room at Buckingham Palace ten months ago, save a semblance of history—and a shower of bullets.

A shiver ran up her spine, the most recent echo of psychological scar tissue that had yet to fully heal. She turned to Becky, always good for a distraction, when a blonde at the next table yelped in laughter. The woman quickly put her hand over her mouth, a fleeting look of embarrassment glossing both eyes. Yet, for all its glitter and gleam, this was still just a cruise ship. A hundred fellow passengers chuckled along with her.

Petr raised an empty glass. "I'll have what she's having."

More laughter from their table, which also included the Carters and another couple celebrating their thirtieth wedding anniversary. They'd all just made it through a five-course meal, dessert and the stale jokes of an ambitious MC. And, of course, dancing. Several couples still occupied the floor, shuffling to the strings of a miniature orchestra.

Allison stole a glance at her phone: 10 p.m. Despite the shiver, she felt a jump in her step. Thanks, surely, to the nap she'd managed on the deck while everyone else scampered ashore for snorkeling and kayaking. The ship had spent the day anchored near a resort on one of the Bahamas' southern islands. She couldn't remember the name, and knew it hardly mattered; clear water, white sand and green palms played the same across the globe. Postcards paled.

A loud clap from Becky jolted her to attention. "The night is young, y'all. Petr and I are heading to the casino."

Her boyfriend raised an eyebrow. "We are?"

"And the more the merrier." Becky stood. "Who's ready for a party?"

Across the table, Erin shook her head with a smile. "Girl, your motor never stops."

"Don't tell me that's a 'no.'"

"Afraid so. The sun took it out of me today."

Sam grinned beside his wife. "So did those pina coladas."

Erin pushed him in mock protest. "You'd have done the same. Those things went down like candy."

"Everything tastes better in the tropics," said Petr, standing himself.

"So how about it, Sam?" said Becky. "There's no greater gift for a wife than waking up to a richer husband."

"No thanks." He hugged Erin with a playful look of seduction. "I think tonight we'll prove why they make those staterooms so small."

Erin grinned. "I guess you missed the part where I said I was tired. The only place you're getting lucky tonight is the casino."

The table shook again with laughter. A moment later Becky swung to Allison. "What do you say, Ally? If you don't come, we all might as well stay home."

Allison shrugged. "Why not?"

Another clap from Becky. "There's my girl!" She edged around her chair. "No time to waste. My boyfriend's thirsty and I've got a date with a craps table."

Everyone else stood. The five of them offered well-wishes to the older couple and began walking out together. Allison made it a mere ten feet before feeling a tap on her shoulder. She spun.

Rick Samuels stood before her, similar suit draped across his shoulders, same smug look in his eyes. He doffed an imaginary hat. "I wonder, Miss Shaw, if I might trouble you for a parting dance?"

Becky had also turned. She stared at the newcomer through narrowed eyes. "I'm sorry, what did you say your name was—Dick? Please excuse us for a moment." She steered her friend away. "This is the guy you told me about?"

Allison nodded. "He's certainly persistent."

"Want me to have Petr and Sam get rid of him?" She glanced his way. "I could probably take him myself."

"He's harmless, Becky. One whirl around the floor won't hurt anything."

"Do you *want* to dance with him?"

"I want to be rid of him. Five more minutes in this room is a small price to pay."

Becky didn't respond. She simply stared back behind a steady gaze, which Allison had no problem interpreting: *why dance with him at all?* It was a fair question. Allison found herself delaying an answer. She read her friend's eyes a bit further. "You're thinking about Jeremy."

"I wasn't, but now that you mention him…"

"Jeremy would want me to stay active," said Allison. "Distracted, even. If he were here, he'd be egging me on." She smiled. "Have another drink at the casino. I'll meet you in time to blow on your dice."

Becky paused for what felt like an hour, then stole a final glance at Rick. "Okay." She gave Allison a quick hug. "Don't do anything I wouldn't do."

"That doesn't exactly narrow it down."

She smiled, then found Petr near the entrance. A moment later they were gone. Allison stepped back toward Rick, who had a grin plastered across his face. "Something I said?"

"She's just being a good friend."

He waved it off. "This doesn't have to mean much. Just two lonely people having a nice dance."

"Who says I'm lonely?"

He was about to answer when the orchestra finished its current tune and abruptly began a fresh one. Rick held out his hand and led Allison onto the floor, slipping his free arm around her waist. She'd meant what she said about Jeremy. Their relationship needed to be built on trust. He could be doing this same thing right now with another woman. *But he wouldn't mean it.*

Neither did she, in a way. For all his good looks, she wasn't particularly attracted to Rick. Becky's unspoken words echoed in her mind: *why dance with him at all?* The answer was simple: he represented every other man—life outside of Jeremy Kent. It was an option, despite her heart's allegiance, she hadn't yet been able to dismiss.

"You did, last night," said Rick, guiding her toward an open pocket of space. "The way you talked about your boyfriend, my guess is you're missing him right now."

She let the comment pass, deferring to silence as they slipped across the polished hardwood. After a moment, she found her voice again. "What about you?"

"You mean, am I lonely?" He smiled. "I was a minute ago."

She didn't laugh, instead probing his steady gaze with her own. There was a real answer somewhere behind that smug expression.

"It's the job," he said, finally buckling beneath the scrutiny. "You're gone all the time. Different clients, locations. I find a pretty face now and then, but no roots."

"Why don't you quit? There's got to be a desk job out there for someone with your experience."

"And miss this?" He looked around. "Or a hundred other tropical spots like it? It'd be hard to say no even if the pay wasn't so attractive. Besides, I'm good at it."

"Speaking of that," said Allison, glancing around the room, "this is a bit of a coincidence, isn't it? I was going to give you the benefit of the doubt on the whole stalking thing, but…"

"I wish I could take credit." He turned toward one of the tables near the corner. Two white-haired men sat clinking half-empty glasses, drunk smiles plastered across their faces. "I go where they go. They're not that different from toddlers, really: aimless wandering, falling asleep in random places. I don't know how their wives do it."

This time Allison did laugh. It didn't last, though, as she felt Rick's hand sliding down beyond her waist. "*Hey.*" She reached back and pulled his arm up. They stopped for a brief second, an awkward island amidst the sea of spinning couples.

"I'm sorry," he said, a patch of red burnishing his cheeks. He tried to resume leading, but she resisted. "Please?"

Slowly, they began moving again. "I thought this was a *friendly* dance?" she said.

"I guess I got caught up in the moment. Waltzing on a cruise ship, a beautiful woman in my arms." He paused. "Don't take this the wrong way, but why limit yourself? You're the kind of girl who could have a different guy every night."

"So, like a prostitute. Thanks, that's the vote of confidence I needed."

Panic flashed in Rick's eyes, then, helpless, he simply began to laugh. Allison surprised herself by doing the same. "See, you took it the wrong way."

The song was nearing its close as they faded toward the back of the room, beside the orchestra. Allison slowed her feet, letting the final chords wash over. Other than her partner's roving palm, this had been fun, refreshing. Worth doing again if—

Rick's right hand stretched down and pinched the center of her left butt cheek. Allison nearly gasped and pushed him away. She pierced the five feet of space between them with a glare of shock and anger. His face held disappointment more than anything. *At his decision, or that it hadn't worked?*

Either way, time to go. The floor remained full, and Rick was blocking her path to the main entrance. Lacking the patience to face another excuse, she turned and strode toward a side exit. A push through its swinging door revealed a service hallway. Stark, with fluorescent lights coating the gray walls and floor. But still plenty busy: servers continued to carry trays to rooms off the corridor; maintenance workers rolled yellow buckets to similar destinations.

No one seemed to notice her. She began walking right, in the general direction of the casino. There'd be a re-entry door somewhere up ahead. The steam was still rising off her brow, cheeks flushed, when she caught a familiar face passing by. It took a second to place, then she recognized the young deckhand from the other night. This time he was smiling, and not alone—chatting, in fact, with two female coworkers. Despite her predicament, she felt a small pang of satisfaction that the kid had made some friends.

Another door came into view on the right. She angled toward it just as shuffling footsteps began crowding from behind. "Allison." *Don't stop.* She kept walking, calming herself, ordering each thought. "Allison, please."

She spun, the anger in her eyes having hardened into resolve. Rick stood before her, huffing a bit, his perfect hair tainted by a few errant strands. He glanced around the hallway, then back at her. "Allison, look…I'm sorry. I thought you were just playing hard to get."

"No, you didn't." She took a breath. "You wanted to see how far I'd let you go. Well, you've got your answer. This ship's large enough for neither of us to see each other the rest of the trip. Understand?"

She didn't wait for a reply and disappeared through the door.

32

Like all westbound planes, the Boeing 777 had raced the waning day and lost. Skimming the sky at 500 miles-per-hour was efficient, but the earth below still spun twice as fast. The sun had surrendered over the eastern Pacific, deferring to a darkness that quickly enveloped Kent's port-side window.

A full eight hours later—thirteen since leaving Pearson—he still had the same view. Fine; the black was simple, allowing him to focus his thoughts. But he'd also been stuck in the same position, and half a day with your knees bent was pushing it. He'd yet to figure out how sitting still could drain as much energy as constant motion.

Either way, there was little else to do but continue biting his tongue with the rest of economy. A worn copy of *The New York Times* lay open in his lap. His overhead light was one of the few remaining on—most passengers' internal clocks were still set to Toronto time, where it was 3 a.m. Pockets of snoring wafted across the large cabin, joining the rustle of blankets to create a predictable red-eye soundtrack.

Forty-thousand feet below, the Pacific Ocean was about to give way to the Philippine Sea. They'd land in Hong Kong in two hours; from there he'd catch an Airbus down to Singapore. Then…what?

There was no patch of land to study, no building to case because he still hadn't cracked the second clue. *Make a stand / Cornering evidence / Cross beyond Portland / Toward your deliverance.* By now the words were teasing, almost haunting. Every time he thought he had an answer, the line of reasoning collapsed and brought him back to square one. Presumably, McCoy, Limon and others were attempting the same thing, and—judging by his dormant text screen—achieving the same result.

But he still had to try. Sometimes actually being there, on the battlefield—which was what this was—made a difference. If nothing else, his internet connection had been good for brushing up on Singapore.

Officially, the territory was neither a country nor a city within one. Rather, like Monaco or Vatican City, it was a sovereign city-state. In this case, a small island off the southern tip of Malaysia and one of the wealthiest places on the planet. Singapore had gone from third-world to first in the blink of an eye. Today it was a global financial center and claimed one of the globe's busiest airports.

History, though, was what mattered. The relevant stretch began in 1819 when the British founded the island as a trading post for the East India Company. It wasn't long before they added their own architectural influence, much of it neoclassical. Plenty of columns and stone.

Some of these buildings still stood today, which, considering the current situation, felt like a miracle. They were stacked along a meager slice of land just across the Singapore River from the city's towering financial heart. But while "Portland" had steered him to the island, it was declining to divulge any further secrets. This third, possibly last stone—if it still existed—likely lay within a radius of about seven hundred feet. Yet the stone itself was barely larger than a credit card. He could search for a hundred years and still come up empty.

A fact worthy of Kent's full attention. It received, though, just a fraction. Every bit of the rest went to his three hundred-odd fellow passengers, because one of them was here to kill him. At least, that fit the pattern. In both Portugal and Canada, there'd been a coldblooded, highly-trained assassin waiting on the ground. If he were on the other side, this time there'd be less delay.

His enemy had the general clues, so it was reasonable to assume, after a century and a half of discernment, that they'd figured on Singapore. They also knew he'd been in Montreal, and that it made little sense to stay in that city. He'd had a gun and would want to keep it at least until he reached the next airport, which meant Toronto was a better option than crossing the U.S. border toward Boston or New York. From there it became a simple judgement of time. Kent was in a hurry; he'd taken the first-available flight.

The scenario on board was a tricky one. It hardly mattered that most of the faces were now obscured by darkness. He'd requested a spot near the back and boarded last to get a look at everyone on his way to the seat. Multiple trips to the plane's middle bathrooms—when he knew those in the rear were occupied—confirmed his initial impressions.

The gender split favored men by about two to one. Nearly every person was between the ages of thirty and sixty, most surely traveling on business. Toronto and Hong Kong were each global hubs. To that end, about half the cabin was Asian, half Caucasian. Both previous attacks had come from the latter group, and Kent expected more of the same. It was always possible, however, that his enemies were working with an international crew. The true test was the connecting flight: how many would follow him south?

Trina Eriksson, asleep in the seat to his right, certainly wouldn't be among them. The fact that Kent knew her name, and her itinerary, was no choice of his. Some people, though—lonely, nervous—couldn't help volunteering information. Like the man at the airport, ignoring her would've drawn too much attention.

She looked to be in her early thirties. Blonde hair, nearly as pale as her skin, capped a tall frame—at least five-nine. She had managed, though, to tuck every inch of it beneath a thin wool blanket. Even with her cashmere sweater and dark slacks out of view, she looked like a model. More than one male passenger had sent an interested glance her way.

Kent made the mistake of offering a simple smile. This provided him unsolicited access, between sips of Ginger Ale, to the pertinent details of her life story. She currently lived in Toronto, but grew up outside Green Bay. Her slight Swedish lilt, and authentic surname, owed to her father flying over from Stockholm as an exchange student. He met her mother at the University of

Wisconsin and that was that.

Trina was in her third year with a graphic design firm that had, just recently, begun sending her across the globe. This time it was a pitch meeting blocks from Victoria Harbor. They never sprang for flight upgrades, but her food per diem was generous and there was always an extra "rest" day built into the trip. She used this to explore, taste the world in small bites.

And bring back souvenirs for her two-year-old daughter. It was a familiar story: casual acquaintance, fleeting night, lifelong result. The father, naturally, was a mistake, but her Natalie remained the perfect surprise. She was currently staying with friends, watching cartoons and waiting for mommy to return with shiny presents.

These facts melted into the back of Kent's mind, sharing space with the list of hockey scores he'd just finished pretending to care about. He was in the process of flipping to the Business section when a slight rustling issued from the seat next door. "Are you a Leaf's fan?"

Kent turned. Trina had been sleeping, and the telltale rasp in the back of her throat colored each syllable. He was surprised she'd risk exposing such a private, if universal, deficiency. But then, it dovetailed nicely with the willingness to share her recent past with a stranger. In her mind, they were already friends.

She straightened and began brushing a few yellow strands from her face. Still no worry over puffy eyes or bad breath. She was staring directly at him, focused, as if nothing mattered more than his NHL allegiance.

"Canucks, actually."

She pulled a lukewarm bottle of water from her purse. "That must mean you're from Vancouver." It was a half-question, but she didn't give him time to respond. "I realize I've been centered on myself this entire flight. And I'm supposed to be *Canadian*. If Parliament found out they'd probably banish me to the east coast." This earned a genuine smile from Kent. "I don't even know your name."

"Let's blame that one on me." He offered a hand. "Evan Graves." She accepted, but didn't respond, clearly waiting for more. "You're right, I am from Vancouver. The suburbs, at least."

She gestured toward his left hand and the absence of a wedding ring. "No family?"

Kent shook his head. "My job keeps me too busy. I keep thinking I'll have time later…maybe I'm kidding myself." He knew he was playing it up, but curt answers weren't enough right now.

She seemed to eye him with a sliver more than platonic interest, but defaulted to the obvious question. "What do you do?"

"I'm a junior exec for a shipping firm. Basically, their glorified errand boy."

She shifted a little closer, the sliver widening to a crack. "How long will you be in Hong Kong?"

Here we go. Kent had never considered himself overly attractive. Maybe it was the quiet setting, or their common "occupation." Maybe Trina was simply desperate. "Not long at all." He managed an ambiguous frown. "I've got a connecting flight to Yokohama."

"Yokohama? You're flying west to head back east. Why not just land in Tokyo?"

"Because that's a direct route from Toronto and five-hundred extra bucks. My company's just as cheap as yours."

"What about your layover?" She wasn't yet ready to concede. "I just mean…in case you wanted to grab a bite with a familiar face. I know a nice little place right in the airport."

It was a smooth invitation. Kent, though, was already shaking his head. "Sorry, I've got thirty minutes to get from one end of the terminal to the other. But thanks for the offer."

Defeated, Trina sank back into her seat and took a swig of water. The flame in her eyes had calmed to a dull ember. She'd be fine, Kent knew. He was likely just the latest mark in a string of aerial conquests. Best guess: she'd won some and lost others.

Nevertheless, the entire episode was flattering. In fact, when they first shook hands there'd been a quiet shock of static—but it was no spark. Here sat a beautiful, charming woman essentially throwing herself at him…and she wasn't enough. Not because she was pushy, not even because he was in the middle of an operation.

Because, instead, of another woman more than nine thousand miles away—one who was just as attractive. But not only that: she was *his* beautiful, *his* charming. Kent hoped Allison claimed the same possession over him. There came a point when you stopped choosing someone and started belonging to them.

Suddenly, the numerous times he'd told her he loved her weren't quite enough. He needed to say it again, and needed her to hear it. Staring into the yawning darkness outside, he honestly didn't know if he'd have the chance.

33

It was nearly midnight when the Airbus A350 touched down on the northern end of Singapore's Changi Airport. Free from the clouds, Kent's view had improved: a full, bright moon lit the tarmac like midday. To the south, the Singapore Strait's warm waters twinkled beneath the gaze of a thousand stars.

Connecting in Hong Kong had gone smoothly. Fording the Pacific, though, came at the cost of nearly a full day, thanks to the flight's length and the time change. Once they'd crossed the International Date Line, Kent could feel his margin for error shrink to centimeters. A mere twenty-four hours remained until the assassination date.

There was, however, a more pressing concern. He judged about a third of Toronto's original passengers had followed him south on the connection. Most had already been eliminated from his radar; that's what the job taught you. How someone tilted their head, spoke to a stranger, carried luggage: these were all clues to a person's ability and intentions—their identity. It was similar to poker, except folding was never an option, and you only lost once.

Three candidates remained. All men, all Caucasian, all alone. The third fact changed, though, as Kent followed the rest of the passengers across the jet-way toward Terminal Three. Once through customs, one of the men—trimmed hair, rumpled business suit—was met by, presumably, his wife and two teenage children. They might've been decoys, but doubtful.

The two left couldn't have differed more. The first, another suit—this one with no wrinkles—cradled a briefcase and had pulled out a cell phone the moment they landed. The other was ten years younger and at least one MBA short. Mid-thirties, long hair, a desert of stubble blanketing his jaw. He was too old to be a backpacker—maybe a photographer, or visiting professor.

Whoever they were, they began moving. In opposite directions. Kent had to decide who to follow. Roles might've been reversed, but he'd stopped at the edge of the gate. There was no way for either of them to do so as well without drawing undue attention. Whoever the guilty party, he wouldn't be an amateur.

So they continued walking, and Kent, finally, made his choice. Based on little more than instinct, he fell in step twenty feet behind the man with the cell phone. Perhaps it was simply that both flights had been filled with suits and laptops; business travel made more sense as a disguise.

Kent kept his gait casual, knowing that the trick wasn't identifying potential threats, but looking clueless while doing so. The concourse, even as the clocks ticked over to a new day, remained busy. Blending in was as simple as shifting behind a young couple here, keeping pace with a group of middle-aged men there.

For five minutes the strategy worked. Then the man pocketed his phone and ducked into a nearby Starbucks. What about baggage claim? He couldn't only have the briefcase. Maybe it was the next stop, after the revitalizing aroma of a Grande Cappuccino.

Kent didn't wait to find out. He continued forward, down a level, toward an awaiting rank of taxis. It was a fair walk, but the man in the suit made no further appearance. Neither did his shaggy counterpart. Eventually sinking into the back seat of a Mitsubishi sedan, Kent allowed himself a breath of relief—if tinged with confusion. Had he been wrong? Was there no killer on the flight? His only choice was to continue forward, without an answer. The vehicle soon exited the airport complex and gained the East Coast Parkway southwest toward the city center.

The drive was mercifully quiet. Kent stole more than one look back, but saw no set of headlights wearing out their welcome. He rolled down his window. Gusts of mild December air—Singapore lay just seventy miles north of the equator—refreshed the cabin, along with a sharp pinch of salt from the neighboring strait.

Downtown came quickly, its vertical skyline stretching into the night. Even in such small hours, the view was striking. Across the Singapore River, comprising the financial center of Southeast Asia, rounded towers seemed to touch the clouds, blazing artificial light and heralding the future.

On the opposite bank, though—just four-hundred feet away—the past lived. Colonnades and stucco, washed white and gold by proud floodlights, highlighted the Colonial District. From Parliament House to Victoria Theatre, history had rarely been so prominent. Save the palm trees, it might've been central London. And it was this preservation that caught the eye in the first place, setting Singapore apart from metropolises like Tokyo and Shanghai.

Crossing the Esplanade Bridge, Kent was tempted to detour toward the buildings for a closer look. If the stone was here, they most certainly held its secret. But, at this hour, the area would be deserted; there was no way to search without drawing attention. He pulled his gaze away. *Tomorrow.*

The cab drove on, past the Fullerton Hotel and the heart of the Central Business District, until they were a good half mile south of the river. After turning left onto Central Blvd., then right to Marina View, he could just make out the Westin Singapore's glass tower. It'd been his destination from the start. Far enough from the city core, large enough to get lost in. He had no reservation, but with over three-hundred rooms, the chances were decent they'd find him space.

The taxi threaded its way toward the covered front entrance and pulled to a stop. Kent slid out with his duffel, paid the fare and left a tip. He offered a few kind words to the driver before turning inside. His Mandarin was sparse, but Singapore had three other official languages, including English.

The modern, two-story lobby came next, its army of right angles somehow welcoming. Kent strode across the expanse, a wall of windows on his left swallowing the night. The clerk didn't look old enough to shave, but his hair was combed and suit pressed. He informed his guest that there was still room available and, a key card and practiced farewell later, bid him upward.

Despite its ground entrance, the hotel only occupied the top fifteen floors of the tower. Kent rode an elevator up to number thirty-five and stepped out onto a silent hallway. Still no tail.

His room was the fifth door down. He flipped on the lights, locked the door and dropped his bag before a king-size bed. *Didn't you just do this, in another hemisphere?* For what it was worth, the space before him was a clear step up from the Belvedere in Montreal. Its requisite flatscreen hung opposite a beige accent wall; with each step the plush carpet gave gently beneath his feet. Every surrounding inch signaled the height of strategically engineered comfort.

He pulled off his jacket and raided the mini-bar for a bottle of whisky. Kent had never been much of a drinker, but sometimes the right dose brought things into focus. Pouring its contents into a glass, he walked toward the floor-to-ceiling window and looked out. Again, just like Montreal. This time he saw more than a busy road.

Beacons of neon dotted the skyline like Christmas lights. Some shone from the roof in blue and red, promoting their company's headquarters; others, below, glowed a mundane white, signifying security lighting, or cleaning crews, or a frazzled suit pulling an all-nighter. Some were surely other hotels, each lit window a glimpse into the solitary world of a weary traveler.

Just like you. He took a sip, the alcohol stinging his throat. Such fatigue was a natural consequence of staring down the barrel of an unsolvable riddle. He possessed no clear path or premonition for tomorrow. It was paralysis by ignorance. The heaviest form of despair.

Yet, it went beyond the words he'd wrestled with on the plane, to the enemy behind them. One coma, two stones, three corpses, but still zero clue as to his adversary's identity. Kent felt like a boxer, waiting for his opponent to enter the ring, all the while receiving phantom jabs to the gut.

Which brought him, inescapably, back to Allison. He took another drink and closed his eyes. He thought of the ring that was no longer in his pocket. If he lived to ask her what he wanted, his identity would no longer belong to him.

It would be tied to another person, the dregs of his abnormal world staining forever her safe, ordinary existence. Did she deserve that? Could they make it work? The choice was ultimately hers, but she'd never have the luxury of making it with complete information.

Kent set the glass down and looked up at the stars. *You're going to have to trust her.* With his heart. As he trusted another, far more powerful, with his soul.

34

Every city in the world had a restaurant like the Philadelphia: second-generation owner, traditional cuisine, subdued lighting. It was the kind of place known to the neighborhood, but still hard enough to find. The kind of place that could keep a secret.

Hassan took a measure of comfort in this as his motorcade trundled down Salah e-Din Street toward the restaurant just after eight p.m. He, after all, was the secret. Not for his mere presence; the Philadelphia had hosted everyone from Jimmy Carter to John Kerry. Rather, for the man he was meeting. It wasn't the kind of rendezvous most residents would understand. Not yet.

The restaurant was located in the heart of town, just north of Jerusalem's Old City. Narrow streets, choked with headlights and blaring horns, grudgingly accepted the convoy. A blanket of clouds obscured the stars, but there'd be no rain tonight. The air was mild and dry.

Hassan might've preferred to come in his own car, or even a city bus. But some things simply weren't possible. Soon his Audi A8 angled up to the curb along E-Zahra Street. He waited as the accompanying Toyota and Lexus SUV's spaced themselves strategically along the boulevard. It was a relatively quiet night, but they were steps from the Muslim Quarter. Shin Bet wasn't taking any chances.

Eventually his head of security, Aviv, alighted from the Audi's front-passenger seat and pulled the rear door open against the curb. Hassan stepped out with a nod and was quickly ushered toward the restaurant. A moment later, down a flight of steps, a back entrance brought him to a drab anteroom complete with card table and chairs. A dusty, yellow lightbulb buzzed overhead. It was perfect.

He stepped inside, followed by Aviv. The rest of his security, practically an army, was positioned at strategic points within the restaurant's corridors and courtyard, as well as along the surrounding streets. A guard was also stationed in the kitchen, accompanying Hassan's personal chef. The pretense was to ensure, in an Arab restaurant, that the meal remained Kosher; the reality included protection against some harmful substance smuggled into the Prime Minister's food or drink.

It was quite a thing, knowing your life was constantly in danger. Hassan had never gotten used to it. *Is that so bad?*

He sat down, resisting the urge to scan his phone for updates that could wait until tomorrow. Tonight was about simplicity, and communicating directly. He closed his eyes, forcing in a few deep breaths, exhaling the day's stress. He probably should've been more nervous about this meeting, but everything else had gone smoothly. This was merely a natural extension.

Not, however, an easy one to arrange. In fact, this evening was only the latest in a series of concessions he and his counterpart had had to coax from their respective cabinets. The entire peace process was reviled by a number of consultants on both sides, curiously reluctant to dismiss a thousand years of religious hostility. Eventually, though, both leaders managed to charm enough of their subordinates into agreement.

Beyond tonight, and the coming speeches, plans were fluid. What they definitely entailed were legitimate peace talks, perhaps televised and streamed online. Classified information would be avoided, but it was essential to show their audience that they were serious. This wasn't about going through the motions just to grease the wheels for more foreign aid.

The sound of heavy steps revived Hassan. He looked up to find the doorway filled by a man nearly its same size. Omar Khalidi, President of the Palestinian National Authority, claimed a presence without saying a word. But he was more than mere girth. It began with the eyes, wise even beyond his seventy years, kind enough to recognize friendship through a haze of enemies. A three-piece suit smothered his rotund frame, accenting a pair of stout shoulders that hadn't quite relinquished the ghost of their collegiate bodybuilder.

Khalidi studied Hassan before calmly stepping into the room. His own bodyguard followed—just one, like Aviv. More were surely here, posted, perhaps, beside their Israeli counterparts. Undoubtedly a first. If everyone walked away alive, it would be a coup for peace. Part of Hassan wished the world was watching.

He found himself wondering if Khalidi, too, had brought a chef. As for the man himself, there was no reason to search for weapons. Ditto for Hassan. Neither possessed the training to kill cleanly, and both had invested too much time and energy developing this fragile bond of trust to see it torn apart by a cheap attempt at murder. The same went for their security chiefs, whose loyalty, by this point, was unquestioned.

Nearly forgetting himself, Hassan finally stood. Khalidi stopped five feet away, the trace of a smile decorating his lips. "Shalom."

"As-salamu alaykum."

Silence collected the greetings, extending its presence until the older man reached out with his right hand. Hassan reciprocated. "Your grip is as firm as your voice," said Khalidi.

Hassan needed no reminder that this was their first meeting. Khalidi had made the initial overture, a letter through a mutual friend in the business community. The Prime Minister followed with a phone call, which became a series of conversations. Each had its tense moments, but in the end both men were surprised by how much they agreed.

Neither was host, but Hassan, by virtue of arriving first, gestured to the one other chair at the table. "Please, sit."

"I'm glad you came," said Khalidi, lowering his mass into the undersized seat. "My father used to say you never really know a man until you see him face-to-face. That might've been awkward on a stage, out in the open."

Hassan thought of that day, thirty-six hours from now, when they'd be trapped between a hot sun and heated crowds. Security would be plentiful, but imperfect; some agitators might slip through. Would the people turn on their leaders first, or one another? "I think that would've been the least of our worries."

"Well, you're getting a head start tonight." Khalidi looked around. "This isn't exactly your side of the city."

Hassan had to nod. "Though it's still my purview, my jurisdiction. Depending on who you ask."

At that moment, a waiter—wiry, sweating through his white shirt—entered with a tray of drinks. He set glasses of water down for both men, then coffee for Hassan and tea for Khalidi. There would be no ordering from menus tonight. Each leader's courses had been predetermined.

Without a word, the entrant excused himself. Even after the door closed, Hassan could hear the muffled sounds of the kitchen a few thin walls away. He poured some cream into his drink and stared across at Khalidi. "Are we crazy?"

The older man had the good sense to laugh. "Perhaps. But is that not what is needed right now? I'm afraid I see no other way."

Neither do I. Hassan took a sip, eying the man across. Khalidi was right—face-to-face was better. Transparency reigned. It was much more difficult to lie to a man in-person, with all your facial expressions and body language laid bare. Still, Hassan had always felt like a bit of a mark. There was something beneath the surface, coloring their correspondence. He'd only recently realized it. "You were waiting for me."

Khalidi needed no clarification. "In a way, yes. But also for myself."

Hassan proffered the expected furrow of confusion.

Khalidi drained his tea to the lemon. "What we're attempting is revolutionary, Michael. Meeting together, planning for peace in this region—with no western influence. It's never been done. Which means a special combination of leadership is necessary.

"In my younger days, I was the typical firebrand; force, violence were the only solutions. Allah has graced me with the chance to outlive my skewed philosophy. Some call it wisdom. I just know that, now, compromise is our only hope. I'm not any happier than you on certain points; some beliefs cannot budge. But the ultimate truth is that this furnace has a shelf life. If we don't cool it, we will all of us burn."

Hassan processed this, allowing each desperate syllable to crash over him in troublesome waves. Khalidi seemed awfully prepared for such an answer, but his emotion was genuine. "And me?"

"You are my antithesis, in the best sense: young, idealistic, full of energy. Most of all, pure. You've yet to become disillusioned by the broken machine of government." He paused. "Perhaps that is what it takes to meet in the middle—two men at opposite ends of their career."

It was a good sales pitch, one that worked on Hassan. Not that he had any other choice by now. He was already at the table, and there was no turning back. Their joint speeches—you could even call it a rally—had been planned down to the smallest detail and advertised for weeks. They would either calm the cauldron or be the spark that sent it boiling over.

35

Three hours later the night had grown quiet. Hassan was tucked in safely to the upper floor of Beit Aghion, his fortress of a residence ten blocks west of the Old City. He strode softly down a hallway, the weight of the evening still on his shoulders; it'd been productive, but he felt exhausted. And not just from the meeting with Khalidi. This fatigue had been building, its source hard to pin.

He longed to forget it—even for a moment—and knew just the place to do so. Soon he'd reached the desired door and gingerly turned its handle. It swung inward without a creak. Beyond the threshold, bathed in the paltry glow of a small night-light, his daughter Talya lay sleeping.

He leaned against the doorframe and took a deep breath. The world seemed to slink away, and for the promised moment he was no longer his country's leader but simply his child's protector. It was a big enough job. She was such a small figure on the mattress, chest rising and falling to the peaceful rhythm of secret dreams, hands clutching a ratty stuffed animal who's name he'd recently forgotten.

Talya would forgive him. That was the difference between children and adults. 'Grown-ups' kept a grudge, even if it had to be passed on to future generations, or across national borders. He'd studied the teachings of Jesus enough to know that the man, for all his faults, had some good things to say. "*Truly I tell you, unless you change and become like little children, you will never enter the kingdom of heaven.*" If only life were simpler.

He stayed a minute longer, still as a statue, soaking up the room's perfect innocence. Then, like the end of his own dream, it was time to go. Hassan pushed off from the wall and pulled the door closed. The walk to his own bed was a short one. He found Leila sitting against the headboard, legs beneath a down comforter, scanning a magazine. She didn't immediately set it down, allowing him his bearings.

Hassan closed the door and shrugged off his jacket. Then he turned to his wife. By now she'd traded the human-interest articles and perfume adds for his face. Her own, a mask of departing worry, cradled the slightest smile of relief for her husband's safe return. He was not surprised—indeed, pleased—to find her still awake.

"How can such an ugly world contain something so beautiful?" said Hassan, nodding toward the hallway.

The smile widened. "She asked where you'd gone. I told you were meeting a new friend."

He found a grin on his way to her side of the mattress. "A little generous, but close enough."

"Does that mean tonight went well?"

Hassan leaned in and gave his wife a kiss, then slumped on the edge of the bed. "As well as possible. Though I'm afraid Omar isn't the one who'll need persuading."

She placed her hand on his. "Everyone doubted you, Michael. Remember? Your cabinet, security, the Knesset. And me." She paused. "But you've convinced us all. You'll turn everyone else, too. I know it. God has chosen you for this moment."

Hassan noticed the slightest crack to her exterior, as if she believed what she'd said, but didn't want to. He offered another kiss by way of gratitude.

Leila had left the magazine open in her lap. She now closed it and set it on a nearby nightstand. Hassan began taking off his shoes. "I'd like to come to the speech."

He stopped, laces half undone. They'd discussed this before, but the evening's sentiment had clearly emboldened his wife. "Darling, you know you can't. Even if it were my decision. Aviv has you and Talya out of the city the entire day. You're a prime target for retaliation against the peace efforts."

She was already nodding, resignation lighting her gaze. "And the sharpest attack on you would be hurting someone you love."

"Yes."

"Well what about the other way round?"

This was delivered with far more volume than necessary, each decibel grating the still air. Hassan glanced reflexively toward the door, thankful for the thick wood. He then turned back to Leila and saw the tears in her eyes. Their source dawned a moment later and he berated himself for missing the obvious.

Since he'd first spoken with Khalidi, she'd been his closest advisor, enduring every twist of his gut as if it were her own. He thought about the stress and fatigue he felt just five minutes earlier; now he knew he wasn't their only target. She just did a better job of hiding the pain.

But suddenly there was nowhere to put it. No distant date on which to cast a cargo of omens. The dreaded future, always just over the next blessed horizon, was now today.

The most powerful man in Israel had never felt so helpless. He'd spent so much energy suppressing physical assault to his loved ones, a mental and emotional front had hardly been entertained. Such as it was, he could do little to stem the flood of fear his wife now felt inside. Except survive.

Hassan leaned in again, this time wrapping his arms around Leila and squeezing tight. "Nothing's going to happen to me. I swear."

She quickly brought her lips to his ear. Her voice, just above a whisper, carried the sound of fresh tears. "How can you make such a beautiful promise in such an ugly world?"

36

Kent closed his eyes, letting the morning sun wash his face. It was a pleasant sensation, made more so by floor-to-ceiling windows magnifying each warm ray. He let a thin smile toy at the corner of his mouth; the contented wanderer, ready to embrace a new day.

That was the role, and he'd settled into it between bites of a seafood omelet. His post required a fair amount of acting, much of it—like this—rather subtle. But rarely had he had such an obvious audience: today, a collection of business travelers dotting several nearby tables in one of the Westin's four restaurants. This establishment, on the hotel's thirty-second floor, featured a clear view of Marina Bay and the South China Sea.

Kent pretended to enjoy it. He could feel the eyes on him, tinged with envy as their owners stabbed at fruit salad and parfaits. The reason for jealousy was simple: they were in suits, bracing for work, and this stranger—seemingly one of them—wasn't. Kent, instead, wore a navy polo and khakis, with a pair of sunglasses tucked atop his head. A slate of brochures rested on his table. The tourist guise would be necessary later, and thus had to begin now.

A pang at his side brought a slight interruption to his grin. He recovered quickly, thankful that the wound had begun healing, and that full hearing had nearly returned to his left ear. But they were reminders of a price paid. That was the other element at play: every junior executive with a line-of-sight was seething at the assumption that he'd covered this trip with airline miles.

A vacation in Singapore for free. On the contrary, he was the only one in the entire city who could write the check.

Fifteen minutes later Kent was holding tight to a pole in the middle of one of Singapore's Mass Rapid Transit cars. As streamlined as London's Tube, the MRT wound its way beneath the city like an obedient snake. He checked his watch: nearly nine a.m., the tail end of rush hour. Inside, though, the cabin remained packed.

Half its passengers wore the pressed clothing and long faces of professionals headed for the office. The rest were split between those lucky enough to have such a sunny day free, and tourists. In every case, enough Caucasian skin mixed with Asian to give Kent proper cover. He added to the guise by scanning a brochure on the city's architecture; an overpriced camera, bought back at Pearson, hung from a strap around his neck.

Kent could feel the birth pangs of exhaustion fraying the edge of his psyche. He'd managed just a few hours of sleep. The walk toward the station had been uneventful, and the car was clean; no sign of Cell Phone, the Professor, even Family Man. But vigilance against an invisible enemy was draining. It meant expending nearly all of your energy on hollow threats, knowing full well the real one could strike at any moment. Like wading through a Vietnamese swamp, or clearing houses in Fallujah.

Two stops later he reached his destination. Half the car spilled out the doors ahead of him. Some were hurrying; others consulted maps with confused faces. Kent chose somewhere in between, allowing a relaxed, curious gait to lead him back toward the sunshine.

He stepped out the front entrance of City Hall Station and began strolling southwest along North Bridge Road. Quickly, though, St. Andrew's Cathedral brought him to a standstill. He lifted his camera and started snapping. There were enough fellow pedestrians out to make the show necessary, but he was hardly pretending. The church—covered in white stone, its Gothic spire reaching toward the clouds—would've been at home near Jane Austen's Pemberley, or in Puritan Massachusetts. Anywhere but present-day Asia.

He continued on. North Bridge soon met Coleman Street, where he turned left and eventually reached St. Andrews Road. One more right turn and his goal was in sight. The Colonial District lay two-hundred yards ahead, its simple warren of streets and bright stucco looking for all the world like the darkest maze.

Kent knew he was walking directly toward the moment of truth. The assassination date was a mere fifteen hours away. And, despite the two previous stones, they still knew absolutely nothing of consequence. Tomorrow's killer could be any one of the world's seven billion people. Fail to find the third piece, and every sacrifice up to this point—including Baker's—would be for naught.

The National Gallery of Art stretched the entire block to his right; behind it lay the Supreme Court. On the left, a large open field, known as the Padang, fed directly into the Singapore Cricket Club. History continued to close in as he spied, up ahead, the unmistakable façade of the Parliament building. To its left stood the Arts House, itself the original Parliament building and now host to concerts and exhibitions.

Kent eventually angled toward Connaught Drive, stopping every few feet to take a picture. He smiled at his fellow tourists, but the sour hole in his gut gained mass with every step. He shuffled the words of the riddle through his mind: *cornering, evidence, Portland, deliverance.*

A short walk down Old Parliament Lane came next, then a left turn onto Empress Place. Soon Kent lost sight of the skyscrapers beyond the river and was completely enveloped by Palladian arches and stonework. Feeling, for a brief moment, like Sydney Carton or Sherlock Holmes, he broke from the architectural reverie near the front façade of the Victoria Theatre.

A look around. This was it, ground zero. *And you have nothing.* Yes, he'd maintained his own façade as a tourist, and had spotted no tail all morning. But every ounce of spycraft had suddenly become useless. This mystery was like a piece of simple, maddening trivia—you either knew it or you didn't. He didn't, and he wasn't alone. But, standing here, the bright sunshine sending down its mocking rays, he felt the failure more acutely than anyone else.

He made his way toward the river's edge, passing the Dalhousie Obelisk on his left. The monument was named after an Indian Raj who'd visited the island in 1850. Kent couldn't help but give it a second look, Place Jacques Cartier flashing through his mind. Could the hiding place be another statue? The short answer was *yes*. But it could also be a dozen of the city's other buildings. Or none of them.

This last possibility was too discouraging to contemplate. Guessing wouldn't work either: there was no time, nor resources, for trial-and-error. He pressed on to the water, not knowing why he was headed that way, all the while battling to maintain an outward show of contentment.

Finally reaching a railing that separated sidewalk from serene current, he glanced across at the Fullerton Hotel. Its location—at the mouth of the river, the site of an old fort—couldn't have been more prestigious. Nothing less would do for the city's premier five-star destination. At least, that's what the brochures called it. From this distance, Kent could easily see the signature fleet of vintage Rolls-Royces decorating its front entrance.

Then he heard it: a faint bell in the back of his mind. Signaling...the river? The cars? No—the hotel. What it used to be. He thought back to the research he'd conducted during the flight. The building originally had more than one tenant, but its bottom two floors were occupied by Singapore's General Post Office. Any post office's chief function was handling the mail: collect, sort...*deliver*.

Deliverance.

Kent gripped the railing tighter. *Cross beyond Portland / Toward your deliverance*. It was a post office, made of Portland stone. In Singapore. He took a few pictures of the skyscrapers across the river to buy his brain some time. The search field had narrowed considerably.

But the Fullerton wasn't the answer. Its exterior was granite, and was only completed in 1928, nearly seventy years after Emile would've stowed the third stone. The oldest building was the current Arts House, but it was never a post office, even when it housed the city's Parliament. Yet, Singapore had been founded over a century before the General Post Office was built. Something had to fill the gap.

He pulled out his phone and sat down on a bench a few steps back. The winded tourist, pausing before his next sojourn. Ten minutes later he'd gotten no further and pocketed the device. Nineteenth-century civic planning in a non-western city—information online was too thin. He needed something more.

Just then a soft breeze rustled the surrounding Rain Trees and kissed the back of his neck. Kent felt an inward shiver and turned. Nothing. Except, perhaps, what he should've noticed much earlier: the Asian Civilizations Museum, resting conveniently beside the Victoria Theatre like an answered prayer. He stood. *What've you got to lose?*

Yet, at that moment, another realization struck and he began walking away from the building. Because it wasn't the right one. The Asian Civilizations Museum was going to give him the entire region's history, before Singapore was even founded. He needed the city itself.

37

A short walk along the Cavenagh Bridge brought him over the river and in front of the Fullerton. From there he took a cab one mile north to the National Museum of Singapore. Still no sign of a tail, nor a single car the least bit familiar. *Something's not right.* His sour stomach, dormant since the post-office epiphany, returned in a sticky wave.

The building had been expanded in back, steel girders and glass canopies creating additional space for touting the national story. But the front façade was much the same as it'd appeared on its first day of service, in 1887: white stone, imposing columns, even a massive dome. On a foggy day, it could've passed for the U.S. Capitol.

Kent stepped through the main entrance and into the air-conditioned rotunda, which doubled as the museum's lobby. Eggshell floors gave way to ivory walls, both gilded by sunlight piercing the dome's ribbon of stained-glass high above. The effect was beautiful, and blinding. He resisted the urge to slide his sunglasses back on and angled toward an information desk.

The museum had only opened thirty minutes ago; it might've still been quiet if not for the field trip of second-graders just exiting the lobby for more rooms deeper inside. Their screams and giggles echoed off the austere surroundings, filling the silence with chaotic life.

Kent was glad for their presence. More patrons meant more faces for the staff to remember, in which case they most likely wouldn't. With any luck the kids would be the story of the morning, and he'd slip away as an afterthought.

Two women stood behind the desk. Both were Asian, but there the similarity ended. One was tall, slim, young—she looked as if she'd just stepped off a fashion runway in Milan or Paris. Her counterpart was a foot shorter and much older. She had the air of a volunteer: plenty of free time to indulge a sense of civic duty and passion for history.

It was this woman who greeted Kent, in perfect English, a genuine smile spreading her lips. "Good morning. Ticket for the museum?" She was happy to be here. Her protégé, probably on the back end of an internship, neither smiled nor looked up from a computer screen that might as well have been her phone. Kent gave her a pass; it was early.

"No, thank you," he said, his camera still a badge of deception around his neck. "I was actually looking for information about Singapore's post office history." The woman raised a slight eyebrow of surprise at such a niche request. Kent conjured a sheepish grin. "I collect stamps, and am something of a postal enthusiast, I guess."

A bit thin, but it worked. The woman nodded toward the exhibits behind her. "We have a full display on the Fullerton Building. You may already know it was originally—"

"Yes," said Kent, holding up a polite hand. "The General Post Office. I'm more concerned with what came before."

This earned more hesitation, though now her confusion was directed inward. "Unfortunately, there's not much to go on. After the British landed here, their navy handled the island's mail. I think…around 1850 a separate post office was commissioned. It moved buildings a few times, and nothing was really permanent until the Fullerton came along. We have a small display that fleshes this information out, as well as a couple pictures. Beyond that, I'm afraid it's a mystery."

"I was hoping to get a sense of the architecture from that period. You're saying, other than pictures, there are no physical remnants?"

The woman was already shaking her head. "No blueprints. None of the buildings have survived."

Kent could feel the hammer dropping. There was no choice now but to look the devil of failure in the eye. Deep down he'd known it all along: he was simply too late. Emile's stone, and its elusive secrets, had been ground up lifetimes ago in the verdant soil of a growing nation. He forced another smile, pretending that the turn in his stomach hadn't become physical pain.

"You might try the Government Quarter," said the woman, the futility of each word made all the more tragic by her cheery tone. "It's not a post office, but the Parliament Building is a wonderful specimen of colonial architecture. Or our museum here. It dates from 1849."

Kent glanced up at the rotunda, for effect. "It's beautiful." He fingered his camera. "I think I'll start with the exterior. Thank you for all your help."

She nodded, her apprentice still a statue beside her. He turned back toward the exit. A million thoughts ran through his head, all of them leading nowhere. He'd break the news to McCoy, who would ask if he was sure. One look in the woman's eyes eliminated any doubt. The entire land area of Singapore was less than a quarter of Rhode Island; there were only so many places for culturally significant buildings to hide.

And, now, there were only so many steps left to take. Security for every world leader, particularly the President, would need to be increased. *Why?* That would be the question from a dozen governments. Kent saw no other choice but to provide a credible answer. Which meant spreading at least part of this volatile scenario to hundreds of virgin ears, with little or no warning before the coming attack. This would, in turn, increase the likelihood of a leak to the press or public. Hysteria would follow. You needed a million bullets to hurt a million people; it only took one to paralyze them in fear.

A laugh sounded from behind. More of a chuckle, actually, and only made audible by the rotunda's echo-friendly dimensions. Kent, curious, spun from the door and began the awkward walk back to the desk. He could see it was the older woman who'd broken the silence; the ghost of a grin still haunted her face. She glanced up and read the question in Kent's eyes. "It's nothing, really. I just happened to remember."

"Please," he said, reaching the stand, "indulge a nosy traveler."

She smiled once more, eventually shaking her head at what was apparently such a trivial thought. "It was on the news, several years ago. A little story about Gerald Chang, the CEO of Crystal Freight. He'd bought a slab of stone that'd been found in the basement of one of our sister museums. Collecting dust since the eighties. Evidently, it'd been saved for a possible future exhibit, then ruled out and forgotten. Until one of the maintenance staff finally dug deep enough to see what it really was. A few curators looked it over and confirmed." She met his gaze. "It was part of the front façade from Singapore's original post office."

Kent had trouble speaking until the pause became conspicuous. "Where is it now?"

She squinted, trying to recall. "The story said he wanted it…for his office, that's right." She nodded in the direction of the financial district. "As an emblem of his company's purpose. Something like that."

"You don't sound too impressed."

"Chang donated plenty to the museum; for that I'm grateful." She leaned in. "But between you and me, he's just another self-absorbed millionaire who does more harm than good with his wealth."

"Don't have to be a local to agree with that."

A moment later Kent had offered more thanks and made it all the way outside. He donned his shades; the sun seemed just a little brighter. *It can't be.* No, it couldn't…could it?

Impossible—that word seemed to fit best. It was why she hadn't initially remembered. The scenario was too far out of left field to be considered legitimate history. And yet, he had to believe it. Somewhere on this island there was a piece of rock that aligned, however imperfectly, with Emile's riddle. *The only piece.* Could it actually hold the stone?

More importantly: could he look his superiors in the eye and admit he'd discarded a lead based solely on probability? What about one of the assassins' victims?

Some answers came easier than others.

38

Crystal Freight—officially Crystal Freight Enterprises, or CFE—had achieved success in Singapore the same way other companies had done so the world over: by finding a chink in a particular industry's armor and stabbing at just the right time. In this case, the sword was service, the chainmail expensive.

Like everyone else, the wealthy took vacations. But instead of buying trinkets and tee shirts, they came home with diamonds and original paintings. Sometimes the cargo was too large for a Gulfstream: statues, exotic animals, vintage Ferraris. Enter CFE. Chang had built a market-leading company out of ferrying foreign purchases back into the arms of their owners.

It was a provision that'd been offered elsewhere for years, but no competitor had ever placed such emphasis on a personal relationship with the client. As it turned out, billionaires liked to be pampered. For a special fee, CFE would even dispatch one of its agents to escort a purchase throughout the entirety of its journey.

The company had gone public nearly twenty years ago, quickly gaining a foothold in the markets. Inevitable offices in London and New York sprang to life. But its headquarters remained in Singapore. Just across the river, in fact, crowning the top five floors of the glass-wrapped Republic Plaza tower.

Kent's only real chance was to gain entry to Chang's office during working hours. This was not only due to tomorrow's fast-approaching deadline, but because the building's overnight security measures would be state-of-the-art. He'd need days of planning and recon just to get through the front door.

Which put him, currently, on the sidewalk, striding north along Market Street toward the city's Central Business District. After leaving the museum, he'd bought a suit and briefcase and retreated to the Westin to freshen up. That'd been lunchtime; it was now 1:30 p.m. He aimed for pockets of shade, the suit's stiff collar already conspiring with the sun to dampen the back of his neck. He could've taken the MRT, practically to the building's front door, but needed the walk to think. Beyond the appropriate attire, he'd yet to formulate a plan.

Hi, I'd like to see Mr. Chang. No, I don't have an appointment. No, he doesn't know me. I'd really just like to see the chunk of stone in his office…No, I'm not crazy. It would only get worse from there.

He stopped at the crosswalk to Cecil Street, waiting with a group of fellow pedestrians for the light to turn. A glance around: two other suits, but mostly the casual dress and vague anxiety of tourists and shift-workers. Kent summoned, without much effort, his own mask of unease.

He reached the far side of Cecil and turned right. Republic Plaza stood just ahead, its zenith stretching high into the cloudless blue. At 280 meters, the building was imposing, but merely tied with two other structures as Singapore's *second*-tallest tower. Compared with the rest of Asia, it barely registered a blip on the vertical radar.

Kent swung left alongside D'almeida Street, nearing the entrance. One-hundred meters ahead, a grass clearing named Raffles Place lay nestled within a ring of high-rises. Still no person, nor vehicle, on his tail. He started to worry that this was too easy and began bracing for the ceiling to cave.

He spotted a burnt-out employee, jabbing a finger into his cell phone between puffs on a cigarette. Next came a security guard, short, looking hot and bored between the building's twin sliding glass doors. Kent wasn't too worried about standing out; between the city's European heritage and its status as a global financial center, he was one of many Caucasians making for the air-conditioned lobby.

It came a moment later, four stories high and covered in polished granite. He'd decided to play the part of a visitor and stopped to admire the space. More familiar entrants streamed past him, like busy ants focused on the task at hand. Most strode toward the right and a row of steel barricades, each with its own digital access point. All waved key cards at the readers, earning a faint beep and passage deeper into the building.

Kent turned left and approached a security desk, where two guards—a man and woman—punched away on hidden keyboards. The woman looked up first. He glanced at his watch for effect, clearing his throat. "Hello," he said, in English. "This is a bit embarrassing, but I've got a meeting with Gerald Chang at CFE and can't remember the floor number."

She offered no words, but forced a smile and began searching her computer for what Kent assumed to be the building's directory. A handful of seconds passed before she looked up. "Mr. Chang's office is on the sixty-first floor, sir. You'll need a pass card to access the elevators."

He nodded.

"May I see some identification?"

Kent fished out his passport and slid it across the counter. She checked it over, entering some data into the computer. He took another innocent look around, finally settling on the man behind the counter. The guard studied him with a practiced mix of courtesy and skepticism. Kent grinned back, filling the sluggish seconds with all the nonchalance he could muster. The woman eventually handed the document back, then placed a plastic card in his hand. "This is good until 6 p.m."

"More than enough time, thank you." He strode away, hoping to blend into their subconscious with the rest of the throng, yet feeling the weight of prying eyes between his shoulder blades. It wasn't these guards he feared, but their colleagues. Dozens of them. One false move and the building could be locked down, any chance at the third stone lost in the afternoon haze.

Soon he'd passed the barricades and squeezed into one of the tower's double-decker elevators. Their concept was simple: two cars, one atop the other, sharing the same shaft. The lower serviced odd-numbered floors, the upper even ones. The design was popular with skyscrapers, where horizontal space was at a premium. It effectively doubled the passenger capacity of elevators without the need for additional shafts.

Now Kent stood inside one, rubbing shoulders with eight neighbors breathing down his neck. He'd officially passed the first stage, but still lacked a plan for the second. There was no free day to case the sixty-first floor, nor a floor-plan to scan in preparation. There was only time—about five minutes, as, one-by-one, each of his fellow passengers alighted through gold-plated doors. With every "whoosh" of the partition sliding back together, a handful of possible tactics was torn from the clandestine playbook. By the time the correct floor lit the elevator's side panel, he was alone, the blueprints for how to negotiate the next thirty seconds as void as the eternity of empty shaft beneath his shoes.

The doors slid open.

Twenty feet of marble tile lay before him, terminating at a matching counter nearly as wide. In its center sat a female receptionist, looking comically small behind such an expansive slab of decoration. Kent took a breath and moved forward, spotting a security guard at a much smaller desk out of the corner of his left eye. There was a distant hum of office commotion, but his steps provided the only sound in the immediate area.

The woman had already noticed him and offered her own smile; it was a touch more genuine than what he'd received in the lobby. *I'm up here. I must be important.* Her hair was done up in a bun, as black as the suit hugging her diminutive frame. Kent reached the counter a second later. "Good day." The words assembled themselves on instinct, one step ahead of his brain. "A colleague of mine is meeting with Mr. Chang later this afternoon and requested I wait for him on this floor."

She stared back at him, pausing for an extended moment, then finally consulted a monitor below. "You are with Hogue and Scarlet?" she eventually asked.

"Yes," Kent breathed, counting his blessings that the CEO actually happened to be in the building.

"Mr. Hogue isn't scheduled to arrive for another hour."

He held up his briefcase. "I have plenty of work to do."

She nodded, gesturing to a waiting area over his right shoulder. "Would you like something to drink?"

"No, thank you." He retreated to a bank of leather chairs, earning an uncomfortable level of interest from the security guard. Kent chose the seat furthest from the elevator and sank down. He might've preferred something around the corner, but at least he was off to the side, out of his two companions' direct earshot.

Now what? He supposed he'd passed the second 'test,' but hardly felt victorious. In sixty minutes, a man would enter the space and profess never to have seen this awaiting visitor before. An awkward exit would be the best he could hope for at that point.

He laid his briefcase on a glass coffee table and popped it open. Inside were a few pens, highlighters and notepads. Props that he'd now have to use. He thought about transcribing his current situation, then reconsidered. Who would ever believe it?

39

The hour passed quietly. Kent, though never completely ignored by the receptionist or guard, was soon tolerated with minimal attention. Enough footsteps—visitors and employees—crossed the marble entry to occupy the eyes of anyone stationed nearby.

Kent glanced at a gold watch he'd bought with the suit: almost three o'clock. Thanks to CFE's wi-fi, he'd learned that Hogue and Scarlet was a UK-based law firm that specialized in contract liability. With Crystal Freight insuring the vast majority of packages it transported, divining the meeting's purpose was simple.

At that moment the elevator doors opened and three men emerged. Kent knew immediately that the lead figure was Thomas Hogue; even if his picture hadn't been on the firm's website, his tall frame and official bearing signaled the presence of leadership.

Kent's heart beat a tick faster as the trio reached the desk. He heard Hogue announce himself in a faint baritone, then pause as the receptionist leaned in, speaking softly. Seconds later Hogue craned his neck in Kent's direction, then back to the desk. There was another pause, awkward for everyone in the room. The receptionist soon picked up a phone and began dialing. Hogue started toward the waiting area, his lieutenants in tow. The security guard watched with mild interest.

Kent stood. Hogue, cradling his own briefcase, closed the gap between them. "Excuse me," he said. "There seems to be some misunder—"

Gripping one of the highlighters from his pocket, Kent jabbed it into Hogue's kidney and brought his mouth to the man's ear. "I'm with you in Chang's office or you're on dialysis for the rest of your life." He feigned a smile. "Laurel and Hardy stay here."

Hogue, expectedly, froze. Whether Kent survived another minute depended on how and when his target broke from the stupor. An aggressive response—*shoot me, then*—exposed the bluff. But so did fear and panic; there was little he could do with a terror-stricken victim, blubbering at his knees.

For the third time, he lucked out. The lawyer took a deep breath, clapping his free palm on Kent's shoulder. "Thanks for coming, Jonathan. Gerald will want to see those figures." He turned to face his men. Kent stayed close, keeping the marker tight on his waist. "H-Hugh, Simon, change of plans. You're staying here. I've called Jonathan in. I'll start with him, then send for you."

Kent couldn't have asked for a smoother performance. It was impressive what the instinct for self-preservation could supply. But they weren't out of the woods yet. "Who is this?" asked one of the men, a fresh scowl matching the disdain in his voice.

Hogue barely paused. "An outside consultant, on retainer. Gerald wanted a fresh opinion for this account." The other man started to protest, but his boss raised an authoritative palm. "I'll fill you in later."

Without waiting for a response, Hogue stepped toward the reception desk as a second woman entered the space. "Good afternoon, Mr. Hogue." She gestured beyond with her arm. "If you'll follow me, Mr. Chang is waiting."

He obeyed, Kent riding his coattails like a corporate phantom. The latter could feel further sets of eyes boring into his back, but what could they do? He'd removed his hand from his pocket to avoid attention. The next moment, they were beyond the entry and out of sight.

They walked in silence. Technically, Kent no longer needed either of his escorts; from here he could find Chang's office on his own. But there was no chance to lock them away without causing a stir. So he followed, past small desks and large meeting rooms, making sure to stay close to Hogue. A handful of employees glanced up as they passed; none maintained their stares. Finally, rounding a corner, they reached a set of heavy wooden doors. The woman rapped softly before opening the partition and ushering her charges through.

Every CEO had an eccentric hobby; Gerald Chang evidently fancied himself an explorer. In almost laughable contrast to the business chic beyond, his office was fit for Indiana Jones. As he and Hogue stepped further inside, Kent spotted cedar-framed adventure scenes hugging the amber walls; decorative wooden crates arranged in a corner, their black-stenciled labels heralding exotic locales; a Persian rug conducting the eyes toward a carved oak desk.

More than anything, though, the concrete slab hanging from the center of the room arrested his attention. It seemed to be a rough cube, about five feet on every side. He could barely see the wire supporting it and figured more than one visitor had hesitated before walking directly beneath.

Later. Kent forced his eyes down, to Chang, leaning against the desk and flanked by a pair of leather chairs. He looked to be about five-foot-ten—tall by Singaporean standards; a slight pudge spilled over his belt. Behind him, a wall of windows admitted healthy swaths of the South Asian sun.

The CEO was on a cell phone but nodded toward Hogue. After a few more words, in Chinese, he ended the call. "Eric." Chang stepped forward and extended a hand. "Thank you for coming on such short notice. My VP's tell me if we don't address this now, it could metastasize." He turned to Kent and paused.

"My second for this meeting," said Hogue, still dutifully playing his part. "Jonathan Smythe. He'll be assisting…in an advisory capacity."

The lie appeared good enough for Chang. He offered Kent his hand. "Please, gentlemen, sit down." He gestured to a sofa on the left side of the room. "I'll have Mila bring us some tea."

Chang turned and muttered the request through an intercom on his desk. Hogue—clutching his briefcase with ivory knuckles—levered himself onto the cushions. Kent knew it would be more awkward to stand later and stayed on his feet. Sidling beneath the slab, he looked up, feigning curiosity.

The stone's surface was remarkably well-preserved, assuming Chang hadn't altered it. Kent ran his eyes across the underside, reminding himself that, even if this was from the right building, it constituted less than one percent of the entire exterior. He continued his scan, knowing the warning clock in the back of his mind had already buzzed, seeing Chang begin to spin away from the desk. *One last section.* He thought he noticed something and strained closer. It almost looked like an 'X.'

Cross beyond Portland.

Now he couldn't move if he wanted to. *Make a stand / Cornering evidence / Toward your deliverance.* He pictured this slab as it might've been over a century ago: part of a building, perhaps eye-level, where one could *stand* and see it. Even constituting a *corner* of the façade. In his line of work, there were no coincidences.

"She's beautiful, isn't she?"

He pulled his gaze away to see Chang strutting forward with a smile. A second's silence clued Kent that the question wasn't quite rhetorical. He cleared his throat, buying time to refocus. "Forgive me. I haven't been in too many offices like this one." He hoped the British accent was passable.

Chang kept his grin. "I'll take that as a compliment." He glanced upward. "The only surviving piece of Singapore's original post office. I had it tested; dates from the 1850's. How I got hold of it is a story in itself."

Kent was about to offer some vague encouragement when Chang turned toward the far wall, near the windows. "See that rope?"

Kent nodded. It appeared to be several feet of coarse hemp, frayed along most of its length, fastened to the wall and looped on a hook. Chang swiveled back. "That's nearly two-hundred years old. Used to unload some cargo shortly after the city's founding."

"You must be very proud."

He spread both arms. "We all need inspiration. I started a company focused on shipping, crossing the world. What better way to maintain CFE's mission than to surround myself with history's own attempts at transportation?"

Chang had begun gliding toward the sofa. Kent followed, allowing the latest question to hang in the air. He wanted no more attention. It was time to slink away, escape into the background. They both sat, Chang in a stuffed chair near Hogue, Kent on the couch's far end. Hogue had opened his briefcase and was leafing through a set of papers.

Chang leaned forward. "Eric, I know you're familiar with the situation. I was going to let you take the lead here. Where do we start?"

Kent stole a look at Hogue's hands. They were shaking. Beads of sweat soaked his forehead, despite the room's air-conditioning. The man was entering shock. Kent hated putting him in this position, but it'd been the only way. And this was the end; Hogue had held it together for as long as could've been hoped. Kent knew he only had a minute or so to make his move. Just as soon as he figured out what it was.

Chang was still waiting for an answer when the heavy wooden doors parted. He turned. "Well that was quick for tea—"

He stood, confusion gracing his face. Kent rose too, knowing immediately that something was wrong. A young woman stepped into the room, but carried no tray or beverage. She also, clearly, wasn't Mila, whom Kent assumed to be the woman who'd led them to Chang's office. The new entrant locked the doors behind her. Kent saw Caucasian skin, but didn't get a clear look at the face.

Hogue now stood as well, the interruption seeming to wake him from his nightmare. Chang moved beyond his chair. "Who are you? What is this all about?"

"Sit down, Mr. Chang." The voice was deep, cold, and one that Kent had heard before—on a plane. Chang stepped aside, confirming his suspicions. Trina hardly looked now as she had then. One glance at her empty eyes explained Chang's obedience.

She started walking toward them, with every step becoming less the mythical young mother and more the actual trained killer. At least, that's what

Kent had to assume. Her hands were empty, but she would be carrying some kind of weapon. He found himself wishing he hadn't parted with the Glock in Toronto.

She was now staring directly at him. "Where is the stone, Jeremy?"

Both men looked at Kent, Hogue slightly less surprised than Chang. Kent shook his head. "I don't know what you're talking about, Trina. And my name's Evan."

She took a step forward. "You wouldn't have come all the way up here if it wasn't in this room. And my name is Kai."

40

All the way up here. How had she known where to find him? Kent would've bet his life—did bet—that no tail existed. His mind raced for a plausible answer, even though finding one no longer mattered. It had to be something he didn't—

The shock. On the plane, when they'd shaken hands. That wasn't static electricity; it was a prick from a minute syringe, injecting him with some kind of tracking fluid. He'd seen the technology, but never anything so covert. How long would the signal stay active? Did anyone else have access to his location?

Questions for a future he'd likely never see.

The tension in the room had only increased. Trina—Kai—remained locked on Kent, her initial query still snapping at the silence. He frantically traced every mental angle for a way out. None ensured retrieval of the stone without collateral damage and too much luck to count on. Then Chang turned toward the entrance, the atmosphere evidently having worn through his discretion. "Mila!"

His shout filled the office, but doubtless fell on deaf ears. Kai's visit was too critical to plan between an AA's bathroom breaks; Mila was either stuffed in a nearby closet or slumped beneath her desk.

"This is ridiculous." Chang, unaccustomed to disobedience, muttered something more to himself in Chinese. Then he started for the door.

Kent took a step forward. "Gerald, don't."

Too late. In the moment Chang swiped past Kai, she pulled a knife from her side, grabbed him from behind and slit his throat. His body immediately went slack, nearly beating the drops of red down to the Persian fiber. Hogue gasped in terror, backing from the couch and tripping over himself toward the desk.

Kent didn't move. The entire room went quiet, he and Kai sizing each other up. There wasn't much comparison: she had the knife, and probably something more powerful tucked beneath her suit. The only reason she'd yet to remove it was the noise factor. But she did now, slowly, eyes on him the entire time.

It looked like a Glock 26, smaller than its many siblings but still capable of blowing his head off. She gripped it without pause, leveling the barrel between his eyes. "One last time: where is the stone?"

Time was running out. Kent had no doubt she'd use the weapon if necessary. Chang continued to stain the rug; he could hear Hogue whimpering behind. What began with a promising discovery had quickly turned to complete disaster. There was no clear escape, only a desperate path of misdirection that delayed the inevitable.

Which, of course, he took. "It's in the crates." Kent nodded toward the corner behind Kai.

She kept her gaze on him, eventually gesturing with the Glock. "Then fetch it."

He started to walk. Thirty seconds to come up with something brilliant. Kent didn't know where she'd gotten the gun, but with it came control. She wouldn't have brought it without a plan to slip away after firing. Once she had the stone, she'd put a 9mm round through his forehead; Hogue would be a formality.

Kent made it to the wood and stopped. There were three boxes, stacked like a miniature pyramid. It would've been easy enough to tear into the top container, but something told him to pick it up and bring it toward Kai. He clutched the edges and hoisted.

It made perfect sense that they'd be empty. But he was expecting a full load and, for an instant, jumped at the lack of resistance. Then he tightened his grip and forced a grimace across his face. *Lift with your knees.*

Upright, he spun and began trudging toward Kai. From her vantage point, the crate had to be a hundred pounds. Other than the stone's actual location, it was the only piece of information he possessed that she didn't. But in a dance like this, it constituted a sliver of tactical leverage.

He could feel the weight of the Glock's aim. At the edge of his peripherals, Hogue, back on his feet, was now braced against the desk. Kent stopped before Kai. Once again, the room fell silent. Still no sound from Mila.

"Open it," said Kai.

"I don't have a tool."

"Use your foot." She stole a glance toward the door. "Quietly."

He bent low, flashing the strain through his lips. If there was any move to make, it had to come now. He might forestall execution by claiming a mistaken box—*it's in one of the others*—but doubted she'd buy it.

He reached the floor, close enough to smell the iron in Chang's blood. He didn't let go, though. Making to rise with a half-jerk, he instead flung the crate directly toward Kai and raced after it.

She knocked it aside with the butt of the Glock, then swung the barrel back and fired two rounds. Delayed just enough, the slugs whistled over Kent's head as he dove into her midsection. The two of them hurtled through the air and slammed against the far wall. Kent heard the gun hit the ground. He whirled toward it, saw he couldn't reach and turned back in time to catch a chop from Kai across his right shoulder. The area immediately went numb, a vague tingle running down his arm.

She stayed on her feet, wincing from the force of impact. Kent once again eyed the pistol. He managed to grip it with his left hand, but had hardly raised it when a strip of fire blazed across his back. He turned to find Kai, knife out, this time stained with his own blood. He arched in pain, gasping.

Another cutting stroke. He just managed to parry, the feeling creeping back toward his right side. But it wasn't there yet; his right arm still lay at his waist. He raised the left, trying to aim the Glock. Kai gripped it by the barrel, tying him up in a tug of wills. This left her with the knife hand free.

She sliced once more, then again, each time Kent just managing to dodge the crimson blade. They danced across the carpet, he retreating a step at each thrust. He held a distinct strength advantage, but with their alternate arms locked, pushing her back brought him no further from the blade.

Quickly Kai feigned a jab, then lifted the steel in a diagonal arc across Kent's chest. It dug just below the skin, lighting a red river from ribcage to collarbone. He grunted in agony once more, but planted his feet. The wall lay at his back.

She reared for a final assault. He felt his fingers in his right hand. As the knife closed for his throat, Kent released his share of the Glock. An instant's surprise flashed across her face. Before she could turn the gun around, he stopped the blade with his left hand, reversed it with his right and used both to drive it into her chest.

Surprise became shock. She managed to squeeze the trigger once, the bullet whizzing by Kent's left ear before he chopped the weapon to the floor. Kai followed quickly, landing on her back with a quiet thud. Her eyes had already begun glassing over.

Kent stood above her, bleeding and breathing heavily. He'd live, but there was no time to rejoice. A loud banging shook the entry doors to his left. Security. A deep voice cut through the barrier in muffled Chinese. *'Are you alright, Mr. Chang?'*

Kent noticed Hogue on his right, feet still planted near the desk. He hadn't slipped out during the fight; fear was a great paralyzer.

More pounding on the doors. They were thick, but the lack of an answer only intensified the air within. Kent knew he had mere seconds before the guard was joined by others and the pounding became more violent. He hadn't yet figured how to escape. One thing at a time.

Bending down, he pried the Glock from Kai's hand and stepped toward the suspended stone. A closer look at Hogue: the man looked a shade paler, brow and collar drenched with sweat. Kent held up his free palm. "I'm not going to hurt you."

Weak words right now; Kent would've had a hard time believing them himself. But they simply needed to hold Hogue in place for a moment longer. He couldn't afford a dash for the exit.

If fully loaded, the pistol would've begun with a ten-round clip, plus one in the chamber. Kai had fired three times. Wasting no further movement, Kent raised the Glock and fired its eight remaining rounds at the point where the stone's support wire fed into the ceiling.

Nothing happened. Outside, the pounding had abruptly stopped, as he knew it would. There'd been a few gasps, but now mostly silence. Another few seconds to work with. Cutting the wire would've been the first option, but it was supporting several hundred pounds of stone; the knife in Kai's chest wasn't up to the task.

Beyond the door, the guard would be waving his comrades close. Kent could almost hear their approaching footsteps, see his final seconds of freedom draining away. But he wasn't leaving without the stone.

Where would you even go?

A sharp tremor sounded above his head. He glanced up. A dark web began sprouting from the ceiling, encircling the wire's entry point. The plaster broke free a moment later. With its tether released, the slab collided with the floor and split into a dozen pieces.

Hogue still hadn't moved. Kent almost thanked him. *Keep calm and carry your briefcase.* Kent kneeled toward the rubble as the pounding resumed, louder this time. He ignored it. Seconds later he spotted the tablet, resting free from a hollow pocket within the stone. Like a lottery winner, he swiped it into his pocket.

Now came the hard part. Escaping meant—

Beep. A sudden chill flared up his spine. He heard the faint sound, then again. *And again.* Emanating from Kai's body. Each ping grew higher in pitch and closer in succession to the last. Like a tidal wave, realization hit him, dropping his heart into his stomach. He scanned the room, desperation coalescing into the shadow of a plan. There was no way they'd get through the door in time.

Kent jumped to his feet and shouted toward Hogue. "The window—now!"

Somehow, the Englishman understood enough to race toward the glass. Behind him, Kent sprinted right. He could hear the countdown in his head; they had three seconds, maybe. Nearly colliding with the far wall, he jerked the rope off its hook.

The rest was instinct. He saw Hogue reach the center of the window, planted his foot on the corner of the desk and leapt toward the sunshine. Halfway there, the rope in his right hand, he clotheslined Hogue.

They felt the boom before hearing it. Instantly, Chang's entire office bent beneath the weight of a rippling concussion. With the heat of a fireball at their backs, men met glass just as it shattered into a thousand pieces. Fresh, terrifying air took its place. Kent slid his left arm around Hogue's own and tightened his grip on the rope. Below, over seven-hundred feet of open gravity began tugging them down.

41

Hogue tried to scream, fear choking away most of his voice. Kent maintained his grips as the rope caught at its full length and swung them back toward the floor below. The explosion spewed out above, singeing the air they'd just occupied. Kent didn't know how long the rope would hold; their arc toward the building might as well have been in slow motion.

The window ahead was intact, but splintered by the blast's proximity. An instant later they crashed into its glass, their momentum just heavy enough to break through. Next came a circular table, collapsing to the hardwood floor under their weight.

The two of them lay on their backs, panting, vaguely aware of the mounting chaos around. The half-charred rope had gone slack in Kent's hands. He pulled its remains inside and sat up.

They seemed to be in an executive dining room. Several tables, identical to the one they'd just destroyed—down to the white linen—dotted what had, moments ago, surely been a peaceful space. Now the walls shook with screams of terror. Dozens of people—most of them staff, cleaning after the lunch hour—tumbled over one another toward a set of elevator doors at the far end of the space.

Kent could hardly blame them. After 9/11, no explosion in a skyscraper ever felt like an accident. He looked up. The ceiling here was cracking too, helpless beneath the pressure of the blaze above. Kai must've brought an explosive, some kind of incendiary fail-safe. Whatever the material, it'd produced a blast ten times larger than any grenade.

Kent rose and pulled up a shaking Hogue. The man was now fully in shock. Yet he paused, abruptly, and fixed Kent with a lucid stare. "Who are you?"

"Forget me." Kent turned his charge toward the crowd and they stumbled forward. No one in the room had given them a second look. Fear continued to soak the air, spurred not just by the immediate danger but also the unknown nature of its source.

Kent was scared too—he still had no idea how he was going to escape the building undetected. This wasn't Montreal, with points of egress in every direction. The only way out was down. His best chance was to join the masses and slip free amidst the descending confusion.

They were thirty feet from the door when a hunk of burning ceiling fell steps to their left. Hogue flinched wildly, but Kent kept him moving; the ground beneath their feet was strong enough to withstand the impact. Ahead, several remaining employees dove toward the elevator. A few others chose an adjacent stairwell.

Twenty feet. The sprinklers kicked on just as a second section collapsed to the right. The chunks of concrete and plaster were immediately doused beneath the spray, but hardly flickered. Fire, like a hungry serpent, crawled from the upper floor through the newly made holes above. Heat radiated from each pocket of flame, thickening the air. Smoke began to build.

Kent pulled off his soaked jacket and bunched it into Hogue's face. "Breathe through this."

Ten feet. They were almost to the door. A young waiter, having spotted them, held it open with a frantic wave. Kent pushed Hogue in front—too late. The roof above them creaked once, then broke free. Their forward momentum wasn't fast enough; Kent had no time to think.

Instead, he jumped straight up and dropkicked Hogue into the stairwell. In addition to saving the Englishman, the action sent Kent back a few feet, just beyond the blazing slab. He hit the ground and rolled away. The ceiling, growing angry, dropped another section beyond the first, forcing its prey deeper into the room.

Kent could now see clearly into what had once been Chang's office. It was nothing—almost literally. Blackened shreds of furniture and fabric were the feeble holdouts, quickly succumbing to sheets of roiling flame. He backed in farther, coughing through his sleeve. There hadn't been time to look down, but he could feel each burning stripe of crimson wrapping his torso. By now, enough of the blood had clotted to keep his tattered shirt an even pink.

The sprinklers continued their deluge, making slow progress. Too slow. Kent blinked, fending off the smoke with watery eyes. By the time a fire crew arrived both floors would be a charcoal shell. The stone in his pocket hardly mattered now as options for escape officially reached zero.

One. The idea flew by, buzzing the tower of his brain like a desperate F-18. He turned farther within, searching the tables. Seconds remained until the entire ceiling caved in. Finally, he found an intact tablecloth and ripped it off its stand. China and glass crashed to the floor, accenting the symphony of destruction.

Kent could now barely see through the smoke. He turned toward the broken window, its jagged light cutting the haze like a beacon. Heart pounding in his chest, he could hear what was left of the ceiling begin to crumble behind. Gripping the sheet in both hands, he raced toward the hole in the glass and jumped out.

The wind was the biggest shock, sucking the breath from his lungs like an alien substance. It burned his eyes, daring him to keep both open. The thick cloth instantly swallowed its available air, stiffening from the strain. It hardly seemed to make a difference. Far below, the green expanse of Raffles Place stretched out like a peaceful par five.

He *heard* the wind now, screaming past his ears with unwelcoming vigor, reinforcing the hostile environment. The improvised chute fought gamely, even making some headway. But he was still falling at too fast a clip. Halfway down, trees and cars continued to rush upward.

Kent's hands cramped from gripping the linen. He shifted his focus, down, toward a growing crowd of onlookers near the edge of the clearing. The bomb had only blown seconds ago, but they were already two-dozen strong. Some had pulled out cell phones, filming his descent.

Five, six seconds until impact. He'd slowed enough now that colliding with the ground would only break both his legs. Which meant arrest, delay, failure. Fates worse than death. *Unless...* He angled right, willing his course toward a tree at the front of the lawn. He could hear the crowd gasping through the wind.

The tree came in line just enough for him to rake his lower body through its upper limbs. A city of fresh welts immediately sang from his shins, but it worked: his drop had been slowed further. The remaining distance was simply a matter of choosing grass over concrete.

He cleared the nearest sidewalk with feet to spare, hitting the ground in a role and releasing the sheet. A glance back up at the building was impossible to resist.

Heavy black smoke continued to waft from both affected floors. Orange flames danced at its edges, hunting down every last pocket of oxygen. Below, the Republic Plaza's main entry coughed out stream after stream of suited men and women. The scene was eerily quiet, most of them wrapped in too much fear and shock to muster the typical hysteria.

Not so for his adoring fans. Several in the pack on the lawn had stayed put, but an intrepid remainder was now rushing, and yelling, his way. Most were surely bent on offering assistance, a few, perhaps, emboldened by the chance to play hero and subdue a possible suspect. Kent didn't have energy for any of them. The tension over the past five minutes—compounding like interest on a bad loan—had now come due, soaking his body in sudden exhaustion.

Then the sirens began their approach from around the corner, and it was time to run.

42

Unlike her fellow passengers, Allison didn't mind the rain. It'd arrived suddenly—clouds moved fast in the tropics. But they carried neither lightning nor thunder, and the drops were warm, drumming the *Blue Countess*'s deck in rhythmic sheets. For its part, the sea stayed calm, an expanse of navy glass stretching toward the midnight horizon.

She was still on the deck chair she'd claimed twenty minutes ago, near the bow. Back then there'd been a dozen other people, mostly couples, trying to squeeze a bit more romance out of the evening. Despite their size, cruise ships rarely offered this kind of intimacy.

But when the rain came, they'd all scampered for cover. *Like normal people.* A few had sent her sideways glances, wondering what kind of woman would welcome a downpour from out in the open. No matter. The air remained humid; she wasn't cold. And she wore only her swimsuit, flip flops and an oversized tee shirt—nothing that couldn't take a little water. The experience was almost relaxing.

On the surface. Beneath her skin, the true storm raged. That was actually one of the reasons she hadn't moved when the sky opened up: right now, each limb held the weight of a mountain. Driving this fact home were a bevy of fresh tears, disguised as raindrops as they fell down her cheeks.

The crying started with a bad feeling about Jeremy. It wasn't the first time. Since they'd been together, whenever he left the country, she couldn't help but assume the worst: tortured in some Syrian prison; drowned in a car beneath the Seine; bleeding out on a lonely field in Africa.

She'd have brushed it all off as ridiculous if he hadn't endured an army of similar threats less than a year ago—with her by his side. They were larger-than-life obstacles that cut with the sharp edge of reality. Yet, he'd made it through them all in one piece.

This, though—the maelstrom in her gut that'd begun swirling an hour ago—was different. She couldn't even conjure a mental picture of where he might be, only an acute sense of panic. *That's all it is.* Fear. There was no sixth sense, no cosmic premonition connecting her and her boyfriend across continents. Just a tendency for dread that, if she didn't reign it in, would literally drive her crazy. Because none of these things—the thoughts, feelings, danger—were going away.

Theirs was a unique relationship. They'd first met amidst a firefight and car chase across the streets of Linz, Austria. Even if he hadn't mentioned the letters 'C.I.A.,' she'd have guessed something close. Which meant, while most women in her position believed their partners really were accountants, she was in on the lie herself.

Did that make it better? It wasn't too late to turn back. She could always end things, say goodbye. There were plenty of alternatives out there in business suits and hard hats. And they were guaranteed to come home every night. The next few decades would roll by as safely as vanilla ice cream: kids, suburbs, carefully insulated vacations just like this one.

But that was never going to happen. She'd known it long ago; every subsequent moment was simply a brick in the long path toward honesty with herself. There was something about the fleeting nature of life—when you found something real, you held on forever. That's what Jeremy was: her reality. She had no idea what direction her road ahead would take, but she knew it had to go through him.

It was more than mere physical attraction. She felt purpose in walking beside him. Other women might've been completely fulfilled honing their skills as a nurse, delivering babies for forty years. It was a worthy pursuit. But

Allison had long felt the tug for something different. As if her heart had been specifically prepared for the unusual.

Loving a clandestine officer was just that. It took a special kind of woman. There would be further doses of sorrow and isolation, which was another reason for the tears: she'd finally come to terms with the consequences of her choice.

But that choice would also provide the chance—however slim—for radiant joy, and a peace that only came from knowing you'd found where you were always meant to be.

43

"And the foreman says, 'wait, I thought you were a democrat?'"

A blue-collared chorus, packing the machinists hall to its faded-brick gills, erupted in laughter. Even the reporters and camera crews lining the back wall admitted a few smiles. The joke was only lost on the Secret Service, who were exempt from amusement, and the man they were paid to protect, who'd long ago lost his appetite for partisan one-liners.

That was an issue. The mere cusp of his bid for reelection wasn't the place for second thoughts. But the game had continued to grow ever-nastier, more personal. *Game.* A word far less innocent than its connotation. He thought of the concussions incurred over a thousand distant Sundays, Jack Youngblood's broken leg, even his own mangled ACL as a linebacker at the naval academy.

Campaigns were little different. Even if you were lucky enough to emerge from the political gauntlet a victor, you spent the next four years licking your wounds. It was a wonder anything ever got done.

"Matthew Billings has been like an uncle to me. I remember when..."

The President, just out of sight stage right, glanced again toward the man at the microphone. He was a stand-up comedian, and he wasn't lying. His father's friendship with Billings went all the way back to high school. Since then, myriad family get-togethers had given the future chief executive ample chance to dote on the budding comic.

Now the same bright boy was a middle-aged semi has-been. Still talented, but prisoner to the persona he'd cultivated two decades ago. It was as if the world of humor had gradually reinvented itself, and he'd been unable, or unwilling, to keep up. His bank account followed suit. What had been posh escapes in Miami and Malibu were, today, a two-story Tudor outside Columbus; the same man who'd filled arenas in Toronto and Chicago was now playing community centers in Toledo and Flint.

And machinists halls in Ann Arbor. Because he'd been available in a pinch. Billings was supposed to be sipping bourbon at Camp David. Instead, at his campaign manager's insistence, he was here. Strange, such urgency a full month before the Iowa caucuses. Except that was the problem.

It came in the form of a private-sector wunderkind with wavy hair and perfect teeth. The man was a decade from AARP-eligibility, but he'd already had a popular run as mayor of Detroit, then disappeared into a real estate conglomerate. Five years and millions in profit later, he was back with a 'new vision' for the country.

He also happened to be from Michigan, which meant the President wasn't even guaranteed victory in his home state. The governor, hedging his political future, hadn't offered an endorsement and no-doubt wouldn't before August. Never mind the unwritten rule of refraining from challenging the incumbent in your own party. His opponent was energetic, brash, not one to buckle beneath the weight of decorum or tradition.

Billings supposed the whole thing would've been a moot point if his own approval ratings had been better. He'd always had more success with foreign policy than domestic issues. Today, so many of his fellow citizens hardly seemed concerned with overseas threats. As if years of safety had somehow formed an impenetrable wall around the country.

"He was a good man then, and, like my favorite wine, has only improved with age."

Two minutes. After that, he'd have to take the podium and continue convincing potential voters that he was the right man for the job. For what it was worth, the fire still burned within. Billings believed in the power of this office.

It was a lot like marriage: the hardest, and best, thing he'd ever done.

"Mr. President." He didn't have to turn. The baritone of his head of security announced itself. "You have a phone call."

He also didn't need to ask if it was urgent. They could each hear the man behind the microphone, mere feet away, nearing the end of his introduction. Now Billings did turn, waiting for confirmation of what he already suspected.

"It's the Agency, sir."

The President nodded. Despite this impromptu rally, his most recent thoughts had hardly been burdened by the political landscape. That honor fell to a cell phone video posted online by a foreign exchange student four hours ago. It showed black smoke and orange flames encircling the upper floors of Singapore's Republic Plaza. In the foreground, what started as a dark smudge soon became a man, gripping a makeshift parachute and gliding toward the camera. He clipped some trees and angled right, skidding violently into the grass.

The phone followed him, temporarily abandoning the building. He shed the mass of cloth, looked around, then began running in the opposite direction. By the grace of God, the face was too distant to recognize.

Billings was led from the stage toward a small anteroom. Along the way he passed the incredulous eyes of his campaign manager and shot a glance back. *I'm the President.* For what he was being paid the man could dream up a stall tactic.

Another agent held the door and handed him a cell phone. He stepped through and was sealed in silence. The space before him was clean, trade-union chic: stained carpet, a metal desk and chair; paint-chipped walls. He sat down and brought the phone to his ear. "Billings."

"Mr. President. This is Peter McCoy."

A pause. "Where's Tom?"

"Sir, we've had an update on the stone. Director Vanning has been briefed, but preferred I fill you in as I spoke personally with Kent."

A moment passed. Billings noticed he was clutching the desk with his off-hand. "So he's alive? He has it?"

"Yes, and yes. He's on a Gulfstream as we speak, heading toward the Netherlands."

The President leaned back, releasing the desk. The pounding in his chest, having accelerated to DEFCON 1, began its tricky journey back to a slow flutter. "Tell me we didn't just start a war with Southeast Asia, Pete."

"You're referring to the video. It's been posted online and picked up by several news outlets, including the BBC. But we have it contained. Kent's face is unrecognizable, and no witnesses have come forward with a detailed description. Tower security scanned his passport, but linking that to the explosion will take too long. Even then, it'll lead to a digital dead end."

"How'd we get him on that plane?"

"He couldn't fly commercial, for obvious reasons. A CFO at one of Singapore's investment houses owed us a favor. He personally met Kent at the airport and ushered him onto the jet. No flight attendant, just two pilots."

Billings allowed himself a deep breath. "And it's going to Holland?"

"Yes sir. The third stone held no clue, only an address. It matches an estate in Het Gooi, a wealthy enclave southeast of Amsterdam. The owner is Edmund van Leer, chairman of Van Leer Holdings." A pause. "He's the sixth-richest man in Europe."

Billings straightened. It was a name he'd heard before. "Are you saying Van Leer is tied to the attacks?"

"We don't yet know. Electronic records indicate the grounds have been in his family for over three-hundred years. We're waiting on confirmation from some older, local data.

"Van Leer runs the company with his brother, Jakob. He's clean on the surface. Vacation homes in Monaco and Curacao, a penthouse in Manhattan. But the estate in Het Gooi is still his primary residence. He gives millions to charity each year, pays his taxes. No criminal history to speak of.

"Then what's our play?"

"We can't be sure of anything without a closer look at that house. Delacroix specifically etched the address on the stone. It has to be there for a reason."

"You mentioned local data. I assume that means we have assets in place?"

"Yes. One team is standing by in Amsterdam, another just outside Brussels. But, Mr. President, I would advise you to consider them secondary options. Kent remains our best chance for success."

"Kent?" Billings checked his watch. "How long has he been airborne?"

"About six hours, sir."

"So he's another, what, six hours out of Schiphol in Amsterdam?"

"Almost exactly."

"It's eleven o'clock here in Michigan, Pete. December 19th has already arrived in over half of Asia. If that list is right, a single bullet could do more damage than a nuclear bomb."

He stood. "I've got to go make a speech in sixty seconds. Which means you've got half that time to convince me why we should wait for an injured, strung-out officer who's barely over the Caspian Sea when we have fresh personnel already in the area."

McCoy exhaled on the other end. "You're right, Mr. President. The day is dawning. Which means we've only got one chance. Kent may be tired, but he's been waging this war for days. If there is a threat waiting, he's the only one with firsthand knowledge of our enemy's skill level and tactics. Failure here means losing the last lead we'll ever have to follow."

"Is this your personal assessment?"

"No sir, Director Vanning's. But I agree, as does DNI Sanders."

A few breaths ago Billings had been ready to end the call and stride out confidently; now he was frozen in place. A cloud of stress had seeped inside, clamping each bone. It was his own fault, really—he'd asked for this four years ago, and was about to ask again today. When it came to decisions, the President never got layups. The Buck followed him well beyond his Resolute Desk.

In the end, like a football coach on fourth-and-one, he went with his gut.

44

After three years in the Navy and five more as a SEAL, Lieutenant Shane Cartwright finally knew what injustice looked like: azure waves crashing peacefully into tracts of white sand; sunshine stretched bright across a cloudless blue sky; seagulls, wings taught, scouting the surf for an early dinner. Guantanamo Bay's Windmill Beach had never been so beautiful.

Or restricted. Not, of course, for the handful of base residents currently enjoying the space a mere fifty yards ahead. Just for he and his men, who probably needed the wind and salt more than anyone.

He took a swig from a bottle of water, biting his proverbial lip. Their presence here made sense, in a twisted sort of way. The brainchild, surely, of some ambitious two-star at the Pentagon, fussing over his uniform and forcing through initiatives that carried the bare minimum of practical significance.

Case in point: an extended training exercise, in which the navy's transportation apparatus would be drilled and sharpened, eliminating redundancies, trimming delays. On paper, it was perfectly rational: what good were Special Forces if they couldn't be ferried to the right place at the right time? But this wasn't just point-A to point-B; it was a global operation, measuring readiness and transfer capability. The appropriate metaphor was a relay race. *And you're the baton.*

Because, thanks to the wisdom of his superiors, it wasn't good enough to execute such logistics minus flesh-and-blood cargo with which to interact. The best part was that his platoon—one of only two selected for travel among dozens of candidates—was to consider this 'recognition for exceptional performance.' They'd just flown from Japan to Pearl, then boarded a second, awaiting C-130 and landed here five hours ago. Cartwright's head spun; his legs were as soft as jelly. None of it felt like a reward.

Which made the scene before him all the more punishing. It wasn't San Diego with his wife and kids—the 'sand' here was really small rocks, mixed with shells and other sea debris—but it beat their temporary barracks, laced with the stale BO of a thousand previous sailors. He scanned the length of the beach, nodding. A few lawn chairs, cooler of Coronas…they could've made this work.

As it was, they had to stay ready to move. Clearance for the next leg, though, had yet to come; apparently there was a maintenance issue with the plane. Which, while proving the point of this entire exercise, didn't make the standing around any easier.

Soon, though—within 24-48 hours, according to brass at Coronado— the training would be over. Cartwright and his platoon would officially be on leave. Then he really could see his family, enjoy some of that overpriced California coastline.

For the time being, it was energy drinks, protein bars, maybe some PlayStation if they were lucky. The Lieutenant took a final swallow from his bottle, eventually turning away from the beach. Spend too much time thinking about something you couldn't have, you almost started to believe you didn't deserve it.

45

Once again, Kent found himself tracing a dark, lonely road. It was in danger of becoming the story of his life.

A life that began as an only-child in the middle of Kansas. After college he'd joined the Army. Then came Special Forces, now the CIA; only a handful of people knew what he actually did. His wasn't a life conducive to partnership. Even a professional like Baker had tasted its bitter edge.

Then Allison Shaw came along. She didn't just add to his life—she completely changed it. He'd seen a new course flash before his eyes, one filled with companionship, understanding and the kind of love neither of them deserved. But he was starting to realize it wasn't enough.

He'd known this, of course. It'd been there all along, haunting the recesses of his psyche like a cruel ghost. She'd stepped into his world so suddenly…he'd managed, for six fleeting months, to ignore the truth. Now—with each cold gunshot, every burning scar—it'd reclaimed its influence. It was no longer fair to let Allison choose her own path. Her only chance for a real life was away from his.

Kent felt a dense weight begin leaking through his heart. Emotional pain had its own set of teeth. His mind drifted back over the past summer and fall, to what he was losing. Many moments they'd had together, and every one they hadn't. "*It's not just wanting her by your side,*" his dad had told him, shortly after his mom passed. "*It's how much you miss her when she's not.*"

Kent jerked the wheel left, barely missing a dear that'd invaded his swath of headlights. His heart drummed in his chest, perspiration blanching his hairline. Then, as quickly as it came, the threat passed. He made it back to his lane, slowly regaining speed. The asphalt continued to stretch ahead, oblivious lines of birch and ash dancing in the shadows. He snuck an internal grin: wouldn't it be something to make it this far only to be done in by venison?

It wasn't all smiles, though. If anything, the last ten seconds underscored the focus needed to survive the next twenty-four hours. Which, in a microcosm, was his life: no mistakes, no accidents and no one else to share them with.

He'd slept an hour on the Gulfstream—miracles still happened. A fresh change of clothes had been waiting on board, along with a first-aid kit. The latter held bandages for his chest and back. Stitches would've been better, but he'd live. At this point, necessity was a fluid concept.

The jet touched down at Schiphol Airport, six miles southwest of Amsterdam, just before 11 p.m. After taxiing off the runway, the copilot wordlessly entered the cabin and activated the stair ramp. A moment later Kent strode forward into the darkness. The immediate area was quiet, save a gust of frozen wind that cut through to his skin. If trained killers didn't get him, the change of climates might.

No customs agent at the bottom of the steps, no tram waiting to haul away his nonexistent luggage. Instead, seventy-five yards distance, he spotted two men through the gloom. They stood outside a pair of dark sedans. McCoy's idea. It was a tad conspicuous, but by now 'Evan Graves' wasn't fooling anyone.

He traipsed across the open asphalt, feeling like a ten-point buck at the onset of rifle season. In reality, the airport's terminal lights were practically specks on the horizon. Each car—a Passat and Peugot—hugged an old hangar that'd seen better days. This was obviously Schiphol's low-rent district.

Soon Kent was close enough to make out his welcoming party with ease.

Both men stood beside the Peugot's hood, tucked in parkas against the cold. Neither shivered nor swayed; they'd been trained for much more than a thankless handoff. Which had to make each wonder what kind of arrival warranted such a reception. They'd probably never know.

Seconds later Kent had reached them. No words were needed. One of the men stepped forward and handed him a spare clip for Trina's Glock—now his—as well as the keys to the Passat. Then they both folded into the Peugot, started its engine and pulled away. The French sedan quickly disappeared around the corner of the hangar.

Kent didn't wait around either. The Volkswagen purred smoothly to life and he was off, exiting the airport grounds toward the A9. From that point it was nearly a straight shot east into Het Gooi.

46

You're close. True for his current drive, truer still for the last handful of days. Though they were beginning to wear the weight of months. His body felt like it'd been chewed up and spit out by some malevolent giant of espionage. Knife fights, chases, snipers, explosions—all, in the end, for a simple address. He couldn't help glancing toward the passenger seat; the third stone lay there like a tarnished pearl, caked in pale starlight. Upon it's ancient face he could just make out the carved ridges detailing words he'd long-ago memorized: *Three Lambeth Pass, Het Gooi, Netherlands.*

On back was the phrase *Odyssey Complete* and the numbers *38, 17* and *22.* The words were peculiar, but fitting, the numbers a complete mystery. He'd have written them off as an archaic detail, but that's what anyone else would've called this entire sequence of stones. Somehow, the truth knew better.

He slowed the Passat along N236, knowing the next turn-off was close. It came seconds later, a slender line of blacktop disappearing within a deep maw of barren timber. Despite the lack of foliage, the moon's natural light faltered; his headlights had to pick up the slack. On either side of the roadway patches of snow dusted the landscape. Wind howled outside his door, testing seams in the glass.

Kent spotted the sign for Lambeth Pass and drove on. Fifty meters ahead, another road jutted off to the right. He swung the sedan down and pulled against the curb, cutting the engine. *Lights off, deep breath*. Only one house was visible through the windshield, a bank of floodlights illuminating its exterior.

There was no movement inside or out. He exited the vehicle as the icy breeze began to dissipate, giving way to near-perfect silence.

He pocketed the stone and began jogging back toward the previous road, then down to Lambeth Pass. He'd only seen half a dozen cars once leaving Schiphol, but was now surrounded by affluence. Which meant police. A patrol, who would know the area and probably what cars didn't belong, might happen to spot the Passat. Even run its plates.

But that hardly mattered anymore. With any luck, this would all be over before local authorities could make a fuss over Mr. Graves. At the moment, his only danger was being seen by passing headlights. He kept a weather eye, ready to dive into the trees at the faintest glimmer.

Finally, Lambeth came into view. He slowed to a walk, the Glock tucked firmly behind his back.

This road was even quieter than the last, with even less homes. Did each of them date from the nineteenth century? It was beyond remarkable that Van Leer's address hadn't changed since Emile carved his clues. What might the Frenchman think if he could see it today?

The lane curved slightly to the left. Kent didn't follow. Instead, he turned to face another track snaking in the opposite direction. He'd studied satellite images on his phone: this wasn't another street; it was a driveway. And at its head, scrawled into a granite post, was the number '3.'

One more glance around confirmed he was still alone. The wind returned for an encore, caressing his jacket in frigid wisps. Ahead, the path narrowed into the brush like a dark tunnel. It would filter out the other side, he already knew, onto a parklike sprawl, hugging a modest lake before curling in front of a neoclassical mansion.

Kent glanced at his watch: it was just after midnight. The present day's countdown began echoing in his mind, then pounding his gut. He started running.

The dense air deadened his footfalls atop the line of gravel. There was little cause for further fear of detection as, earlier, Langley had spied past the firewalls of Amsterdam's leading residential security company. Van Leer's 'No. 3' was number one on their list, but no contract had been set for the grounds themselves. Unless a pack of Dobermans met him at the pond, Kent knew he should arrive unannounced.

Cresting a small hill, smoke issuing from his mouth, he saw the house. It stood about a hundred meters ahead, looking like a forgotten relic of history. Not a single light, inside or out, cut the surrounding darkness. A pinch of confusion joined the tension that always hugged his bones in moments like this.

Fifty meters. He veered to the right, off the driveway and through a sparse patch of pines. Definitely no dogs. He heard little beyond the swift crunch of his boots against the cold earth.

The forest soon opened onto a trimmed lawn. He swung toward the rear of the house, where a four-car garage presented itself beside more grass. Beyond the drive to the right lay a stone patio, but Kent turned left. In front of him stood a small porch, leading to what looked like a servant's entrance.

He slowed, removing the Glock. One step along the antique wood, then another, hoping against a creak. The boards obeyed. He gained the landing, breathing now under control. The screen door was within reach when a fresh alarm bell lit the back of his mind. *This is too easy.* Like an open jump-shot or uncovered receiver—something that only happened when the opposition made a mistake. But he knew his enemy: that wasn't in their playbook.

Still, there was no other direction but forward. He traded the gun for two slivers of metal, propped open the screen and went to work on the wooden barrier behind. Its lock was old, simple. He was through within thirty seconds. Immediately, as expected, a quiet beeping echoed over his left shoulder.

He turned to find a control panel from the security company. It required a five-digit code to cancel the impending alarm. That had been another gift from Langley. Kent punched it in and was rewarded with utter silence.

He was in the kitchen. The only glow came from some timid moonlight peeking through a window above the sink. Everything beyond was pitch-black.

He pulled the Glock back out, using his phone as a flashlight.

Ahead, dual corridors snaked to the left and right. Kent stopped; for the first time, he realized he hadn't the faintest idea what he was searching for.

This home's address was obviously not enough. It couldn't have been, even in 1860. What proof was there tying the Van Leers to the assassination list? Delacroix was no fool: accusing such prominent citizens required tangible evidence. One last time, Kent endured the sinking thought that it was something only Matthieu would know.

You've made it this far. Maybe God had one miracle left.

47

Thirty minutes later he was no closer to discovery. The seeds of doubt had swelled as each room looked prepped for a dormant winter: shutters barred every window; the kitchen's cabinets were nearly empty; white sheets clung to myriad tables and desks, chairs and nightstands with the sheen of lethargic ghosts.

Kent cleared the final second-floor bedroom and turned toward a thin staircase leading up. He'd seen every space, checked nearly every nook and cranny; it all looked maddeningly normal. Just another billionaire's ancestral estate, sleeping through the snow while its owner chose to hibernate in warmer climes. Around the corner a grandfather clock, its chime still active, intoned the arrival of one a.m. He felt the watch on his wrist grow a little heavier.

The staircase might've been terrifying. He did, after all, stand at the center of a deserted house in the middle of the night. The steps ahead were steep, rising through clouds of shadow and, at the very top, a mass of pitch black. Even the floorboards obliged with muffled creaks below his weight. But this wasn't that kind of horror movie—and all the scarier for it. The worst monsters were always, in the end, human.

The third floor turned out to be just as well-appointed—and empty—as the rest of the house. He descended the stairs, frustration building into fear. A discovery that had begun with so much promise was veering dangerously close to a lost cause.

In fact, what if the address on the stone didn't even refer to this house?

What if it meant the grounds instead? That was a nightmare he preferred not to contemplate—no clue could've survived outdoor exposure for over a century and a half. And he'd barely had enough time to search inside—twenty acres was impossible.

Kent reached the second-floor landing and pulled out the stone again, washing it in his phone's fluorescent beam. *Lambeth...Het Gooi...*it had to mean something. He started rearranging letters in his head, trying to find a hidden message. It was fruitless.

The next staircase was down a hall. He started forward, not sure where to head next, slipping the stone back toward his pocket. It didn't quite get there. In the process of angling it inside his jacket, he'd caught a glimpse of the other side. *Odyssey Complete.* Phrasing that had been strange before now felt even more so. *Why those words?*

That's when realization hit, and he immediately made for the library.

Kent strode into its cavernous gloom seconds later. Pale shafts of moonlight edged the heavy curtains, cutting the dark into segments. Sure now that he was alone, he tried a nearby switch and wasn't surprised when it failed to offer illumination. On cue, he noticed the last wisps of his latest breath dissolving into the black above. Electricity and heat had been turned off. Likely the water too. The alarm itself must've been on a separate breaker.

No matter. He was in the right room; of that he was certain. His first visit had been cursory—more concerned with spotting something that didn't belong. Now he took time to admire the main attraction: leather-bound tomes, many surely as old as the house itself, rising as far north as his phone's light could stretch. A stone fireplace graced the far wall. No bearskin at its base, but the obligatory spiral staircase swirled a few feet away.

Kent's first instinct was to check his watch again; he could search for hours and still not find what he was looking for. But then, the Van Leers would've had the same problem. As much as this room was for show, they might've actually used it. And he was willing to bet no member of the family had every book's location memorized. There had to be some kind of system.

It only took him a moment to see he was right. The nearest wall held texts of every size and color, but all had names on their spines like Kant, Hobbes and Aristotle. *Philosophy*. They were even in alphabetical order. Now he simply needed to find the section for ancient literature, or mythology.

There was no signage indicating where one subject ended and another began, but the collective spines told a clear enough story. He continued through the lower level of the room, shifting from history to religion to science. Ten minutes later he still hadn't located the prize. Next came the staircase. He met Shakespeare at the top and began working left.

The library—the entire house—remained completely silent. Kent's only ambient evidence was the shuffle of his own feet across a balcony rimming the entire room. He turned a corner, nearly three-quarters finished with his entire search. Finally, the names began to resonate: Wordsworth, Tennyson, Virgil. *The Aeneid* was at waist level; he looked up, tracing his gaze from one epic poem to another. *The Odyssey* lay just above his head, gold lettering on a green spine, shining like a tree at Christmas.

One more instinctive look around, as if Van Leer might step through the doorway with a pistol, or McCoy with a grin on his face, announcing this was all some elaborate joke. No on both counts. It was just him, these books and one final secret.

Taking a deep breath, Kent reached up and pulled down on the thick leather spine. Nothing happened. He yanked again; still no. The book wouldn't budge. He checked several of its neighbors—maybe this row was stacked too tight—but they all slid freely. Then a curious thought occurred.

Almost ceremoniously, he slid his fingers back to the *Odyssey*'s spine and pushed inward. It barely gave at first, stubborn against the pressure. But then, after half an inch or so, there was a deep, distant grinding. The book began receding within the darkness of the shelf, as if on a track. Kent heard a noise behind and swung his flashlight around. Below, to the left of the fireplace, a panel six feet square slid to the side, leaving a dark void in its place.

For half a second, he forgot the house, the deadline, the danger. "You've got to be kidding me."

He shuffled along the balcony, gripping its railing with white knuckles. The spiral staircase followed, soon giving way to the newfound entrance. Kent stood before it, Glock still firm in his grip. He could see a set of stone steps, leading down one level to a small landing. Its cement floor glowed beneath a yellow bulb, presumably triggered by the panel's opening.

Kent moved forward, descending into the unknown. Near the bottom he glanced left. Set into the stone, about eye level, was a carved recess. Designed to hold…a candle. *Before the bulb.* Which meant this space was well over a hundred years old. His pulse quickened.

The only direction was right. Kent turned to find a short hallway, terminating at a thick, wooden door. Another light set into the low ceiling kept the shadows at bay. He reached the handle and twisted. The barrier swung open without a sound.

Before him lay a modest space—about a third the size of the library, with a much lower ceiling. Oak paneling wrapped matching floors, accented by two large, oriental rugs. More recessed bulbs dutifully lit the space, their minimal buzz no doubt activated by the same sliding panel. This area, like the alarm, was clearly on a separate breaker. Or powered by a backup generator. Either way, it retained the chill of the library above.

Kent took a few cautious steps forward. Directly ahead rested two stuffed chairs and a low table. To the right, beside a built-in bar—fully stocked—stood a waist-high stone slab at least six feet long. He moved closer. Its surface and sides were smooth, polished from use over the years.

But the most interesting feature came at the rear of the room. Here the walls narrowed into a corridor, stretching back twenty feet or so. No furniture, just gilded frames hung evenly around the entire enclosure. Convinced he was alone in this space too, Kent tucked the Glock behind his back and eyed the first one.

If there was any lingering doubt about the legitimacy of the address, the three stones—this entire operation—the sight before him put it to rest. Protected behind tempered glass was the front page of the New York Times. It appeared to be an original copy. The paper was yellowed and cracked, but its headline remained clear: "President Lincoln Shot by an Assassin." The date above read 'April 15, 1865.'

No stopping now. Kent slid to his left, finding, more or less, what he expected: The Cleveland Leader, dated September 19, 1881, detailing the death of James Garfield. This time he merely glanced left, and kept going, wrapping his gaze around the stunted hallway, each frame staring back at him like the dead eyes of a hidden corpse. Suddenly the room felt even colder.

Seconds passed, his mind arranging the last pieces of the puzzle. Emile had finally been vindicated: this space was, indeed, a secret worth dying for. He shifted left, toward the dead end. There was a frame at its center, but he hardly needed to see its specific eulogy; the collective told a more compelling story.

This was a trophy room. An invisible retreat to which the Van Leers, over the passage of decades, had surely disappeared. Where else to revel in the past victories of your ancestors? Or plan the next hit, achieving for yourself equal standing with their memory? These assassinations weren't about ruling the world; they were about changing it. Bringing humanity to its knees and, for a few glorious moments, watching it burn. That was ultimate power.

But what did—

Kent felt a wisp of alien air claw at his neck, and knew he was already too late. He spun anyway, reaching for the Glock in the same motion. Surging directly toward him was a rock of a man, scar above his left eye. A thick blade shimmered in his right hand. He was still a pace or two back and brought the knife up in a final lunge.

Kent had his hand on the pistol, but would never get it out fast enough. By going for the gun, though, he'd left himself no time for anything else. His mind could only send the command to evade, each muscle far too slow to receive the message in time. Like a serrated torpedo, the weapon surged toward his heart, cutting the distance in milliseconds.

Crack. A familiar sound reverberated across the chamber, shaking the surrounding frames. At the same time, a bullet he couldn't see drove through his assailant's backside into the rear of his heart. The man—and his knife—went no farther.

The body dropped, revealing a man with a gun on the far side of the room. He stood in silhouette, face dark below the dim lamps. Then he began walking forward. Kent thought about reaching for his Glock, but abandoned the idea once the shooter stepped into the light.

James Baker stowed his own pistol, glancing down at the corpse he'd created. "That might wake the neighbors."

Kent, heart rate slowing, stepped over the body. He knew the smile on his face wasn't professional, and didn't care. "Thanks for finally showing up."

"Figured you'd had enough time in my spotlight."

Now Baker smiled too, before spreading his arms and embracing his friend. After a moment, Kent turned back to the man with the knife. "Nice shot."

"Big target. You think he was part of The Family?"

Kent was nodding. "One way or another. Some ties are thicker than blood." He swung back to Baker. "But not, I guess, thick enough for you to tell me you were conscious?"

"McCoy's orders. It's the critical hour—he didn't want you distracted."

"Distracted? What am I, an amateur?"

"Maybe just human." Baker waited a moment, then stepped past his partner toward the frames. "Are these what I think they are?"

"A regular wall of infamy." Kent gestured toward the first of several cases that'd yet to be filled. "At least we know the date of the next paper."

Baker was a few feet down, staring at The Daily Telegraph announcing the death of Mahatma Gandhi. "If only there was a pattern, some connection between the newspaper used and the place and time of each kill. This entire wall is random." He checked his watch. "We're down to hours now."

Kent looked around the room, refusing to believe this latest discovery could somehow yield another dead-end. "It has to be here."

But not…*here*. He stopped, thinking. This abbreviated hallway—even the bar and chairs—was about celebration, after the deed was done. But what about the planning before? Each assassination clearly bore the mark of extensive research. Where better to conduct such sensitive preparation than in a hidden, controlled environment?

Kent stepped over to the slab. It didn't seem to fit with the rest of the furniture. In fact, despite the ceiling's glow, it remained in half-shadow. Moving closer, he found a switch on the wall to his left and flipped it. Additional illumination buzzed to life within the near corner, easily lighting the rest of the stone. But still shining on nothing of interest. The surface remained bare, the slab's near side void of any drawers or cubbies. There weren't any on the far end, either.

But a safe was. Its forged black metal stood about three feet tall by two wide, set into the surface like a custom cabinet. Kent edged closer, his heartbeat regaining life. A combination dial and silver handle sprouted from the right side; the rest of its face glared back, imposing. It was a very old device—hints of rust played along each sharp edge—but still appeared solid.

Kent knelt down, knowing this was the moment of truth. All of Emile's courage, every ounce of his and Baker's blood, came down to what lay in this safe. A second later he felt his partner's presence over his shoulder.

"That thing's ancient," said Baker. "Probably predates the Civil War."

"I still can't see kicking it in." Kent turned his head. "Any ideas?"

"Just a question: why? This room is secret enough. What's the benefit of having this thing?"

"You don't think, at some point, a cousin or some party guest pushed *The Odyssey* in by chance and found this room? Can't exactly have incriminating documents laying out in the open."

A light flickered in Baker's eyes. "And nothing else in this room points a finger. The chairs, the bar—it's just a glorified man-cave."

"Albeit with an assassination fetish.

"What's a billionaire without some eccentricity?"

They both stared at the lock, willing its springs to give way. Kent had considered his gun, but quickly discarded the idea. The safe before them was as thick as a rock. Bullets would only bounce off.

Baker gestured back toward the dead body. "Guess I could've shot our guy in the leg. Romanced the combination out of him."

"You've been watching too many TV shows. Besides, my heart thanks you. I—"

Kent reached toward his chest. Not where the knife's tip had grazed him, but into his jacket pocket—for the stone. In the end he didn't need it, the digits long ago seared into his memory. *38-17-22.* He started spinning the dial.

Emile must've found his way down here in secret. If the Van Leers even suspected he was aware of the combination, or simply the room itself, they would've changed venues. Which meant whatever lay behind this door was the kind of secret worth killing for.

A final click echoed through what had suddenly become a silent room. He swung the heavy door open and peered inside. It was out of the lights' optimum path and darker than the rest of the slab. But he could still easily see two metal shelves. One was empty; the other held a thick manila folder. Kent reached in, pulled it out and set it on the slab. They eyed one another, then flipped it open.

Maps, balance sheets, letters, diagrams. At first glance it all looked innocent enough. But they kept flipping pages. A note about a meeting point at Ben Gurion Airport outside Tel Aviv; specs for a compact sniper rifle; past motorcade routes and response tactics for Shin Bet, the security force for the Prime Minister of Israel.

Kent felt his blood run cold. He finished scanning a record of minutes for a recent session of the Knesset and turned. Baker held up a perfectly defined close-up of Michael Hassan's face. "It's almost like they're announcing the target."

Kent shook his head. "All this distance, and we probably could've guessed."

Which only made the sour lump in his stomach rot further. The entire Middle East was a perpetual lake of gasoline; this would be like dropping a blowtorch in its center. No matter where it happened, the killing would quickly go public. Kent imagined a perpetrator from Gaza, or maybe Tehran. Threats would be made, missiles aimed, and the dominoes would fall. The only question would be the size of the grave.

Baker checked his watch. "You catch the headlines between all that frequent flying?"

"You're talking about his speech."

A nod. "It's nearly 3 a.m. in Jerusalem. That puts Hassan on the podium in nine hours."

"You think that's where they'll do it?"

"Wouldn't you?"

"Security'll be oppressive."

"And it isn't any other time the PM leaves Beit Aghion? You know the Israelis—their default setting is that someone's trying to kill them."

Kent set his paper down. "That's because it's usually true."

48

Despite the Audi's tinted windows, and a pair of closed eyes, Hassan could see sunshine pouring through. It was no comfort. The light represented the world outside—reaching for him, tearing at his psyche. Soon he'd have to let it in. The A8 swung north along King George Street, edging its way toward Zion Square. Within minutes he'd be on a stage, beneath the searing sky.

And above a volatile crowd. That was partly why he'd risen this morning with a nervous swirl in his stomach. He'd been lobbying for this day so long, there hadn't been time for butterflies. Now the wait was over, and all he had were idle thoughts. Perspiration, despite the German sedan's powerful A/C, began collecting at the nape of his neck.

The other cause for his anxiety came even earlier. The phone beside his bed had rattled to life just after four a.m. Through Leila's mumbled, comatose objections he'd cinched himself up on his elbows and gripped the receiver. It was Josef Azoulai, the Director of Mossad. Hours earlier the CIA had uncovered evidence confirming the likelihood of an assassination attempt on his life today.

Hassan had paused, exhaling slowly. He probably should have been shocked. This was more than the vague threats of violence that readily accompanied such a controversial event; it was expert intelligence directly pertaining to his itinerary. But at the end of the day—figuratively speaking—he'd always known he'd be risking his life for this speech, one way or another.

As expected, Azoulai took the opportunity to urge him to call off the gathering. The CIA had identified the suspects and were following several leads concerning their location. They'd briefed the Mossad on their investigation and were in the process of transmitting the details, both agencies comparing notes. It was only a matter of time. The speech could be given weeks or months from now, after the atmosphere had cooled.

Hassan said no. It would happen today, unless or until they pinpointed the whereabouts of the potential assassins. Israel's citizenry had been promised reconciliation, a vision of the future. To deny such a gesture at the last moment would be to destroy any existing goodwill and sabotage all he and Khalidi had worked for. There would be no point in continuing.

The next hour had been spent in his study, fielding calls of protest from select Knesset members, Neri, even Matthew Billings. Hassan wondered if he'd been the last to find out his own life was at risk. Billings was especially adamant. Throughout his first term, he'd advocated for increased solidarity between the United States and Israel. Now the American election cycle had begun, and the assassination of an ally's head-of-state was a black eye for any incumbent.

More important than all of this, though, were the national security implications. Israel's government, by virtue of power and tradition, served as a stabilizing force throughout the Middle East. Cut off its head, even for a moment, and pockets of control would be seized by the most violent bidders. Every town from Cairo to Kabul would suffer the resulting tremors, with the aftershocks extending much farther.

"This isn't just about Israel and Palestine," the President had said.

"With respect, Matthew, neither is the speech I'm about to deliver."

Hassan's answer still hung in the back of his mind. Had he been right? *Too late to turn back.* Or, as it happened, to think any further. They'd arrived.

49

Normally McCoy needed coffee—lots of it—for moments like this. Over the years his body had acclimated to the caffeine, requiring more and more to reach a focused high. Not today. Adrenaline was enough to keep him alert. Even though the clock on the wall was still inching toward five a.m., and he hadn't slept in twenty-three hours; even though the room he stood in was as dark as a movie theatre. Because today wasn't normal—even for the CIA.

Technically he'd gone home. Last night, around nine. Vanning's orders. *"You're no good to me a zombie."* Kent and Baker had only relayed their discovery two hours prior. Intel was still being analyzed, sent to Mossad. But the pipeline had been firmly established; McCoy wasn't really needed. His pride disagreed. *I haven't always been a suit.*

In the end, it was all for nothing. He'd ended up nursing a frozen dinner in front of *The Tonight Show*, barely giving either the time of day. Darkness and silence didn't fare much better: atop the sheets, eyes open, he'd spent the remaining time trying to pierce the future with a level gaze.

Five hours would just about do it. He could see the sun, the dust, the crowd. *Five hours.* By the time tonight's third-shifters clocked out, he and his colleagues would've averted disaster, or…he couldn't bring himself to face the alternative. So much would go wrong so quickly. It was almost unfathomable.

At least he had a good view. McCoy stood at the top of a large room in the depths of Langley, rows of technicians sloping down toward a wall of video screens. Each pixel captured a piece of the scene: Jerusalem's Zion Square, filled to bursting by a mass of potent humanity that continued to swell by the second. Muslims and Jews alike, shoulder-to-shoulder beneath the blazing sky, spilled into Jaffa, Ben Yahuda and Herbert Samuel Streets, all of which had been shut down for the occasion.

They certainly weren't alone. Shin Bet had augmented its Protective Security ranks with personnel from other departments, along with agents from Mossad and Aman, Israel's military intelligence directorate. This was all in addition to the CIA's deployment, which included officers from Beirut, Damascus, Riyadh, Istanbul—the list went on. McCoy didn't like having so many high-value assets in one place. With any luck they'd be back home by sunset.

A host of news agencies were also present, rimming the square like a bitter garnish: CNN, the BBC and more regional and local outlets than he could count. Space restrictions made vans and antennas a pipe dream, reducing most of their complement to mere reporters and cameras. Some had multiple teams in different spots to offer additional vantage points. In fact, a few of the feeds McCoy now stood watching were from the media. Every angle counted.

He took a sip of lukewarm Aquafina. Three rows down another senior officer stood beside a female technician, working with her to adjust a camera feed. McCoy studied the man—fiftyish, balding, but muscular and fit. *Your replacement*. Not really, though. McCoy was a handler; he ran field officers, who in-turn ran agents. He could've done this today, but there were others more suited to the necessary tactics and logistics. Another look, this time at the entire room: dozens of experts clicking, typing, sweating. Suddenly this had become much larger than Kent and Baker.

The two of them would be late, anyway. No more private jets. Heck, even if they wanted to hitch rides in a pair of F-16's, Spangdahlem Air Base in Germany was a four-hour drive away. It was commercial or nothing. Their 737, accordingly, was set to land at Ben Gurion in about ten minutes. From there it was an hour drive to Jerusalem.

Meantime, a team of cleaners had been dispatched to the Van Leer residence in Het Gooi. Kent and Baker had wiped their own fingerprints, but altering security footage from an army of exterior cameras and disposing of yet another corpse would take too much time. McCoy was just wondering how a clandestine agency could leave such a large footprint when he nearly jumped out of his shoes at the sight of Vanning by his side.

The director was shrugging off his coat, eyes on the screens. "Anything yet?"

McCoy recovered after a second. "No, sir." He glanced at his watch. "Ten-till in Israel. Let's hope he doesn't get cold feet. I don't think this crowd is built for surprises."

Vanning didn't smile. "Assets in position?"

"As close as possible. Between ours and theirs, the front rows are covered. But, as you can see, they're packed pretty tight. Not much room to shift around, look for shooters. The other problem is perimeter security. Police have barricaded both ends of Jaffa and are checking entrants for weapons, but..."

"But it's thousands of people filtering into a crowded square, at the speed of anticipation." He turned toward McCoy for the first time. "Like a cracked hourglass."

McCoy found himself nodding. A few grains of sand always slipped through.

50

No riots, stampedes or gunshots—Aviv was already inclined to consider the event a success. Never mind that Hassan and Khalidi had yet to take the stage. For a sea of Israelis and Palestinians to stand shoulder-to-shoulder in prolonged, relative peace bordered on the miraculous. He supposed it was the calm of curiosity: the crowd before him seemed to have a sense that they were about to witness something unprecedented.

Of course, this was the best-case scenario. Preparations for the worst had also been made, but would never be enough to cure the eddy of dread swirling within his gut. From behind a pair of sunglasses, at the left end of the platform, he surveyed the scene before him. It was different every time; people in the crowd didn't move, but somehow—a turn of the head, the angle of sunlight—their faces seemed to change. He shifted his gaze from one expression to the next, mentally cataloguing those warranting future attention.

Every moment or so he looked up. Sniper fire had been their chief concern from the start. Several multi-story buildings hugged the square, boring down on its proceedings like stern judges. *What will be your verdict?* Aviv's job was to ensure acquittal. Each structure had been scoured more than once over the past week. Today, balconies and windows were clear; multiple security officers patrolled every floor. Still, Aviv kept a sharp eye out for errant shadows, glinting metal—anything that didn't belong.

"*Thirty minutes to change the world.*" That was Hassan's go-to answer in justification of such a dangerous appearance. Aviv had protested numerous times, but stopped once he'd noticed the gleam of determination in his superior's eyes. At that point there was no changing the man's mind. Hassan was a dreamer, but possessed acute powers of persuasion. Aviv almost found himself looking forward to the speech.

He thought back to the faces in the crowd, and remembered one more in his pocket. No need to take the photo out; it'd been memorized long ago. *Edmund van Leer.* A Dutchman's pale skin would've been easy to spot in such a mass of olive and copper. But then, their friends at Langley had said the man often used intermediaries to carry out his deeds. Which narrowed the suspect list down to *the entire square.*

A few sharp words buzzed into his earpiece, renewing focus. Aviv felt a jolt of adrenaline shoot through his veins before discreetly raising the microphone in his sleeve up to his mouth. "Copy." One final breath. "Here we go, everyone."

A moment later the square nearly shook beneath the thunderous weight of both boos and cheers as Michael Hassan and Omar Khalidi stepped onto the stage. 'Stage' was too descriptive, really. The cement dais was merely a raised entryway for the Herbert Samuel Hotel, from which the two heads of state had just emerged. The inn had graciously agreed to temporarily close its bottom two floors, reducing by a sliver the anxiety which Aviv had been grappling with all morning.

Part of the crowd began chanting in support of…Khalidi, it sounded like. Others remained silent, their own masks of worry stretched tight amidst the surrounding crush of humanity. Still others waved small Israeli flags, sold by a vendor at the edge of the barricade.

Hassan and Khalidi now turned toward one another, reached out and shook hands. The proportion of positive to negative emotion stayed the same, but increased exponentially. The square was deafening now. No gunshot or explosion, though; if Aviv were a terrorist, he might've chosen that moment. *One test passed.*

Finally, both leaders began motioning for the crowd to quiet down. Khalidi held his arms above his head. Once the decibel level settled, he gestured toward his counterpart. Hassan nodded and, with a deep exhale, stepped up to a wooden podium. Leaning toward its microphone, he began to speak.

51

Kent strode through the concourse of Ben Gurion Airport with yet another new duffel bag slung over his shoulder. He'd bought it in Amsterdam and filled it with clothing he was never going to wear. Such were the conditions of anonymity.

He'd been just as concerned with blending in here as he was on the plane, but quickly saw there was no danger. The majority of people in view—tourists, business travelers, airport staff—were either looking up at a television screen or down at their phone. All of them, he knew, were watching the same thing.

Hassan and Khalidi had taken the stage moments ago. A rare energy now warmed the surrounding air, even here at the terminal. There was a sense that history was being made. Kent moved past a crowded bar and stole a glance at its TV: Hassan was squinting through the afternoon sun, his words, translated into English, scrawled across the bottom of the screen. Kent increased his pace, reminding himself that history could go both ways.

Soon he was out the door, into his own sunlight and searching for Baker through the corner of each eye. They'd reversed roles from Lisbon, Kent dawdling at a gift shop while his partner found their contact in the parking lot. A junior case officer was supposed to deliver two Berettas and a dusty compact, then catch a taxi back to his hovel in Tel Aviv. Moments later Kent found a white Hyundai idling beneath a palm tree.

After a final look around, he tossed his bag in the back, then eyed Baker in the passenger seat. "I'm driving?"

"Kid put the rental agreement under 'Evan Graves.' No sense taking chances if we get pulled over."

"Is that what you're expecting?"

"Twenty-four hours ago, I was in a peaceful coma. Life's full of disappointment."

Kent slid behind the wheel with a smile. "Almost sounds like you mean it."

Baker reached for the radio. "Ask me in twenty minutes."

They were circling away from the airport on Ha Teufa Boulevard when the BBC's local signal filled the small cabin. A female interpreter was speaking in English, voice soft enough to admit Hassan's Hebrew in the background. *I know some of our differences are absolute*, she was saying. *But that doesn't have to mean violence. President Khalidi and I believe there is a way beyond every barrier, if each of us, as stewards of this sacred land, would take a single, trusting step.*

"He can certainly deliver a speech," said Baker.

Kent only nodded, gunning all four cylinders toward the ramp for Route 1. Baker's comment, he knew, was merely an attempt to distract from the obvious: this drive wouldn't be pleasant. Over the last several days they'd each sacrificed, and nearly died, to reach this particular moment; now the fight was beyond their control. They could only listen as others attempted to avert disaster.

The translator continued, Hassan's words tantalizingly clear in the background. *Over the next few weeks, President Khalidi and I will be unveiling a joint set of proposals aimed at securing the peace and livelihood of every resident of this region.* A segment of the crowd had begun to raise its discontent with the prevailing message, and this last point brought a fresh, stronger wave of jeers. Hassan raised his voice to counter the noise. *But we cannot do this without you. Without one another.*

There was a pause, during which a passionate cheer rose from the crowd. Kent assumed this was Khalidi's cue. He could almost see Hassan stepping aside, gesturing for the Palestinian leader to take the podium.

An instant later, two loud cracks—they could only be one thing—echoed through the square. A panicked roar followed immediately, then several more gunshots in close succession. All of this before the interpreter could grunt into the microphone, choking back her own shock.

Another female voice, presumably a reporter, quickly stole the air. *Oh, my G—The Prime Minister is down! Michael Hassan has been shot!*

52

For the briefest moment, the Situation Room knew true silence. Then its dozen souls reacted much like the crowd they were watching. Chief of Staff Scott Foster was the first to jump out of his chair, hands on his head, gaping at the horror before him. Others followed, cursing, gasping—some louder than others—as the scene in Zion Square played out on a bank of video monitors. All shook with the dread that comes from having your worst fears realized. This wasn't merely the loss of one life; it was the instant destabilization of an entire region.

The screens ahead held not only news footage of the event, but also several feeds from CIA officers planted in the crowd. Each view showed the same thing: a pair of flashes at the foot of the platform, followed by Hassan falling backward on the far side of the podium. An army of security guards materialized on the stage. Half blanketed the PM; the other half fired into the crowd, presumably at the shooter. At that point the mob had transformed into a frothing hurricane. A few of its members tried to rush the stage; most tore through one another toward the square's exits. In the resulting tumult, every transmitted visual had been corrupted by severe angles, human obstructions or black screens altogether.

They were blind. But no longer frozen in shock. The room quickly became a hub of activity. Some people flipped open computers, others dialed cell phones or strode into an anteroom, where a small army of military and intelligence support personnel were monitoring the same scene with even more data. Bill Dyson, the National Security Advisor, picked up a secure landline for Langley.

The only person who didn't move was the president. This was the one time when, owing to a ream of emergency protocols, the government almost ran itself. Every security sector across Washington had been drilled on the next ten minutes until those in its ranks were blue in the face. Soon, Matthew Billings knew, the vice president and speaker of the house would be ferried to predetermined locations on the chance that this assassination wasn't isolated.

As for his own safety, he could do no better than this very room. It lay beneath the surface of the most protected building on the planet. Its four walls, close enough for him to touch, would guard against nearly everything. Except the duty that lay before him.

Billings took one more glance at the space's other inhabitants, still moving, sweating, swearing. He remained motionless. A president's job wasn't to gather intel, or scan for threats, or reestablish comms; a president's job was to decide. To make the choices no one else was permitted to make, because only he had been elected to make them.

Billings felt his stomach begin to swirl. Were you allowed to get nervous as the president? Moments from now fresh information would arrive, particular options advised. *The Buck Stops Here.* Had Harry really known what he was getting into? The President comforted himself in the knowledge that this, at least, wasn't like Hiroshima or Nagasaki. Was it?

53

Kent, knuckles white on the steering wheel, weaved through tangles of slower-moving traffic in desperate spurts. It wasn't easy. Route 1 was clogged with distracted drivers, reeling at the news most of them had just heard. Some were still screaming at their radio; others sat in stunned silence, or cried, or called home to commiserate with loved ones. Several cars had pulled off to the shoulder.

Inside the Hyundai, the feeling was mutual. They'd failed. There would be no pouting, but each man felt acutely the special weight of helplessness. For its part, the BBC had few further details. The last news they'd received was that, while Shin Bet agents had converged on the Prime Minister, the terrified crowd began stampeding toward the exits. Reporters had apparently cut their feeds to avoid getting trampled. Baker cycled through the dial; no station had yet recovered.

Did it really matter? Hassan's life had been stolen, and with it—surely—any chance for lasting peace. Volleys of blame would soon be launched between the Knesset and PLO. It would start with pointing fingers, and end with pointing things more powerful. Today would simply be lost in the madness; after a conflagration, no one ever remembered the spark.

Kent consoled himself with the fact that they could still make the hunt. It was a thin chance, but catching whoever did this—alive—might lead them to Van Leer. He eased the peddle down slowly, coaxing a few more horses from beneath the meager hood.

Seconds later, Baker's phone rang. It could only be one person. He fished the device from his pocket. "This is Jim." There was a slight pause. "In the car with me." Now a longer one. Suddenly, he straightened in his seat. "What?" More listening. Kent kept both eyes on the road as they buzzed by an exit ramp. He strained to hear McCoy's words, but could make out nothing concrete.

Finally, Baker said "We'll call you back." He hung up and turned left, staring across for what seemed an eternity.

"What?"

"Hassan's alive."

Kent felt his heart rate spike. He took a breath, then swallowed. "How bad is he?"

Baker was shaking his head. "You don't get it. He was never hit."

"The killer missed? Those shots were close."

"They weren't shots—they were blanks. Hassan just tripped back, in surprise."

The next five seconds passed in a blur, and suddenly Kent could see the end game clearly. He slammed on the brakes, sending the Hyundai skidding toward the shoulder. Baker braced himself against the dashboard. "Whoa!"

A pair of nearby Renaults were just as surprised, their drivers blaring a frantic salvo across the asphalt. A moment later the Hyundai jerked to a halt. The passing horns quickly became memories. Kent kept his hands on the steering wheel, staring into the distance. All of the puzzle pieces had finally, instantly, locked into place. Just in time for the two of them to fail again. *We're too late.*

Baker was saying something. Kent fought through the haze to hear: "What the heck was that?"

Go anyway. He ignored his partner, jamming the car into reverse and angling back to the off-ramp. More passing drivers offered their objections. Baker's knuckles were white now too, but he stayed silent.

They reached the entrance to the ramp, Route 6, and pushed forward again. A mile down Kent had corralled his thoughts enough to speak. "I'm sorry."

Baker had soon recognized the gravity in his friend's gaze. "Just tell me where we're headed."

"To the coast."

54

Leila Hassan had never before experienced such an extreme range of emotions in so small a period of time. It started in the kitchen, where she stood chopping artichokes with her husband's voice echoing over her shoulder. The television was around the corner—just close enough to hear clearly, while sparing her the anxiety of a direct view. It was hard enough to envision what *might* happen.

Thus, the chopping. Her mother had taught her to cook at a young age and she'd never looked back. Even at Beit Aghion, with a chef on staff, Leila frequently prepared the evening meal. The process was calming; it kept her hands busy and her mind focused. Or, like today, at least lowered her heart rate to a manageable level.

She'd just given up expecting the worst when the shots came. They might as well have actually been in the house they were so loud. Her knees went weak at the same time the crowd began to scream. She could hear commotion in the next room, where half of her security detail stood glued to a flatscreen. Bracing herself against the wall, Leila felt her way around its edge and spied their expressions: shock, horror, anger—all the requisites. She passed a mirror but didn't dare look at her own face. Instead, she inched toward the TV for a better view, heart breaking a little more with every step.

Eitan, the group leader, spotted her first and stepped forward. "No, Mrs. Hassan." He gripped her shoulders, gently, and guided her over to a nearby chair. She made a show of struggling, but could already feel the shock spreading through her veins. A moment later the broadcast was muted and another agent was on a cell phone. Eitan stood barking orders into his wrist for the perimeter team outside.

Between numbing waves Leila noticed a third guard walking toward the bedrooms. *Talya*. Thank God, she'd been watching a movie. Couldn't have heard. Safety protocols meant the guard had to check on her daughter, but Leila motioned—pleaded—for him not to alert Talya of what had happened. He nodded.

She sank back into her chair, realizing a secondary disaster had just been averted. But she'd have to tell Talya eventually. That conversation, right now, was too difficult to imagine. Instead, she zeroed in on the cell phone, praying for a miracle that, inevitably, didn't come with the call.

It came with the next one.

Five minutes after they'd been told no information was available, Hassan himself rang back. The phone was handed to Leila, now gasping for breath, who listened to her husband through streams of tears. She only heard a fraction of what he said; her head was still spinning. Something about a blank gun, and a fake shooter who only wanted to prove a point. He'd tell her more when he got to the house. With each of his words, her face regained three shades of color.

Eventually she handed the phone back to Eitan, who told Aviv their location was secure. Then the bedroom door had creaked open and Talya skipped out. Her movie was finished; she wanted a snack. As if nothing had happened. Once again, Leila thanked the Lord.

Into the kitchen they went. Talya was soon munching away on a bag of Bamba chips. Leila realized she needed a glass of water herself. The shock still lingered, numbness and nerves twisting together from the pit of her stomach down through her toes. She took several gulps, then, after a deep breath, went back to chopping. The rhythm and concentration would be like therapy.

The TV remained off, the house now quiet. A natural buzz persisted among the security team, but most had returned to their posts. She could hear Eitan on the radio, confirming the all-clear one final time with the perimeter detail; they didn't respond at first. Outside, the Mediterranean continued flirting with the shore, its eternal motion somehow reassuring.

Eitan tried again. There was still no answer. *That's odd.*

55

Kent careened west down Highway 431. "Hassan still has that place on the beach, right?" It'd been in the notes of a past briefing.

"Yeah, I think so," said Baker. "Belongs to his family."

"Call McCoy back. Tell him to warn the security team at that house."

"Security team? How do you even know anyone's there?"

Kent revved around a Kia SUV and stole a glance across. "Hassan's not the target. His family is."

Baker stared back at him for a long second. "You can prove this?"

"At the end of the day, it's a hunch. But nothing else makes sense."

Another pause. "Go on."

"The packet in Amsterdam pinpointed a place—Israel—but never a victim; we assumed Hassan. What if we were wrong?" He jabbed a finger at the radio. "What we just heard wasn't failure, it was diversion. A false victory to lower Shin Bet's guard. Like the explosion that draws EMS personnel in for a second, larger blast."

Baker narrowed his eyes. "But why his family? The entire assassination list has been about changing the world with a single kill. Trading a head of state for his relatives isn't nearly as impactful."

"Isn't it?"

Kent saw Baker's mind begin to spin, circling the same realization his own had seconds earlier. Killing a leader was tragic, but it was business; the kind of act that almost always had its roots in politics or ideology. Killing family—especially a wife and young daughter—was personal. On the level of statecraft, it accomplished nothing. Its sole purpose was to cause pain.

The true target, of course, was Hassan himself. If Kent were the Van Leers, he'd plant blame at the scene, implicating a neighbor: if not Palestine, then Syria, Egypt—there were a dozen candidates. Suddenly, a prime minister known for his temper would be faced with the dual threats of grief and fear. Sound judgement was an impossibility, even with the wisest counsel. His citizens would only fan the flames of revenge, their equal fury stoked by the intimacy of the attack, as if their own family had been killed. Soon the pawns of an inevitable war would gather at the borders, drawing gunfire, grenades and missiles—maybe even the kind that needed codes.

It would be ten times worse than Hassan's own death.

Baker had pulled the phone back out, but paused. "What makes you think his wife and daughter are at that specific location?"

"If I were Hassan, today I wouldn't want my family anywhere near large crowds; too easy for violence to break out. That eliminates Tel Aviv, even Beit Aghion in Jerusalem. But I also wouldn't want them too far away, which keeps them in country. The house on the Med is the most logical choice."

"But still based on a hunch."

"You have a better idea?"

Baker stared back at Kent, then, finally, slid his finger across the phone's screen. "You know McCoy can't call the house directly. By the time word filters through the right channels, it'll be too late."

"It's already too late. But we have to try."

Baker brought the phone to his ear. "Maybe they can get a bird out there."

"Doubtful. IAF probably has Apaches on standby near Jerusalem, for the speech, but that's a twenty-minute hike. Blackhawks at Palmachim are closer, but by the time they're prepped and manned it'll be the same delay."

"Fake an assassination on one side of the country," said Baker, "then do it for real on the opposite border. Just after the all-clear has been sounded, when security lowers its guard, and just far enough away from reinforcements." He shook his head. "They thought of everything."

"Except us." Kent kept the pedal down, coaxing the last few horses from the Hyundai's engine.

56

At first Leila was confused. They sounded like rain, rocks—anything but bullets. Then shouting filled the living room, and Eitan burst into the kitchen. "Let's go!"

Leila instinctively squeezed the knife in her hands as Talya rushed over and grabbed her leg. She quickly traded the weapon for her daughter and turned to Eitan, who motioned for them to crouch down. He had his pistol out and led the way toward the main entrance.

In an instant, the house had become a war zone. Gunshots—dozens, hundreds—echoed through every square inch of the once-peaceful space. Four agents huddled between sofas in the center of the room; two more lay on the ground, immobile. Banks of windows along the front and back walls had been shattered. The group's focus was in each direction, as if fire were coming from everywhere.

Eitan gripped her arm tightly and shouted toward the center. "Omer, now!"

A second guard scuttled to their position, then the door. Leila knew the drill; the chief objective was to remove the principal—she and Talya—from the threat. Omer swung the door open to a gust of hot air. Leila looked around, but could see no shooter along the relatively flat horizon.

A black Audi careened around the side of the house, bumping from the driveway to a bed of gravel closer to the entrance. Leila shielded Talya from a spray of rocks as the car skidded to a halt. "Inside!" yelled Eitan.

As if to underscore his urgency, a pair of bullets zipped in from the surrounding sand. One drove into the stucco behind them, but the other caught Omer in the forehead, dropping him instantly. Eitan forced her into an even lower crouch and turned toward the car. It was fifteen feet away. They took one step before an explosion from underneath flipped it onto its hood and engulfed the cabin in flames. The sound stunned Leila more than anything, knocking her back and making her head spin. Talya—until now a mask of shocked silence—began to scream.

Eitan quickly dragged the two of them back inside, where the gunshots continued. Leila had no idea who their attackers were, but pictured an army. Where did it come from?

They were back at the edge of the living room. Two more agents were down. The remaining pair paused for the slightest moment as Eitan hurried his charges across the room, toward Plan B. It was the most dangerous route, but also the quickest.

They were halfway there when a large bullet sliced through the neck of one of the guards with a sickening 'whoosh.' He dropped to his knees, clutching his throat, the flow of blood soon coating each knuckle. Leila froze in terror, shielding Talya's eyes. She would've stayed there if Eitan hadn't shoved each of them forward.

Their destination was now just a dozen feet away. Little larger than a closet, the bomb shelter was lined with steel walls and a door several inches thick. Leila focused on her breathing. They seemed to move an inch at a time, like a dream. She clutched Talya with all her remaining strength.

Then the flash grenades came. Two of them, rolling across the hardwood floor with insidious calm. Leila knew enough to cover her daughter's ears; Eitan covered hers. A second later the room ignited like dawn. She fell down, the scene tumbling. First the bullet-riddled walls swirled beneath her feet, then the skylight set in the roof. The sofas would've come next if Eitan hadn't lifted she and Talya off the ground and flung them the remaining feet into the shelter.

"Stay inside!" he said, coughing through the smoke. "Lock this behind you!"

Eitan started swinging the heavy door closed. Leila had just enough time to see the final agent near the sofas fall before she and her daughter were plunged into darkness. She could feel her heart racing and took several deep breaths to slow it. Talya continued to cry, lungs ragged. Leila reached up and flipped a switch; a paltry light buzzed to life. She immediately stretched forward and locked the door. She then cradled Talya in her arms, whispering lies into her ears that they were going to be alright. After a moment she spread her palm over the little pair of lips, careful to keep the nostrils clear. Talya continued to tremble, but eventually grew quiet, out of fatigue more than anything.

And with that, the house returned, eerily, to the silence it had known just moments before. Not a sound stirred beyond the steel door. Leila pictured Eitan, behind a chunk of broken furniture, poised for a platoon of mercenaries to breach the house walls. Did he—or someone else—manage to call for help? Would anyone get here in time for it to matter? She thought of Talya, then discarded the nightmare.

More silence, followed by the soft crunch of boots on broken glass. Leila held her breath. Suddenly three—four—gunshots rang out; shouts of rage were replaced by a dying moan, then the telltale sound of another body crumpling to the ground. She knew it was Eitan; her stomach rang hollow. They were completely alone.

Leila's survival instincts kicked in. She scolded herself for leaving her phone on the kitchen counter, but doubted there'd be reception through the steel walls. A glance around the room revealed little else of use: blankets, bandages, some food and water; enough to wait out an aerial attack, but not if the bombs were coming specifically for you.

The same silence returned, until the same boots clicked across the hardwood, nearing her position. It certainly didn't sound like an army; she detected one pair of footsteps, maybe two. That was no comfort. The agents guarding her and Talya were some of the best in the world. If a mere pair of soldiers had dismantled such a defense, they were far beyond regular military.

Her last hope was, of course, the door itself. Such a dense, airtight barrier could withstand anything but a direct attack. That's what came next. It sounded like a drill or blow torch, flaring to life on the other side of the barrier, near the handle. Talya remained quiet.

Suddenly Leila surrendered to the inevitable; the next three minutes passed like a formality. Slowly the steel on her side began to melt away, until a grapefruit-sized hole was cleared directly below the lock. Then a hand—a *Caucasian* hand—slipped through the opening and disengaged the latch. The door swung outward a moment later, revealing two men in tan fatigues.

The first thing she noticed, beyond race, was their age: neither was young. Which made their recent victory all the more astonishing. They shared the same blonde hair and sharp facial features, which meant they were probably related. One—toned, wiry—stood behind his muscular counterpart, unfurling what looked like an Iranian flag. The other, in front, calmly removed a black pistol and pulled the slide back.

Talya had finally stopped shaking, mesmerized by the sight. Compared to the bedlam minutes ago, the men before her meant peace. Her mother knew better. The only thing that scared Leila more than the gun was their eyes: gray, empty—devoid of feeling. They didn't so much look at her and Talya as through them.

The man in front cocked his head sideways. "I think you've frightened them, Jakob."

"Force of habit," said the second one, without looking up from the flag.

The first man gazed at each female in turn. "This will only take a moment. Small price to pay for eternal infamy." He raised the barrel directly between Leila's eyes. "I'm almost envious."

Crack.

57

The baseball-sized rock broke the last remaining window and rolled to a stop against one of the corpses in the living room. Kent hated announcing his presence, but, sprinting toward the house, he'd seen Edmund van Leer leveling his Ruger for the kill.

He was now only ten feet from the entrance. Both brothers immediately turned at the interruption, delivering a hailstorm of bullets. Kent, in the same moment, dove through the front door and skidded across the tiled foyer amidst through avalanche of dust and debris. He sprang behind the nearest wall, pinned down at a tough angle.

The shooting stopped. "Is that you, Jeremy?" *Edmund.* "So you've solved the puzzle. Congratulations."

A beat of silence followed. Kent tried envisioning their next attack, then realized he wasn't the target. Instantly, he shifted the Beretta to his left hand and swung it around the edge. Edmund was about to complete his assassination when a sea of rounds tore into the drywall above his head. They were close enough to send him ducking behind an upturned dinner table.

Kent spun back, knowing he'd bought himself a breath, hoping Leila was smart enough to keep Talya right where they were. He had to get in better position. Another burst of covering fire and there would be time to—

A flashbang thudded onto the floor beside him. Kent leapt into the kitchen a split-second ahead of the explosion. White-hot light surged behind as he met more tile and broken glass. And another grenade. This one clinked directly toward him. He kicked it away, but it still burst close, shocking his senses into submission.

A distant part of his brain—beyond the screaming in both ears and flames behind his eyes—told him he had to rise and draw more fire; another part told him this was suicide. The latter notion might've won out if he'd had more time to think. As it was, each previous second was forgotten with the next and he stepped, half-blinded, into the living room.

Jakob van Leer held a third grenade in his left hand, but lifted a pistol with his right; Edmund, at his side, did the same. Neither man hesitated, nor displayed any emotion. Kent, stumbling forward, could barely grip his own gun, much less aim and fire. Shards of lightning continued to ring through his head. He needed a miracle. Both brothers paused in surprise, for the slightest second, at such fruitless sacrifice.

Then the heavens opened.

Two gunshots sounded as the skylight shattered above. Glass fell like rain, followed closely by Baker's poised frame. He had his gun up and buried a bullet between Jakob's startled eyes. Edmund had the presence of mind to roll away from two more shots. Baker tried to brace himself but landed awkwardly on a cedar coffee table, splitting it in half.

Edmund popped up near a loaded bookshelf. He'd lost his gun during the roll; it was too far to retrieve. Instead, he braced himself against the wall and tilted the bookshelf down. Baker could only gasp as hundreds of pounds of leather and wood crashed over him like a wave.

The entire process had flashed before Kent's eyes in seconds. He'd wanted to shoot, but didn't trust his aim with Edmund so near Leila and Talya. Now Edmund dove back for his gun, and the time for thinking was over. Kent sprinted across the sea of corpses. Edmund crouched directly in front of the bomb shelter—no safe shot. In a single motion, Kent lowered his gun and clotheslined Edmund just as he was raising the Ruger. They somersaulted into the far wall together, pistols clattering out of reach.

Each man scrambled to his feet, Edmund dusting himself off, Kent shaking the cobwebs free. They stood feet apart, measuring one another. For the briefest moment time stood still. "Winner take all," said Edmund, almost smiling.

He was right: this was for everything. Survive and Edmund could still complete his assassinations. Kent was the only thing standing between his opponent and ultimate success.

"Or you could just surrender," said Kent.

"You don't know me as well as you shoul—"

Kent was already charging. Edmund abandoned his words and, swiping a knife from his belt, flung it forward. Kent dropped to his knees, arching back. The blade whistled past his left ear, skinning a layer of flesh off his shoulder. He rose with an uppercut that caught Edmund beneath the chin. As the big man staggered back, Kent pursued with a kick to the gut before chopping into his throat. Edmund crumbled to a knee. Instead of hitting the floor, though, he swung a heavy boot that upended Kent. Then the other heel came down like an axe onto Kent's stomach, while a third kick burst into his jaw.

Both men rolled back, breathing hard. The room reverted to silence. From the corner of his eye, Kent noticed Leila creep from the closet toward Baker's position. He forced himself up, abdomen on fire from the recent blow. Edmund kept pace and soon they were each on their feet.

Round two. Kent parried an initial jab, but caught its follow-up in the nose. Momentarily stunned, he saw a third, heavier punch just in time and strafed left. Edmund's momentum carried him past and the two men tangled once again, scissoring to the ground.

The hardwood floorboards were a practical armory, holding a sea of pistols for an equal number of prone shooters who'd long ago lost the ability to squeeze the trigger. It was a marvel neither Kent nor Edmund had yet been close enough to grab one. Now Edmund was, reaching for Jakob's gun less than three feet away. Kent lacked the angle to lunge for the same weapon; no other lay close enough to matter. He was an open target.

Reacting on a sudden instinct, he spun toward the broken cedar table. Baker's Beretta was already in the air, released from Leila's hand like a winning horseshoe. Kent caught the handle, swung back and fired three rounds just before Edmund could squeeze his own off. The bullets carved a tight circle through Edmund's chest. He fell back, gun clattering harmlessly to the floor.

Kent crawled over to the table, wiping a layer of sweat and grime from his forehead. Leila was struggling with the bookshelf, her own body smeared with dirt. He motioned her to shift down and, a moment later, they both pried the heavy wood off Baker. Kent scanned his friend's legs, covered in books, then saw his chest rise and fall evenly. But both eyes remained closed. Kent's first thought was another coma.

This time, though, Baker grunted to life. Rustling his limbs, he fixed Leila with a wide gaze, then turned to Kent. "Good news?"

Kent nodded, unable to mask the hint of a smile—for his friend's life, and the entire operation. It was finally over.

Leila, temporarily blinded by focus, remembered herself and sprang to fetch Talya. Kent began helping Baker up. They'd just made it to their feet when the two females returned. Kent had a better view now and caught the heavy streaks of red ringing Leila's eyes. Her entire security force—men she knew and trusted—lay dead before her. This had been a bad day. And yet, she and her daughter were alive.

"You're American?" She'd directed the statement at Kent, in English. "CIA?"

Kent was too exhausted to summon the company answer. "Yes."

He was about to thank her for saving his life when a patch of movement sounded from Edmund's direction. He rushed toward the noise, Baker following. Edmund—too far from a weapon to be dangerous—lay flat on his back, a sphere of deep red staining his fatigues. His eyes were nearly closed, lips spread in what appeared to be a dying grimace. Once Kent crouched down, though, his stomach went hollow. The man was laughing.

Edmund's gaze cleared slightly with the two of them in view. "You can't save her."

"Too late," said Baker, nodding toward Leila.

But Kent wasn't listening. The hole in his gut had just doubled in size. "My cousin…" rasped Edmund. "…will kill…without my word. Call the ship…she dies faster…" Now Edmund focused in on Kent, the smile broadening as he took his final breaths. "It was worth it to see your face."

His life officially ended a second later. Kent hardly noticed, and fell to his knees. Edmund's body, along with the rest of the room, receded into oblivion.

Until this moment, Kent had fooled himself into thinking Allison was safe. As if mere geography could shield her from his enemies. Now the truth had become his worst nightmare. For Edmund to be willing to speak, his cousin had to be expecting an abort call shortly—within two or three hours. Kent was currently over six thousand miles from the Caribbean. Math alone painted the odds of Allison's survival.

For a second, he entertained the fantasy that she could escape. There would be security on the ship. If he got through to the captain…*you'd still be kidding yourself.* This cousin, whoever he was, came from the same family that'd just eliminated over half a dozen Shin Bet agents. Cruise rent-a-cops—even local law enforcement, if they were on an island—would be no match.

Kent felt his world collapsing—every desperate idea for escape shot down the moment it grew wings. Baker could only grip his shoulder; there was nothing to say. The tightness in his chest threatened to suffocate, and the truth became clear: the only thing worse than failing to save the woman you loved was knowing it ahead of time.

58

Another perfect day in paradise. Allison pushed her sunglasses atop her forehead, soaking up the blue sky, and stepped off the ship onto a long, wooden dock. Ahead lay Grand Turk, one of the largest Islands in the Turks and Caicos chain. It was similar to each of their previous stops, but shone a bit brighter for being the last.

"Ready to snorkel?"

Becky skipped up beside her, looking cute in a straw hat and orange top. Allison slung a leather bag over her shoulder. "You lead, Captain Nemo."

"Don't encourage her," said Petr, stepping forward with Sam and Erin. "She's already done it twice this trip."

"Hey," said Becky, "the fish and coral are different on every island. Can I help it if the best action's underwater?"

"You could sure help my portfolio. I was hoping to get out of here without blowing our first kid's inheritance. Guess we'll just tell him Mommy got in over her head."

"Already with the dad jokes." Becky gave him a frisky jab. "You're a natural."

It was barely nine a.m., but the island was packed. They were nearing the end of the dock, where a duty-free shop led into the heart of the cruise terminal. Passing through unscathed, they reached a makeshift square, itself surrounded by more shops selling everything from jewelry to clothing to fine art. A few restaurants also stood close by, their bartenders already busy popping caps on Landsharks and Coronas.

Erin stepped forward. "Remind me again where we're supposed to go?"

Becky pointed to the left without breaking stride. "The tour office is just down the beach."

"*Allison.*"

The voice came from behind. Allison recognized it immediately. She spun around, feeling her friends do the same. Rick stood near the entrance to the duty-free shop, long hair rustling in a slight breeze. He wore a blue polo and khakis; a far cry from his previous suits, but his presence still made her tense.

By now everyone in her party knew what had happened on the dance floor. Upon seeing who'd spoken, Petr and Sam took a step forward. Neither man was physically imposing, but Allison appreciated the gesture.

Petr opened his mouth to say something when she gripped his arm. "It's okay."

She turned toward Rick. "I just want apologize," he said, glancing from Allison to each of her companions. An awkward silence filled the handful of feet between them. "Face-to-face, if you're willing. It'll take thirty seconds."

She thought she saw sincerity in his eyes. Did he deserve a chance to make amends? Becky strode to her side. "Let's go, Ally."

"In a minute," she said, gaze still trained on Rick.

"You can't be think—"

"Thank you," she said, spinning toward Becky, then the rest of the group. "For looking out for me. But it's just a few words. I think they'll bring me some peace."

"Ally," said Erin, "not to be blunt, but isn't this the definition of asking for it?"

"I don't think he's going to try to fondle me in front of five-thousand people."

"He did in front of two hundred," said Becky.

A long pause followed. "Look," said Petr, "it's her choice." He calmly faced Allison. "You know this is all just friendly advice."

She nodded, managing something close to a smile. "Thanks. Just…buy yourselves a tee shirt or something. I'll be with you before you know it."

She turned around before any doubt materialized on their faces. In reality, she wasn't that nervous. Something about being beneath daylight, out in the open air, made the situation less daunting.

Rick squinted her way. Behind him, people continued to stream through the store in both directions. His clients, once again, were nowhere in sight. Allison realized she'd yet to actually see him speak to either couple. "Do you mind?" he said, motioning a few feet to the left, where another shop created a small patch of shade. She shook her head and followed. It was still visible from most of the square.

They stopped in the center of the shadows. "You've got some good friends," said Rick. His voice was softer, free of its arrogant edge.

"What about yours?" She nodded toward the bar. "Thirsty already?"

He almost laughed. "Too thirsty last night. They're still sleeping it off."

She said nothing. He took the cue. "I'm sorry. For the ballroom, for everything. Truly." He exhaled, scanning the square, coming back to her. "You've probably guessed you're not the first woman I've danced with on a cruise ship. But I'm no sexual predator. Everything is always consensual.

"I don't know what it was about this time. Your initial rejection, maybe? Made me want to try harder." He lifted both hands, as if wiping away the last comment. "It doesn't matter." Another breath. "We'll likely never see each other again. I just didn't want you to leave thinking I was something I'm not." He reached out his hand. "Truce?"

It wasn't eloquent, but it was honest. She accepted, shaking his palm with a firm grip. A moment later she let go, and they were no longer adversaries. Just a pair of tourists who happened to bump into one another.

"I never asked: what's your boyfriend's name?"

"Jeremy."

"Well," said Rick, backing away, "Jeremy really is a lucky guy."

Ten seconds later he was gone, lost in the throng of vacationers still spilling from the ship. Allison remained still for a moment, allowing herself, for the first time, to be flattered by his attentions. Then she turned back to her friends. Most of them were out of sight, having taken her shopping advice. Only Becky remained visible, leaning against a tree on the far side of the square

Allison began walking toward her. The area was busy, but would be even more so later that afternoon, when a second cruise ship pulled into port. With any luck, they'd be gone by then.

She'd moved alongside a circular fountain, near the center of the open space, when the echo of running footsteps reached her left side. She turned, curious, to find a young man jogging out of the duty-free shop. He was holding something above his head. Then she looked closer and remembered she'd seen him before. Twice. It was the blonde deckhand from the ship. Another second passed before she realized he was trying to flag her down.

The object in his hands was a pair of sunglasses. Once he got within twenty feet, she could hear him: "Miss…miss…you forgot…" She continued squinting through the sun, hardly believing an hourly worker, probably making minimum wage, would take the time to track her down and deliver a pair of cheap shades she'd obviously dropped. She made a mental note to shout his name up the company food chain, then started reaching for a tip.

Now just a few paces away, he slowed to a walk. He was breathing a little heavily, but still managed a smile. Allison found some cash and fished it out. "Thank you so much," she said, shaking her head. "What's your name?"

"Toby."

"Toby. I'll make sure to put in a good word for you."

He stopped within arm's length. "Thank you." Before handing over his find, he wiped a streak of sweat from his brow. It was only then that she realized her sunglasses had been on her forehead the entire time. A pang of alarm flashed deep within her brain. Too late.

Most frightening of all, the smile stayed on his face as the crew member swung a silver blade around in his free hand. Allison saw the knife headed toward her ribcage but had no time to move, or scream. She felt the agony of steel piercing skin, then heard two heavy claps of thunder.

An instant later swirls of blood clouded her vision, matched by a level of pain she'd never before experienced. The last thing she remembered was falling to the ground before everything went black.

59

"We've got to stop meeting like this."

For the first time in more than a week, McCoy guessed, the president cracked a smile. It was a cheesy joke, but, under the circumstances, he figured he'd give his commander-in-chief a break.

If Vanning, to his left, was thinking the same thing, the noncommittal grin draping the corners of his mouth offered no clue. That, McCoy knew, was how the agency-head had managed to remain on so many senators' guest-lists over the years. "When someone gives you a line they think is brilliant," he'd once said, "let them keep thinking it. Smile, nod—you never know where it might take you."

Today, it'd brought them back to the Oval Office. Outside, the scenery was still more fall than winter. A late-afternoon sun sliced through the Rose Garden, all but ignoring the space's myriad Christmas decorations.

Inside, the mood was nearly as bright. No longer would Matthew Billings be remembered as the president who allowed the Middle East to go up in flames. Gathering himself, he stepped behind his desk and motioned Vanning and McCoy into two chairs opposite.

"Thanks for getting here on such short notice. I wish I could spare more than twenty minutes, but I've got dinner with the Japanese ambassador. Delaying would turn too many heads."

"We understand, sir," said Vanning. "As you know, the worst is over. But there are still several loose ends."

At this he turned to McCoy, who addressed the president. "We have tentative containment in both Jerusalem and the coast. It's still unclear how, but Edmund and Jakob van Leer likely recruited the shooter in Zion Square." McCoy checked a folder in his lap. "His name was Adir Peretz. Worked as a waiter at a café in the city; mid-twenties, no family. No history of violence, either, though he had voiced strong political opinions in the past on social media. So far, the press seems content painting him as a lone gunman.

"As for the Van Leers themselves, they were, officially, never in Israel. Hassan's government offered to dispose of the bodies. It gets tricky as Edmund was one of the richest men in Europe. His absence will be noticed."

"Plan is," said Vanning, "to put a couple corpses in his house in Curacao and burn it to the ground. We'll adjust the flight logs from Amsterdam, make it look like a real trip."

Billings nodded. McCoy was a bit surprised he didn't protest, but the president knew as well as them that options, and time, were tight. Just about anything was better than the world learning the truth.

"What about Kent and Baker?" Billings asked.

"Ghosts, like the Van Leers," said McCoy. "Eight Shin Bet agents died in that firefight. Story is a pack of Israeli nationalists—furious over Hassan's plans for peace with the Palestinians—knew the whereabouts of Leila and Talya Hassan and attacked. It was a war of attrition. The last agent alive killed the final attacker before succumbing to his own wounds."

"I assume," said the president skeptically, "that we have the human collateral to prove this?"

Vanning broke in again. "It's better if you don't know the details, sir. Suffice to say the Israeli military secured the scene. There is no evidence to cause the public, or the press, to second-guess what transpired."

As if running the meeting himself, Vanning then gestured for McCoy to continue.

"Eight hours ago, Dvir Cohen, a senior member of the Knesset, was stopped trying to board a private jet at Ben Gurion Airport. The flight had only been scheduled the night before. Mossad considered this strange and brought him in for questioning." McCoy suppressed a smile. "You can imagine, sir, how comfortable they're capable of making a detainee feel.

"Cohen broke an hour later. In exchange for fifty million dollars—since confirmed by wire transfers—he'd disclosed the location of Leila and Talya Hassan and secured for the Van Leers, through numerous channels, an array of weapons including sniper rifles, machine guns and flash grenades."

"As practiced as the brothers were," said Vanning, "that's how two men were able to subdue eight well-trained agents so quickly."

"And Cohen?" asked the president.

"Health problems," said Vanning. "Fortunately, his doctor's records nearly prove it. Convalescence at an undisclosed location, then forced retirement. Beyond that is subject only to his government's imagination."

Billings took a deep breath. "Anything else?"

McCoy straightened. "Just the Van Leer's estate in Het Gooi, sir." He scanned a different page in his folder, then looked up. "Our team on the ground found an additional room—more of a large storage closet—adjacent to the secret basement. Seems there was a lever hidden behind one of the framed front pages that granted access.

"The new space is a goldmine. Letters, maps, illustrations. Some go back more than a century, and all appear to tie the Van Leer family to the assassinations in question. But that's just a first impression. It'll take weeks to catalogue every item, months to analyze and interpret the data."

"Obviously," said Billings, "they can't do it on-site."

McCoy nodded. "We're readying the documents for shipment. But it's not as simple as stuffing FedEx boxes. Most of the papers are yellowing, some old enough to fall apart. It's a delicate process. Team should finish within the next eight hours, have the cargo back to Langley by this time tomorrow.

"Fortunately, we still have free reign at the house. Local police have no reason to take a closer look. Van Leer even dismissed his domestic staff for a full week. Our guess is he was planning on disappearing for some time after the assassination."

"Which plays into our plans for Curacao," said Vanning.

The president sat, waiting for more. Nothing came. Slowly, he turned his head from Vanning to McCoy, then back. "Good work." He then stood and both men followed. Billings didn't move, didn't step from behind his desk. Instead, a thin glaze fell over his eyes, turning his look distant. "Curacao...why couldn't it have happened there? Or Holland? Anywhere but Israel." He sighed absently. "I'm going to have to fly over there, show my support."

"Not for at least six months," said Vanning.

The president's gaze instantly cleared, because he knew why. Each of them did. Amidst the perpetual powder keg that was the Middle East, Israel had somehow lowered to a simmer over the past few years. But no matter how close peace had actually been, today it was little more than a dream.

While Hassan's assassination was unsuccessful, significant damage had been done through the attempt. Riots flared up in Jerusalem and Tel Aviv. Hassan and Khalidi went on TV to finish their original message and urge restraint, but their citizens were no longer listening. The unrest quickly spilled into cities like Damascus, Beirut and Amman. Tomorrow the region was now likely to be less-stable than today. Despite its recent gains, the area had returned to its own combustible status-quo. McCoy scolded himself for finding comfort in such familiarity. Yet he knew he wasn't the only one.

"Sometimes," said Billings, "I feel like I'm barely surviving today only to do the same thing tomorrow. Plenty of people in my line of work would call that failure."

Vanning glanced toward McCoy, then back across the desk. "In our line of work, Mr. President, we call it victory."

60

Allison heard the beeping before she opened her eyes. She recognized the sound immediately—a heart monitor, over her left shoulder. For a split-second she wondered if she was back at work. Had the past week all been a dream? Then pain told the truth, throbbing near her abdomen and bringing her back to the square, the deckhand…the knife.

Her heart rate began to increase, the beeps behind multiplying. She opened her eyes to escape the memory. And found herself, indeed, in a hospital. She lay in a private room, its surrounding walls a spotless white. Matching tile reflected the abundant florescence streaming from a paneled ceiling. To her right, a soft breeze filtered into the space through turquoise shutters. Despite her state-of-the-art surroundings, she couldn't help imagining a similar kind of room from over a hundred years ago: oozing natural light, cotton and silence; always showing up at the end of sad movies.

Allison continued panning left. She soon saw that the door was closed, and that she wasn't alone. Not technically. Kent slumped beside her in an uncomfortable-looking plastic chair, asleep. The joy of seeing him crashed against the weakness in her bones. She didn't move, didn't speak. He hardly looked like he could do any better. A bandage covered a gash over his left eye; the rest of his face wasn't much of an improvement. He looked like he'd aged a year since she'd last seen him.

They'd done this before—her lying awake in bed, watching him sleep in a chair. Eight months ago, in Austria. They'd been the most terrifying days of her life, and also the most exhilarating. *Easy to say for a survivor.* Yet she'd do it again, because it marked the beginning of their adventure together. One that, up to and including today, the world seemed set on destroying.

A sudden pain cut through her stomach. She twisted in response and banged her foot against a bar at the end of the bed. Kent's eyes, a little bloodshot, popped open. Allison's discomfort passed quickly, and for a second the two of them stared at one another through the rebuilding silence.

Eventually Kent let a tepid smile creep onto his face. He straightened and rose out of the chair, bending over her. "How do you feel?"

Her own grin was a bit wider. "Better now."

He looked like he wanted to move in close, but, as before, simply pressed his lips to her forehead.

"You won't kiss me for real?" She meant on the lips. It was a special code of theirs.

He acted like he hadn't heard her. A glance toward the monitor, then his watch. "Doc's got you on Percocet. Might be time for another dose."

Allison let the evasion pass, propping herself up on an elbow. She tried to picture the damage the knife had done, already feeling safer with Kent by her side. "What happened?"

He hesitated. "You need more rest."

"Please." The medicine was, indeed, wearing off; she felt wide awake. "Tell me."

He took a deep breath. "The man who…attacked you didn't work for the cruise line."

"Who was he?"

"A friend of my enemies. He was following their orders."

"Which were?" Even as she asked, Allison knew the answer. "*To kill me.*"

All at once she felt the weight of such a violent reality crash down upon her. The room began to swirl; thick tears blurred the edge of her vision. Kent held her close this time, whispering into her ear. "I'm so sorry. It's all over now."

They remained still, intertwined, in the center of the sterile space. Allison didn't know how long it was, but finally she stopped shaking. Kent released her and sat up on the edge of the bed. She rubbed her eyes and cleared away a few wet strands of hair. "Thank you."

He shook his head. "It's my fault."

"Hardly. You saved me."

"Not exactly." She stayed silent, drying her eyes. "I was too far away," he continued. "But there happened to be a platoon of Navy SEALs stationed at Guantanamo Bay. Cuba is only a ninety-minute helicopter flight from Grand Turk. They landed just in time."

"And shot my attacker," she said, remembering the claps of thunder.

He nodded. Allison didn't notice the hint of grief on his face, so busy was she piecing the puzzle together. She scanned the room, studying its walls anew. "Where are we?"

"At the National Hospital in Cockburn Town."

She sifted through the bits of their cruise itinerary still clinging to memory. "The capital of Turks and Caicos?"

Another nod. "We're three miles north of the cruise terminal. They stabilized you on the *Empress*, then moved you here." He checked his watch. "It's been about twenty-four hours."

"What about Becky? The others?"

"At a motel nearby. Jim has been keeping them calm."

"Jim is here?" A strange wave of comfort—that wherever in the world Kent had been, he hadn't been alone—filled her chest.

"He's been telling them about our car accident." Kent gestured to the bandage on his face. "How we finished our meetings early and planned to fly to the island ahead of time and surprise you, then wrecked our rental car on the way to the airport."

"You two think of everything." Suddenly her breakdown felt hours old. Allison could sense herself starting to relax. This entire ordeal, so abruptly thrust upon her, was at last coming into focus. It'd been a close call, certainly, but she couldn't escape the notion that they'd dodged a collective bullet.

As if in protest, another jolt of pain sliced through her abdomen. "How bad is it?" she asked, gesturing down.

Kent wore part of her grimace himself. "Like I said, the SEALs got there just in time. But surgery was successful, stopped the bleeding long ago. Now it's just a matter of recovery." He glanced around, forcing a smile. "I suppose there are worse places to wait."

She grasped his hand. "Can you wait with me?"

He squeezed hers back. "Of course." *But…*

This last word he didn't say, didn't need to; she could feel it. For the first time she noticed the melancholy hiding behind his gaze. A hollow fear sprouted in her stomach. "What's wrong?"

Kent opened his mouth, surely to object, then closed it. She already knew him too well to believe anything other than the truth. Besides, he'd never been one to sugarcoat. He tried again, looking her in the eye. "When you leave here, Allison…I can't follow."

Another mission. "How long will you be?"

"No, you don't understand. You and I…we have to end here, in this room."

She should have seen it coming—one of those moments that retrospect would prove obvious. This was the second time in nine months that she'd needed invasive surgery to repair an attack wound. Both had come as a result of her connection to him. There was only so much pain that either of them could take.

Allison sat up a little more, hiding a terrified heart behind what she hoped was a confident stare. "I chose this life, Jeremy. Remember? I knew full well what I was getting into. No number of hospital rooms is going to make me change my mind."

He glared back at her for a long moment, as if committing a receding image to memory. Then he slipped his hand out of hers and gently rose from the bed. By now his eyes had begun to glisten. "It's not your lack of strength, Ally. It's mine. I have to watch you fight for your life in a lonely bed, knowing I was the one who put you there. Every hurt you escape today is a fear I carry tomorrow. And next time, there won't be a SEAL team on standby."

He slowly began backing away. "You deserve a long, peaceful life. Get promoted, marry someone stable. Start a family."

"I see," she said, the fear in her chest turning to anger. "I lead a safe, bland existence so you can feel happy for me and sorry for yourself."

"I never said 'bland.'"

"Do you love me?" she asked, shifting to the edge of the bed despite the pain.

"That's not the point right now—"

"Do you love me!"

"Yes! Can't you see it on my face?" He jabbed a pair of fingers at his heart. "This is killing me!"

He was almost shouting now. She'd never seen him this keyed-up without a gun in his hand. Allison calmed herself before speaking. "Then why do it?"

Following her lead, Kent deferred to the gathering silence before responding. "Because I'm afraid." He let out a heavy sigh. "There, I said it. I can take body-blows, Ally, bullets…I can't lose you."

She slid her bare feet onto the cold floor and pushed off with wobbly legs. Kent's eyes went wide and he moved to help. She waved him back. "I understand. I really do. But when you find the kind of thing we've got, when you're blessed with it…we'll search the rest of our lives and never come close again." She shook her head. "You'll just have to add my safety to your prayers. I'm not going anywhere."

She wanted to walk to him, but couldn't escape her IV. As if reading her mind, he stepped back to the bed until they were face-to-face. She wasn't finished. "You're not the only one who's afraid, Jeremy. So let's face our fears together. Isn't that what this life's about?"

During the long pause that followed, whatever defenses defined his point of view—fortified over the past days and weeks—broke. "Where'd you come from, Allison Shaw?"

"I'm more concerned with where I'm headed."

"In that case…" He turned toward a small table beside his chair. On it rested a half-empty water bottle. He screwed its plastic cap off and detached the circular seal. Then he swung back and slowly dropped to a knee. "Will you marry me?"

Allison suppressed a shiver as an errant draft cut through the back of her gown. She felt dirty, her hair was a mess and the beeps continuing over her shoulder were several strings short of a violin. In other words, it was all as it had to be—and in a strange way, perfect.

She nodded, unable to keep fresh, and far more welcoming, tears away. "Yes."

With a smile, Kent slid the makeshift ring on her finger. Then he stood, wrapped her in his arms and kissed her—this time for real.

ZACH FRANZ studied journalism in college before moving on to pen over seventy-five monthly film reviews for two St. Louis area outlets. He published his first novel, "Racing Orion," in 2021. These days, he's always on the lookout for the next great story. When he's not writing one, he's likely reading, watching a movie, or cheering on his favorite hockey team, the Blues. Zach lives with his family in the Missouri countryside and would welcome your feedback at zdfranz@gmail.com.